Praise for *Impossible Saints*

"*Impossible Saints* [should be] required reading for school-girls in a post-religious world."
— *The Times* (London)

"Fascinating...Whimsical flights of fancy [suggest] that everyday life is both more sacred and bizarre than we might imagine. A rich account of a woman who leaves her convent to find the joy that lies at the heart of all existence...lively and probing."
— *The New York Times Book Review*

"This gorgeous book weaves the lives of 10 would-be saints into the story of a nun who takes a priest for a lover and writes books that are censured by Church authorities...in a world in which the spice-filled air of ancient Mediterranean lands mixes with the damp chill of old and modern Britain. In her irreverent saints' lives, [Roberts] shows us canonization as it might have been if the church were overseen by a matriarchy that celebrated human energy and desire."
— *Publishers Weekly* (starred review)

"Told in a smooth style that expertly details several distinct historical settings...These are broad, often startlingly sexually explicit caricatures of emotionally driven females whose intensity alone, it seems, sanctifies them. Insouciant and entertaining...The Vatican will not be amused."
— *Kirkus Reviews*

IMPOSSIBLE
SAINTS

Michèle Roberts

IMPOSSIBLE
SAINTS

A Harvest Book

Harcourt Brace & Company

San Diego   New York   London

Published by arrangement with The Ecco Press

Library of Congress Cataloging-in-Publication Data
Roberts, Michèle.
Impossible saints/Michèle Roberts.—1st Harvest ed.
p.   cm.—(A Harvest book)
ISBN 0-15-600659-6
1. Christian women saints—Fiction.   2. Fathers and daughters—Fiction.
3. Religious fiction, English.   I. Title.
PR6068.0155147   1999
823'.914—dc21   99-12591

Text set in Garamond
Printed in the United States of America
First Harvest edition 1999
A C E D B

AUTHOR'S NOTE

Although this novel was partly inspired by the writings of Saint Teresa of Avila, it is not about her in any direct way. My character whom I've named Josephine is precisely *not* Teresa. I was also inspired by the lives of the saints recounted by De Voragine in his collection *The Golden Legend*. Thanks to Pat Reuben for pointing out to me the story of St Marin. Thanks to the British Council for inviting me to different parts of the world, trips which sparked off bits of this novel. Thanks to Marina Warner for taking me to see, in Cologne, St Ursula's church and its Golden Chamber, and for pointing out the similarities between the story of the life of St Dympna and the fairytale called Donkeyskin. Thanks to Gillon Aitken and all at Aitken & Stone, and to Lennie Goodings and all at Little, Brown. Thanks to my husband Jim Latter, my family and to all my friends, whose love and encouragement means more than I can say.

for Reg Roberts

Contents

IMPOSSIBLE
SAINTS

THE GOLDEN HOUSE

The golden house was where the bones were kept.

The golden chamber. A room inside a room, like a jeweller's nested box. The golden house was a chapel built into the massive side wall of the cathedral in the centre of the city. You wouldn't know it was there. You would think the low door at the end of the aisle led back outside, another exit, to sunlight and smoky, glittering air. Instead, when you put your hand on the cold iron latch and lifted it so that the pointed door swung open, you pitched forwards down two steps into that gold house full of bones. Thinking to go outside, you went in, to that disorderly house full of dead women.

Deceptive, that place. Four-square, a vaulted ceiling, the walls looking, at first glance, with their tiers of plush-lined boxes, as though they composed a theatre, each little gold-encrusted frame revealing the torso of a beautiful golden-haired woman in gold clothes. Look again, and you saw stacks of doorless cupboards, fretted and gilded, choc-a-bloc with statuesque sculptures in wood. Oak and cherry and walnut: take your pick. Wooden busts of women with carved crimped curls, curved thin smiles, spots of rose painted on their cheeks.

These gilded ladies staring out of their gold windows like captured portraits each had a label, a name: St Paula, St Barbara, St Petronilla, St Thecla, and so on. Saints with a history, a pedigree, who could be looked up in books and their stories checked. The golden legend of their doings ran round the four walls of the golden house. Inside each woman: a few bones. Each golden girl was a small container for relics. A little bone house. Shake her like a pepper pot and she'd rattle out her tale, some bone dust.

Above these rows of reliquaries, these dead dolls, on another level, were displayed the bones of the nameless ones, the women with no identities. Nobody knew to whom these scrap bones belonged. They had been sorted and classified simply according to shape and appearance, then made into a mosaic, which ran all around the top two-thirds of the chapel, and reached the ceiling, filling in the arches of the vault. The mosaic was constructed of square wooden frames, each packed tight with a particular arrangement of bones, that, placed together, formed a precise and repeated abstract pattern of straight lines, rosettes and mandalas. Only on a second glance did you realise that what you were looking at were massed tibias, fibulas and femurs, with here and there a skull and crossbones for added decoration, or a prayer super-imposed in bone letters in a language nobody could understand.

Isabel brought her granddaughter to see it. The child, frowning and black-haired, imagined the architects of this place as busy cooks inventing recipes, sorting and arranging, putting certain bones into the gold cupboards as you'd put joints of meat into larders, and setting some aside, to be boiled down for other uses, soup perhaps, or glue. They were artists, surely. Sitting cross-legged on the floor, each with a lapful of bones, braiding them together like crochet, re-articulating them into fantastic shapes, making them speak like poetry. Fitting them into the square trays, according to the designs they'd worked out, then slapping these up on the walls, a gold mesh nailed across the front to stop the bones, wired into place, from falling out or being pecked by the pigeons who sometimes flew in.

Bone pictures, arranged row on row, so that your eye could travel over them vertically or horizontally or both at once. You could see all the layers of bones, and you could see each individual bone; the part and the whole. The patterns were severe and mysterious. No one could say what they meant. What you saw was the overall dance of shapes. The beauty of the bones.

– Parts of Josephine ended up here, Isabel told the child: and parts of her did not.

THE STORY OF
JOSEPHINE

Nine months after Josephine's death and burial she was dug up again. They discovered that she was still herself. Josephine.

Then they dismembered her. Jo. se. phine.

She died before she had completed her life's work. She had scarcely begun it. She was in transit, on her way towards achievement. Death plucked at her sleeve and said: stop here. This is as far as you will go without me. From now on I shall walk at your side, and I shall come to lie with you in your bed and hug you to me.

Josephine had been ill for some months with cancer. The doctors had not diagnosed it until too late. But, in any case, they did not know how to cure this disease which flourished in secret like mushrooms sprouting in the dark woods, coming up through the layers of fallen leaves. They prescribed purging, cupping, bleeding, blistering and cutting, but she sent them away. She died in her cell, a tiny bare room in the convent of St Joseph's she had so recently founded. She lay on a bed made of packing cases nailed together, between sheets donated by friends. Eucalyptus burned in the brazier in the corner, to take away the smell of sickness. Flies tumbled about, bumping against the small casement window, buzzing.

Thirteen sisters, the number she had stipulated in her Rule for the Reform, lived in that little ramshackle house where she died. A baker's dozen, she called it. Twelve apostles plus one. The *one* in this case was Maria, whom Josephine had named as prioress to succeed her. The nuns, squeezed into the confines of the cell, knelt at the foot of the bed, watching. Josephine's bedding was soaked with sweat. She whispered that she was worn out. So exhausted that death must be very near.

The other persons in the room were Lucian, the nuns' chaplain, who came to give her the last sacraments and anoint her with the holy oils, and her niece Isabel, her attendant in that last year and her constant companion. Isabel was the outsider. She wore the brown dress and black veil like the other sisters, but she was not professed. Josephine had told her to wait, till she was completely sure. She had promised the girl her rosary, as a last gift. Meditating on its mysteries, Isabel would be helped to make up her mind.

Josephine refused confession and holy communion, murmuring that she did not need them now. She consented to be marked with the holy oils, Isabel could see, simply so that she could say goodbye to Lucian as he bent over her. Sister Maria held out a crucifix for her to kiss and Josephine pushed it away.

In the end, hers was a peaceful death. Lucian paced up and down. He stumbled in and out. The rattling sound of his beloved friend's breathing upset him so much that he could not stay still. Sister Maria commanded Isabel to leave the room, to go and get some food, lest she faint after so many hours keeping vigil. She wanted her gone, in case she suffered or felt frightened. Isabel did not want to leave her aunt. Just as she put her hand on the latch of the door Josephine opened her eyes and looked anxiously up. Isabel went back to the bed and said: here I am, now you can rest easy again. Josephine was like a child to hold. So little and light. She laid her head on Isabel's arms. She leaned forwards into her embrace. She gave three small moans then blew her breath out for the last time and died.

On the following day the nuns washed the body, dressed it in a clean, new habit, and wrapped it in cloth of gold. Expensive, heavy stuff. Magdalena, the woman who donated it, meant it as a symbol of her own importance. She had endowed the house when first it opened, paying the nuns' rent for the first year. She sincerely loved Josephine, but she did also love to see herself as the powerful and generous benefactor. For the nuns, the golden cloth symbolised the care and reverence with which to treat the body of their Foundress. The cloth was like their hands, touching her tenderly.

Isabel took Josephine's rosary and attached it to her own

belt. She took care to do this in full view of the others, so that she could not be accused, later, of deviousness or stealing. She had not taken a vow of poverty so she could possess it. It was light, and weighed little. The beads were golden-coloured. The crucifix was missing. Perhaps Josephine had taken it off. When a person dies that you have loved, it's true you want to clutch onto a bit of them. Isabel was going through a period of doubt and confusion about her future as a nun. She was not much given to praying. But she vowed that for Josephine's sake she would use her rosary and pray with it, as her aunt had said she should.

The gold sheet covered the body completely. Isabel tucked in the ends. Maria, the prioress, swung her hammer and fastened down the coffin lid with iron nails. Plump of body, she had long arms which were muscled and strong. She wielded her hammer with energetic grace, banging the nails securely into position, so that, as she put it, nothing should disturb Josephine until the trumpet call at the Last Day.

Off went the body, out of the house, in that long wooden box, made of cheap wood and not adorned in any way. It lurched across the tiny courtyard, carried on the shoulders of six of the sisters. Some of them were so much shorter than the others that the coffin tipped to one side, and then to the other. The sisters did not keep step very well. Josephine would have laughed at the lack of dignity with which she was got to the church. Maria, the prioress, walked in front, and all the rest behind, carrying candles. In the bright daylight you could hardly see the flames.

Father Lucian was waiting for them in the chapel, formerly
the cowshed. He must have been crying in the night for his
eyelids were puffed up and purplish-red, like bruises. Even
his cheeks and nose looked swollen and thickened by tears.
His entire face was flushed a dark pink from weeping. He
seemed ashamed of these signs of grief. He told Isabel they
indicated insufficient faith. Josephine, he was sure, was in
heaven now, in a place of joy. He should be giving thanks to
God. But he told the girl he felt stricken with wretchedness.
All his bones ached, he said, as though he were about to
come down with an illness, and there was a tearing pain
inside him, as though his heart and stomach were slowly
being ripped in two, and his eyes were burning, and his
knees wanted to give way. He whispered all this while Isabel
got out his robes and helped him to put them on. He went
through the Mass clumsily. He croaked out the words and
sang the responses in a small harsh voice.

Magdalena, the woman who had endowed the convent,
was not allowed to attend the burial, for the ceremony was
considered as being held within the enclosure. It was just for
the nuns. But she sent two workmen over to take charge of
making and sealing the tomb, and Sister Maria, not wishing
to offend her, let her have her way.

The site chosen for the coffin's bestowal was on the far
side of the nuns' grille, a niche in the wall behind the altar,
in the small space reserved as the public part of the little
chapel, where the local people knelt when invited in to
hear Mass. A sort of stone cupboard, shallow and open,
wider than it was tall, which looked as though it might

have been the cows' manger. Once the coffin had been wedged into this space, the workmen weighed it down with a great heap of earth, rubble and sand. Then they bricked up the entrance. And across the front of this they built a further screen, of blocks of stone, with one panel marked with a cross.

Isabel stayed on at St Joseph's with the nuns, for she did not know what else to do. Sister Maria said she might remain there as long as she needed, until she made up her mind whether to enter or not. All those years that she had lived with Josephine, her father had sent money from the Far Country every month, to cover her board and lodging, and that would continue, until she needed a dowry, either for marrying or becoming a nun. She lived as one of the professed, with a cell of her own, but as she had not taken vows, and so was not enclosed, she could be sent out of the house on errands, to take messages or letters. Isabel liked these walks through the city, and she liked feeling useful. In the hours which the Rule prescribed for the nuns to spend in their cells, working and praying, she sat on the floor and thought over her life, and wondered what would become of her.

Nine months after Josephine's death, Isabel first, and then all the sisters, noticed a change in the atmosphere in church. A sweet smell had sprung up near the altar. It drifted about and tantalised their noses. It wasn't incense, for they were too poor to burn any. It was more like fresh flowers. A warm giddy breath as of spring tumbling in under the chilly draughts of October, under the cold winds of approaching winter that were already sweeping down from the mountains and driving along the streets.

The fresh scent, so delicate and yet so heady, made Isabel think of flowers that were impossible. Pictures rose in her mind of blooms she could never have seen. Except, perhaps, in her infancy in the Far Country. Did she ever really see them? Striped and spotted orchids, pink and cream and mauve, white lilies whose petals were thick as wax, whose throats gushed such sweetness you thought you would faint. Such a caressing perfume. It enveloped you and you couldn't break away. Climbers starred with yellow, vines dangling bell-shaped scarlet blossoms that closed round your fist and sucked at it, whorled clusters of dark blue petals that dropped wreaths of powerful fragrance, intoxicating as opium, on the evening air. Magdalena grew medicinal plants in her garden. None of them, Isabel thought, remembering, smelled quite this honey-rich.

The breath of flowers, tender and voluptuous, lingered and did not go away. The nuns scented a miracle. At recreation, crammed round the table in the kitchen, they discussed the possibilities. Was it just the smell of loss, of their own longing? How could they be sure?

Father Lucian said there was only one way to find out. He came at night, with his friend Father Peter, and Isabel went down to let them in when they tapped very discreetly, with a pre-arranged pattern of knocks, at the street door. They each carried a lantern, and they had also brought, under their cloaks, pickaxes, shovels and chisels.

Breaking open the tomb was slow and difficult work. The

nuns kept the chapel shut for two days. They wanted no rumours starting up. In this city gossip jumped from person to person faster than a flea. By the second night the task was completed. The stone cupboard gaped wide as the heap of rubble was shovelled away and the coffin tugged out. The lid had been smashed in by the weight of sand and earth thrown on top of it. Lucian prised out the nails and heaved it up. The nuns pressed forwards to look.

The wood of the coffin had rotted, and stank of mildew. The cloth of gold wrapper and the brown habit in which Josephine had been buried were falling to pieces. But the body, though it was stained with the earth that had penetrated into the coffin, was as fresh and whole as though it had been buried only the day before.

The face was a little bruised by the rubble that had fallen on it once the coffin lid had given way, but it was intact. Isabel reached out a finger to stroke earth and dust away and found Josephine there, undamaged. She had to put up her hands to trap her tears but through her crying she went on looking at her. Josephine could not be disturbed by anyone's grief. Her shut eyelids swelled like eggs. She lay in calm repose, beyond the reach of suffering and of pain. She was free. She was herself again, and she was transfigured. Isabel's beautiful aunt.

Sister Maria declared: this is a sign sent by God. Nine months in the cave of the tomb. A miraculous pregnancy followed by birth! Born backwards, into life! A kind of resurrection!

All the sisters now took lit tapers and encircled the coffin as though it were a cradle and they the godmothers arrived to bless the child. They bent over it and looked in. Wax from their raised candles splashed down and dripped onto Josephine's face. Her eyelids became coated with wax. Her lips got stuck together, masked with opaque white. A sliver of wax parted them, fragile as paper, like a communion wafer. Wax discs formed on her fingernails, wax dots dropped on her hands folded across her breast. As though each sister set a seal upon her: you are mine.

Lucian and Peter waved the community back. They needed to confirm that the corpse was indeed incorrupt. So they put their noses deep into the coffin and sniffed Josephine's flesh. They announced that it had not decayed. Lucian said it smelled of clover, of carnations and roses. Father Peter thought lilies, with a trace of violets.

Then they tore away the shreds of gold cloth and the tattered fragments of habit, to reveal fully the naked body underneath. They had to do this, in order to be sure. So although Isabel let out her breath in a hiss of shame, like many of the other sisters, to see Josephine so exposed, she kept her head up and went on watching. She felt disgusted with herself, but she could not resist the force inside her that said: remember what happens. Remember exactly.

Lucian whispered in surprise at how firm and full Josephine's breasts seemed to be. He put out his hand and touched them. The flesh, the nipples. Peter did likewise. Springy as the fat on good meat, he said: like fresh beef suet. Then Peter got out the butcher's knife he had been carrying with him, which the others had not seen before this, because he had kept it concealed in the inside pocket of his cloak, and cut off Josephine's right hand.

He did it so fast, and with such authority, that no one protested. Not Lucian. Not the prioress. Who were the nuns, to think they had the right to stop him? Lucian could have done so, but he was in too great a daze of astonishment and grief, ever since the coffin had been opened. He did nothing. He looked on, like the rest.

Peter sawed off Josephine's hand at the wrist. The blade's edge seemed razor-sharp. It sliced through the skin then scraped on bone. There was no blood, just the ooze of some yellowish juice. He severed the joints and tendons with no bungling and no mess. Then he chopped the little finger off the hand. That looked easy, like taking off a carrot top, the knife coming to rest against his thumb. He wrapped the finger in his handkerchief and put it back into his pocket with the sheathed knife, and wiped his hands on his cloak. Isabel was sent running to fetch an old linen coif. Peter wrapped the hand in it and placed it in the box he had brought with him.

The nuns took the body away and washed it. They rinsed off the earth and dirt, clothed it in a new habit, and brought it back into the church. They sang Matins and Lauds. The scent of spring flowers now permeated the entire house.

Peter presented the boxed hand to Sister Maria. So that she would have a relic of Josephine. It was a warning, she knew. The Church authorities would not allow an incorrupt body, which was the sure sign of a saint, to remain in this convent of St Joseph's, which was tiny, poor, and obscure.

They would arrive, and demand the body. They would hold it, like treasure put into bank vaults for safe-keeping, against the day when Josephine would be officially declared a saint. Then they would decide in what great church to display her body to the faithful.

For the moment, however, Lucian insisted that Josephine's body be left in the public part of the convent chapel, so that the local people of the parish could come in and pay her their respects. The nuns were to keep vigil, day and night, two by two, on their side of the grille.

The corpse was accordingly placed in the open coffin on a sheeted bier. Pilgrims arrived in a ferment of curiosity to see it. Sister Maria let them in five at a time. There was room for no more in that cramped space. They pressed and jostled each other to get a good view. They approached their lips to the hand, the feet.

It took the nuns several days to realise what was happening. Some of these kisses were greedier and less reverent than others. Some of the faithful were feasting on Josephine. Taking bites out of her. They scurried off with little chunks of her flesh concealed in their cheeks or under their tongues. The sisters watched them scamper furtively away, then discovered their little excavations. The fingernails of the left hand, the toenails of both feet, the eyebrows, the eyelashes, the end of the nose. Someone had torn open the habit and bitten off the nipples. Someone else had nibbled the earlobes. The mouth was badly bruised.

The prioress barred the chapel door against the rabble of angry pilgrims. She would not even admit Magdalena, the benefactress, who had tried to protect Josephine's body by having it so well buried. That lady said she would inform the church authorities all around of what had happened. The nuns were not fit to guard the body of her friend and she would see to it that they had it no longer. She complained bitterly to everybody in the city. She accused the nuns of betraying her good faith and abusing her generosity and wasting good cloth of gold.

Sister Maria was commanded by letter to prepare to give up the body to the Cardinal, who was sending his soldiers for it. The Cardinal was a keen collector of relics and was not about to let this one slip through his fingers. He was planning to build a splendid chapel to house his collection and display it to the faithful. An incorrupt body was just what he needed as a centrepiece. So he wrote in peremptory tones to the nuns of St Joseph's, bidding them prepare their Foundress to be fetched the next day.

Sister Maria gathered the nuns together in the kitchen, which functioned as Chapter-House and meeting-place as need arose. Her sallow face glistened with indignation, and her clasped hands leaped about in her lap.

She declared to her sisters: the body of our Mother belongs to us all, not to the Cardinal.

Sister Maria, normally that most placid and obedient of nuns, was extremely upset. Her black eyes gleamed, and she kept checking herself from uttering certain words which rose to her lips.

Sister Maria's plan was carried out that night. Lucian and Peter procured themselves disguises, so that no one could say they had seen them in the vicinity and accuse them. They dressed up as merchants, and took a room in the same side alley as the convent, in a house a little way along towards the main street. They leaned out of the window, waving a blue handkerchief, to signal their safe arrival and entry. Sister Maria then sent for Isabel and told her that since she was the only one who could leave St Joseph's, not being bound to the rule of enclosure, she was to help them.

The two priests came down to the convent, at the far end of the alley, under cover of darkness, and Isabel let them in. Josephine's body was in her cell immediately above the kitchen, in the grain loft which had been converted to nuns' sleeping-places, and Isabel led them there, showing them how to climb the steep ladderlike staircase. She went up nimbly, then stood above them holding a candle, while they came up. They made just enough noise that any nun questioned the next day would be able to say that her dreams had been disturbed, perhaps by burglars.

Peter and Lucian carried Josephine out of the convent, holding an arm each, and Isabel followed. Dressed in a cloak, the body looked like a live person. Anyone glancing their way would have said the two merchants were helping someone ill or drunk. But nobody saw. The corpse was stiff and light. They escorted it along the street, into their lodgings, and propped it up against the wall in one corner. To see Josephine leaning there like an old mop or broom caused Isabel horror and anguish. Also she felt frightened at seeing a dead body stood up in that way, in the wrong place for it. As though it were a clown's stilt and might start hopping about. Her anxiety increased when she found out what Peter, on the instructions of Sister Maria, was intending to do. Isabel, helpless through fear, did not try to prevent him. She watched Peter lay the lifeless form on the table, and undress it, and she took the bundle of discarded clothes and hugged it as though it were Josephine.

Peter cried, afterwards, and confessed to his two helpers that it was the worst thing he had ever had to do in his life. His future was marked by this act, and his reputation, and his name. While he was at it, however, he looked merely as though he was concentrating. He told Lucian and Isabel he had been to a butcher's on the other side of the city to buy a joint of pork, and had watched closely what the butcher did. The miracle now seemed to be that his knife sank in as easily as though he were slicing up melon, or cheese. Arms, legs, hand, feet, he cut them into neat pieces, some small and some tiny. He divided the ribs, and took out the heart. He left the head intact. All these bits he put into grain sacks, then rolled these up into neat parcels which he secured with string. Isabel was a witness to all of this as was Lucian.

When the Cardinal's men arrived at St Joseph's the following day to take away Josephine's body, Sister Maria, weeping loudly, spoke to them through the closed door. She cried that the convent had been robbed in the night and the body stolen. She hinted, through her noisy tears, that Magdalena, their vengeful patroness, who had, most likely, kept a key to the house after the nuns moved in, was the most obvious suspect, since she had loved Josephine with too possessive a love and could not bear that the poor, undistinguished convent of St Joseph's should be her friend's last resting place. The soldiers saw that there was nothing here for them to do. They went away empty-handed, to ask the Cardinal for fresh instructions.

Sister Maria's plan was that relics of Josephine would be distributed around the country. Every church that asked for one would get a piece of her. Her right hand would remain at St Joseph's, and they would have a very beautiful monstrance made in which to display it. Sister Maria made a list of the parts of the body and what to charge for them. The price would vary, of course, according to what bit people wanted. Peter and Lucian would travel around delivering the relics. It would all be done, necessarily, with great secrecy and discretion. But since incorrupt bodies were rare, they would be able to get rid of Josephine's very fast, and to obtain an excellent price. The prospect of this money provided great relief to Sister Maria. The convent would now be on a secure financial footing. She dreamed of a great future. In her prayers she addressed Josephine with impatience, bidding her hurry up and perform the necessary miracles so that they could get her canonised.

What Sister Maria did not foresee was the plotting of the authorities to have the convent investigated as a possible hotbed of disobedience and heresy, and thoroughly searched, since the body was undoubtedly still on the premises. Nor did she sufficiently take into account the threat posed to her plans by Isabel, who knew so much more about Josephine than Maria liked. Sister Maria believed she was acting in God's best interests, like one of her heroines in the lives of the saints. She was convinced that virtue would prevail, because in *The Golden Legend,* the collection of saints' lives she read to her sisters every day over dinner, it always did.

THE LIFE OF
SAINT PAULA

St Paula was a matron of Rome and a pillar of the early
Church, an ardent disciple of St Jerome.

Once she had borne her husband a son she was able to
stop having children. She had four daughters already and
that was quite enough. She learned to regret that she had
ever got married and enjoyed sex. She learned to mortify her
flesh, to give away most of her wealth to the poor, to eat and
dress badly, and to rejoice when her husband suddenly died
and left her a widow. To have been a chaste and continent
wife was to be confined to the lowest rung of the ladder
leading out of the filth of the world up towards heaven.
But now that she was a widow, Jerome instructed her, she
had made some progress. She had advanced to the second
rung.

She had married off three of her daughters to suitable

young Romans of good family. Blesilla, Rufina and Paulina were all settled. The youngest girl, Julia Eustochium, who was only ten, was still at home with her mother. Paula kept her little daughter out of harm's way. Julia never went to parties, weddings or funerals, and never saw a man, apart from St Jerome who often dropped round to discuss theology and exhort Paula to further efforts of virtue.

— Ascetics are the athletes of God! he proclaimed: the more you dominate your senses and your desires, the more you ignore your body, the closer you will get to God!

— Why? asked Blesilla, who happened to be visiting her mother that afternoon and so was present at the holy man's conference: why?

Jerome frowned at her.

— Don't interrupt, he said.

Paula blushed for her daughter. She stood over her and slapped her face. Blesilla burst into tears and rushed out of the room, thereby missing St Jerome's reply.

— Suffering and evil enter the world through the medium of the body, its cravings and desires. More specifically (he coughed) sexual intercourse introduces original sin into the world. The sin of Adam and Eve is passed on through conception and birth. The moment of becoming human marks us as corrupted, lost. Also, sex leads to death. How much happier we would be if we had no bodies and never wanted anything! If we never had sex we would never have to die. Therefore, virginity is the best path, for holy virgins will live for ever and see God. Whereas those who give in to their bodily urges will burn in hell for evermore!

He began to describe the torments reserved by God for the damned.

Little Eustochium pressed closer to her mother. She put her hand in Paula's.

– I'm going to stay a virgin, she declared: I'm going to live an ascetic and enclosed life and offer it to God.

Overcome with joy, Paula hugged her. St Jerome smiled and blessed her. Blesilla stood outside in the hallway, angrily pleating the skirts of her gold chiffon tunic between her beautifully manicured fingertips. She loved the way her fine clothes swished about her when she walked, the caress of silk and linen on her skin. She loved having her hair done, and going to the baths for the afternoon, and lying in bed making love with her young husband. She knew that Paula and Jerome believed she should give up all these pleasures in the interests of gaining a reserved place in heaven, but life here and now was too dear to her. She consoled herself for her mother's harshness by stopping at the confectioner's on the way home and buying herself a large box of crystallised figs.

Soon after this, Blesilla's husband died of a heart attack. She was only twenty. She was robbed of the person dearest to her in the world. They had spent a great deal of time in bed together, experimenting with all the ways they could discover to give each other pleasure. They invented new caresses every day. They had a host of private sexy pet names for each other. His body was imprinted on hers. They had lived inside each other. But now he was torn out of her. She felt that his death had ripped her self away. They used to lie in bed talking, when they weren't making love, for her young husband was unashamed of his preference for her company, and thought of her as his best friend. Now Blesilla had no one to talk to. No one else could understand how she felt, for most men at that time did not consider women their equals and did not believe that friendship with them was possible. Her husband had been exceptional.

– It's all very well to mourn your husband, Paula told her pale and silent daughter: it's right and proper to show your grief as a widow should, but you mustn't go too far. You mustn't overdo it. Excess of grief is a sin.

– Your sister may be ten years older than you, Jerome said to little Eustochium: but you are her superior. You're a consecrated virgin, and she's just a widow. Let's not be ashamed of our holy arrogance! As a virgin, you are, technically, superior to your mother as well. Your crown, my dear, will be the brightest. You are the flower of the women in your family.

Blesilla started paying frequent visits to her mother and small sister, just for something to do. She hoped that a change of scene might occupy her mind and console her. In this state of near despair, her health weakened by sleepless nights spent weeping, she fell under Jerome's influence.

He was cunning. He listened patiently as she rambled on and on. He regarded her kindly, and did not interrupt. Quite soon she found herself wondering whether it wasn't her fault her husband had had that heart attack. She had seduced him too often. She had worn him out.

Jerome sympathised. Blesilla collapsed. She knelt before him, sobbing, and begged him to tell her what to do.

Jerome showed her that her suffering was due to an excess attachment to things of this world. He persuaded her to give away her expensive clothes and to dress in sackcloth over a hairshirt, to cut off her beautiful hair, not to bathe and care for her skin, and not to want to be clean.

– What you don't have, Jerome explained: you don't miss.

Blesilla learned from her mother how to fast and do penance. Lost, and lacking in direction, she copied her mother in all she did. Similarly, she obeyed Jerome in everything. All the passionate energy she had spent on loving her husband, and then on grieving for him, she now poured into ascetic practices.

She was fascinated to discover that there was no end to self-mortification. You could never do enough. There was always another step that you could take. Another privation that you could embrace. Once you were in, you could not stop but had to go on. It was exactly like a seduction. She, who had been an adept in the arts of love, pushed herself, day by day, to go further and further along the path of self-abnegation. Instead of loving her body she fought it. Instead of desiring to be given pleasure she rooted out that desire and wished only for pain and punishment.

– I am in training, like an athlete, she declared to her mother and sister: I have a race to run, that finishes only in heaven. I am God's athlete and by His grace I shall win the race.

At first she confined herself to the austerities Paula showed her. From her daily meals she eliminated everything that tasted good, such as oil, meat, fish, eggs, cheese, honey and wine. She gave away her bed and slept on a mat on the floor. She took just three hours' rest a night. She sold most of her goods and gave the money to St Jerome for his charities. She gave her house, carriage and slaves to her husband's family.

Her likeness to her mother became pronounced. Both were so gaunt and haggard they could have been mistaken for one another. Both had unkempt, unwashed hair, shabby and ill-fitting clothes, and deepset eyes blazing with zeal.

Blesilla thought to herself: if only I try hard enough I will be able to regain, to some extent at least, my former state of virginity.

For she felt it intolerable that little Eustochium was purer, and therefore holier, than she.

In her desperate efforts to attain that impossible purity, which would bring peace with it and a cessation of her suffering, she redoubled then trebled the number of penances she piled on herself. Jerome, watching her, marvelled at her determination and persistence. He boasted of her all over Rome. He praised this mere woman's great soul. He called her his female man of God. Pointing out her growth in modesty and obedience, he spurred her on to ever harsher ascetic practices.

So now Blesilla ate only every other day, when she took a little bread moistened with water, and a beaker of milk, and she managed to cut her hours of sleep down to two. She rejoiced in the ugliness that her new life brought her. Her hair began to fall out, and her eyelashes. Her fingers and toes turned purplish-blue. She smelled bad because her digestion and bowels no longer worked properly. Her bones stuck out in a way that was terrifying to see if you weren't used to it. Luckily Jerome and Paula were. They thought it was normal that a woman who fasted almost constantly should be so thin.

Little Eustochium stayed away from her sister and hid herself in her books. She had begun to study Hebrew, in order to help her mother in her researches on the Old Testament, which Paula had begun in the hope of aiding St Jerome. Remaining a virgin was all that she required of herself for the moment. Her life was quite harsh enough, in its lack of amusement and company, for her not to need to perform extra acts of heroic virtue. So Eustochium became a cheerful, shortsighted bookworm, full of eccentric little habits that bothered no one. Since she was not destined for marriage it didn't matter that she was rather opinionated, that she got the slaves to do her sewing and mending in order to have more time for reading, that she read the pagan philosophers in books smuggled into the household under the loaves in the baskets brought in from the bakers, and that she wrote epic poems. People left her alone.

Paula had begun to be a little concerned about Blesilla. She began tentatively to suggest to her that she should not overdo it.

– You grieved too much when your husband died, she scolded her: and now you're punishing yourself too much. It's a form of pride to drive yourself to such extremes. Please, eat something. Have just a mouthful.

But Blesilla knew that food had teeth and could bite

her. Food was dangerous and fierce. In the garden of Eden the apple had jumped off the tree and leapt at Eve and forced itself down her throat. From that first sin had come all the ills of the world: suffering and death. The only way to conquer that inherited stain of original sin was not to eat.

The devil hid in food and tempted her. Food wanted to choke and throttle her, to swell her up and make her explode. Food mocked her. Food was disgusting, because eating it meant you then had to shit.

Blesilla girded herself for the fight. She was a warrior for Christ, wasn't she? Very well then. She would transcend her hunger. She would no longer feel it. She would train herself not to need food at all. That was her goal. Not to have to eat.

She began by further mortifying her appetite. As soon as she realised she enjoyed the taste of the salt she sprinkled on the bread she allowed herself every other day, she stopped eating salt. She only took stale bread now, preferably mouldy. There was a huge delight in feeling her appetite shrink as her body did, in tightening her belt another notch, week by week. There was a kind of voluptuousness of non-feeling in this, in discovering and mastering one weakness in herself after another. She invented further refinements of deprivation. Now she hardly drank anything at all. She swallowed a few drops of water just once a day.

She felt tight, like a twisted rope, very reined-in, very powerful, with cutting edges she was constantly drawing closer together. She held herself towards the world like a razor, a sharp wafer of purity. She lay on the ground like a dog, curled up, and would not speak. She gave that up too. Nor would she look at people when they came and knelt beside her. She pretended not to hear what they said.

Jerome said: don't overdo it, my dear.

Paula was frantic. She tried to tempt Blesilla to eat. She brought her trays piled with steaming dishes of delicious and fragrant food. But the smell of roast meat made Blesilla throw up. She turned her head away from bowls of grapes, plates of delicate pastries, the crystallised figs she had once loved. She shook her head at her mother as though Paula were trying to murder her. She shut her eyes against her, brought her knees up to her chin, and put her hands, blue bruised flowers of bone, over her face.

Eustochium shut herself in her room and studied furiously. Her sister was dying and it was her fault. She had preened herself on being a virgin, in a state of incorrupt purity. She had shown off. She had failed to understand what her sister was going through. She put her head down and howled onto her blotting-paper.

– This is all very edifying, my dear, Jerome said to the still, prostrate form at his feet: but you mustn't go too far. That would give scandal. We don't want people thinking Christians are extremists. We're still only a young church. We've got our reputation to think of.

Blesilla died without him noticing, while he was still talking.

She won. She proved her capacity to attain complete purity and complete peace of mind and complete absence of suffering.

Her body was as light as that of a small child. The woman she'd been had completely vanished.

At the funeral Paula wailed and tore her hair. She beat her fists against her head and ripped her cheeks with her finger-nails. People whispered that it just went to show that Christianity was a dangerous religion. Mothers shouldn't let their children get involved. These cults always meant trouble. Blesilla had gone way out of control, abandoning the duty she owed to society, her in-laws and the state. The finger of gossip and blame pointed at Jerome. His reputation as a spiritual director was severely damaged.

Jerome left on pilgrimage to the Holy Land. He hoped that things might die down during his absence. By the time he came back, the scandal and the accusations of impropriety would have been forgotten.

A year later Paula followed him. She was sterner than ever now, drier, bent, like a piece of old, well-seasoned wood. She had redoubled her own austerities as a way of asking God's pardon for neglecting her daughter and letting her die. All she desired now was to expiate her faults, see the Holy Places, and live like one of the venerable fathers in the desert. Eustochium also believed that it was her own fault that Blesilla had died. She accompanied Paula on her pilgrimage in order to share her life of penitence.

Paula's son was only five years old. On the quayside he wept and kicked in the arms of his older sister Rufina, who was crying as bitterly as he. The other sister, Paulina, stood next to them, weeping inconsolably. Both sisters were heav-ily pregnant. Their husbands hunched behind them, unable to offer any consolation for the departure of the two paragons of holiness.

Paula's heart was breaking at leaving her children behind, but she accepted her suffering and offered it up to God as proof that she wished to serve only Him. She was a stoic matron of Rome. She had mastered herself at last. She did not show the pain she felt, but turned away from the ship's rail and went below, followed by Eustochium.

Joining up with Jerome in Bethlehem, Paula founded and endowed a large double monastery, for both men and women, as was common in those days. She ruled over the women's half with compassionate strictness. She taught her young charges to fast.

– It's your souls I'm concerned about, she used to admonish them: not your stomachs!

Eustochium devoted herself to her mother, and never left her side, sharing her cell and trotting about after her all day long. When Paula died, she left Eustochium nothing whatsoever, as a lesson in holy poverty. She gave away all her remaining wealth to others. St Jerome inherited a large share of her money, which he used to finance a trip back to Italy.

Eustochium was left to run a large monastery on no income. Grumblings arose, as the monks and nuns became hungrier and hungrier week by week. Fasting was one thing, they complained: but starvation was quite another.

So Eustochium disbanded the monastery, and turfed out all the discontented inhabitants to fend for themselves. She sold the buildings at a small profit, paid off all her debts and disposed of all furniture and pots and pans, then packed a small rucksack and went off travelling and was never seen in those parts again.

Paula's tomb, just outside the monastery, in a small domed structure built of brick, remained a local shrine for many years, until it was looted by grave-robbers and the coffin opened, the contents tipped out and the bones scattered.

The story of
Josephine

Josephine wrote her first book under obedience to the Fathers, her confessors. It wasn't her idea but theirs. They set her to write it as a kind of test. She was in danger of being denounced as a heretic. She was known, in her early days as a nun, to experience raptures and visions, to claim, in her later ones, that her inspiration came directly from God. She did believe God was with her in her room when she wrote. She experienced God's presence as a powerful tingling across her shoulder blades, a shivering. She was touched by fear and bliss together, then God gave her a push and she jumped off the edge. This was the moment when she had to have faith, that the angel would bear her up on strong wings. Then she began to write.

Her confessors asked her certain crucial questions. The ones posed by the Inspectors to every suspected heretic. They ordered her to answer them. It was a written examination.

She wrote her book for them, in order not to be condemned as one of the Others, one of the Enlightened, or Illuminated, and burned at the stake. That was her likely fate at one point, in her early twenties. She wrote her *Life* for the Inspectors so that they could judge her.

The book came out of her. She and the book were the same flesh. She and the book could have been flung together onto the flames and consumed. Shrivelled to cinders, to black ash.

She escaped by not telling the truth. Not telling the whole truth. You could say she protected herself from accusations of heresy by lying and dissembling. By speaking the language they understood. Being careful to use the words they used, the concepts they were familiar with, that they had designed. She kept one step ahead of them in the game and did not let them suspect. The sentences she wrote knelt down. Her prose was modest, humble and grateful. It lowered its eyes and kissed the ground. She referred to herself as 'this unworthy woman', 'this great sinner', 'this woman, the worst of all'. The priests were used to women bowing and genuflecting in front of them, beating their breasts and apologising for presumption and uttering formulae of limitedness and humility. Josephine's self-abasement could have been read as boasts and irony and mockery but was not.

She succeeded in not being labelled a heretic. She escaped with her *Life*. The book was banned from circulation for a few years, while it was read by the committee of Inspectors, but then it was pronounced harmless, and allowed to be read, to be copied and sent round. It was declared quite suitable for girls and women. Appropriate to feminine minds.

Twenty years later Josephine decided to write another *Life*. As she had lived a secret life, so she would write one. This second book would be like the sister of the first, a younger sister kept shut up, about whom little or nothing is known. She does not appear in the biographies. Her absence is glossed over, no gap showing, no ripple to mark the trace of her passing. Her footsteps in the story are smoothed out and filled in. Yet all the time she's there, breathing quietly under the surface of the prose, poking her finger through from time to time, like a ghost longing to be let in. Because when you read Josephine's official *Life*, the one that saved her from being burned at the stake, if you read it very carefully, you start to get a smell, almost, of something awkward, something missing, a bulge under the graceful phrase here, a crack in the grammar there, one sentence that tails off and another that hastily starts, something left out, shouting from the margins, in the gaps in between.

The second *Life* was written between the lines of the first. Josephine wrote it for her niece Isabel, in case it might be useful to her. She bequeathed Isabel the book, though it took the girl some time to discover its hiding-place.

She wrote it at night, sitting on the floor of her cell, near the window, resting a small square of paper on the bread-board, borrowed from the kitchen, leant against her raised knees. It was a good desk, the breadboard. She mixed and minced words on it, patted them into the shapes of story.

She wrote by lamplight. She put the oil-lamp on the low stone window-seat, so that the yellow glow just reached the page. Within the darkness of her cell the lamp built her a tiny radiant house. Inside which she dreamed, searched for words, waited with giant patience for the next phrase or sentence to arrive. These were the happiest moments in her life, when she dissolved and forgot herself completely, when inspiration seized her by the scruff of the neck, when currents of language poured through her, molten gold, when that feeling she called God, burned and shivered and danced up and down her spine.

When she was writing she felt completed, doing what she believed she was meant to do, and no one watching her, which made her very content. Her lap was filled with treasure and pearls. Words fell on her and fed her like manna.

She started the second book because of her new visions. In one, she was a worm, with a job to do. She spun silk sentences round and round to make a case of words. Inside the golden cocoon of writing she died. She died to her self, her old life, her former way of stringing sentences together. She dwindled down into darkness, knew nothing, was extinguished.

Then it seemed to her she was in her cell, watching the cocoon crack open. Out struggled a creature with great wet, dragging wings that were stuck together. It twitched and flared. Shook out flags of billowing colour, reared its head.

Josephine was as skimpy as a child, shrunk into the corner, in the angle of walls and floor. The butterfly enlarged itself, moment by moment. Elaborately whorled and scrolled edges to its wings, long fluted wing-tips, a black fur belly, long feelers. It crackled with energy. It wanted to fly. It reared and flapped above her. Josephine knew it was about to smother her, that she would suffocate in its embrace. Like the baldaquin above a bed, that ornate gathered ceiling of puckered and fringed cloth, falling on her face in the middle of the night so that she woke up screaming, convinced she was going to die. Not a nightmare but real. The great wings beating above her, the hot pulse of its desire, so close, the fireball eyes staring into hers.

The butterfly filled the tiny room. It trembled. It was ready. At last she realised it had come out of herself.

Before everything, God was. There was nothing and no one before him. God was a man. An invisible one. A spirit with no body, but male nonetheless. He walked in the darkness, so softly that you could not hear him open the door and pad over to the bed. He stood there, listening to your breathing, while you lay stock still, and you knew it was God.

Josephine's father Ferdinand made sure all his children knew their prayers exactly so that they could practise their faith properly and address God in the way that he had laid down through his son Jesus Christ.

– Show me you know the Our Father, Ferdinand said to Josephine one day.

His knees, rounded and bony under fine cloth, were level with her face. She stood in between his shoes, which captured her lovingly and held her. He was so enormous, so tall, like a ladder to paradise, that she hardly dared peep at him. He smelled of eau de cologne, lemony and sharp.

Underneath was his own smell, tobacco and sweat and wine, faint and warm.

The point was to have got the Our Father off by heart. Not to need a prompt. God had dictated this prayer and liked to hear it said off pat.

– Our Father who art in heaven.

She could not go on. He was not in heaven, was he? He was down here, seated in the big black wooden chair ornate as the bishop's throne her mother had shown her in church, large as the confessional into which her mother vanished while Josephine held her breath and longed for her return. Ferdinand towered over Josephine. His black sleeves stretched out on the carved arms of the chair. Pleats of thin lace flopped onto the backs of his brown hands.

– Blessed be thy name.

He frowned down at her. He clutched the curly claw edges of the chair arms with his ringed hands. The jewels stood up in their settings like raspberries and blackberries. Each jewel was clasped inside a little gold crown.

– Hallowed be thy name.

She had used the wrong word. Blessed was what you called Our Lady. Her mother stood behind her. She could feel her willing her to get it right.

– Thy will be done. The kingdom come.

– Sorry. Thy kingdom come. Thy will be done.

The kingdom was where the king lived. Josephine's father was the king of the country and of the house and of the family. Much of the time he was invisible, like God.

– Give us this day our daily bread.

– Um.

– Forgive us our trespasses as we forgive those that trespass against us and lead us not into temptation but deliver us from evil amen.

The great hands planted themselves under Josephine's arms, drew her up. She was whisked into the air then set upon her father's knee. He popped sweets between her lips. A crunch of aniseed. Liquorice encased in crackly sugar sent a flood of sweetness into her mouth. Her father's eyes were gleaming when she dared to look at him. His red mouth smiled inside his curled black beard. His face swooped over hers and he kissed her. She breathed in his lemon animal smell. She was triumphant. She had performed well and made him love her. Her mother stood patiently by, hands folded across her swollen belly, and watched. She was the audience now, with Ferdinand, for Josephine's acting of the plays and stories she made up, gestures, words and poses carefully selected to make her father laugh and applaud. She felt he egged her on to do anything she wanted, but at the same time she delighted in being able to give him the entertainments he thought were exactly right. Her talent, which she developed very young, was to understand how to please those who watched. She skipped and danced for her father and fed on his compliments, his pride in her artless coquetting, her instinctive grace, her innocent girlish tricks. She was his queen, he told her. She was his joy.

Josephine's mother Beatrice gave birth to fifteen children in twenty years and died of this. She shaped babies and turned them out, like chair-legs or spindles on a lathe. She seemed to be busy making copies of herself and Ferdinand, all of which were not bad, but none of which was perfect. She hadn't yet got it right. So she had another go. She produced baby after baby, as though one of them would, finally, be adjudged her masterpiece. Josephine could not understand why her father was not satisfied with her alone, given how much, he frequently told her, he adored her. She could not understand why Beatrice kept delivering babies to her husband as though they were loaves come piping hot from her oven and he the baker checking their quality.

Ferdinand was a man of strict chastity, Beatrice explained to Josephine. Once he had made her pregnant he left her alone and lived in continence. If she wanted caresses rather than babies she did not get them. Josephine did wonder whether her mother had time to know and love all fifteen children. Surely to some of those infants, ten of whom died before the age of reason, she must have felt indifferent?

Beatrice withdrew, in any case. The servants kept the children clean and fed, and Josephine, being the eldest girl, supervised the amusements of the younger ones. They all played in the garden and joined forces with the gang of cousins who lived next door. They flowed back and forth between the two houses via the gate in the wall. Josephine had more freedom than many girls did, for her mother thought she must be in good hands if she was with her cousins, and imagined that she spent most of her time looking after the little ones. In fact, Josephine left them by themselves as often as she dared in order to trot round after her cousin Magdalena and copy everything the latter did. Whatever Magdalena decided must be right, whether this was standing Josephine on the window-sill with her drawers down and her skirts over her head and inviting all the other children to come and have a good look, or making up long dreamy stories about the love affairs she would have. Josephine held her breath and felt bewildered at becoming an object in a secret exhibition, but she listened to the stories with shivers of feelings which had no name.

Beatrice went out only to attend Mass or visit relatives. She took the house with her when she left it. Battlements of black veils, a portcullis of cloaks. She swayed across the street on high wooden pattens, to keep her black velvet shoes out of the filth and mud, and entered a closed carriage. When she was at home, she confined herself to her room. She lounged on the floor on a tapestry-covered cushion and read historical novels. Trash, her husband called them. Foolish and impossible adventures. Silly tales for silly women about love and chivalry. Fantastical romances with happy endings about brave knights and exquisite ladies.

Beatrice had her own code of honour, like a brave knight. She never grumbled or complained about her life. She endured what she referred to as her trials in heroic silence, with a smooth brow and a smiling face. She wore her pain on the inside. She had no need of hair-shirts or spiked belts for mortifying herself. We may not be allowed to go to battle with the heathens and win glory that way, she used to tell Josephine: and we may not be allowed to voyage to the Far Country to convert the pagans to the One True Faith, but we

have plenty of battles to fight here at home, against self-love
and pride and needing to stand well with others.

Beatrice might have won those battles with herself she
chose to wage, but others, in which she was enlisted to fight
whether she liked it or not, she lost. She was always ill, either
pregnant and sick or recovering from labour and childbirth.
Bad news would make her feel even weaker. Terrible things
happened in the world outside the house, and when she
heard of them she would shudder, she would yelp with distress. She was a severe justice. She believed firmly in the
punishments meted out to wrong-doers and criminals. She
explained to Josephine many times about the tortures await-
ing the wicked in hell. When she was told about the heretics
called the Enlightened who were going about the city
preaching their false doctrines against the Church, she
turned pale and gasped: hanging is too good for them, they
must be burned.

As Josephine grew older, and learned to read, Beatrice
would let her daughter sit with her in her room. Here she
had an ebony chest, inlaid with ivory and fastened with brass
bands and brass clasps, in which she kept her books. The
lock and key were also of brass, polished to a sheeny gold.
The inside was lined with a thin layer of sandalwood, pale
and shining as brown silk, which kept out moths and other
insects. The contents were arranged in trays stacked one on
top of another. In the top tray Beatrice kept her prayerbook,
her books of devotion, and some collections of saints' lives.
Josephine had to read these over and over, until she knew
them almost by heart, for of course there were very few

religious books published in the vernacular. Most of them were written in Latin for priests to expound from. So Josephine read the stories of saints in *The Golden Legend* many times.

In the second tray of the chest Beatrice kept her copies of novels. Each one was wrapped in a silk scarf of a different colour. Red, blue or green. Josephine was allowed to read anything folded up in blue. The others were forbidden. The books smelled deliciously of sandalwood when you took them out. Parcels of words tied up in silk cloths and silk ribbons. She imagined words lingering in the chest's corners like husks of cardamom, gratings of nutmeg and mace. Words spilled like beads, that you could sift between your fingers. Words that stuck under your fingernails like tiny jewels and were scented and sharp.

When Beatrice left the house to go to church she took some of these novels with her, hidden inside her slashed and puffed damask sleeves. She had invisible pockets there, in which she kept her smelling-salts, rosary, and a few coins. She would greet her friends at the back of the church. They stood in a cluster near the marble shell of the holy water stoup, dipped their fingers in, dabbed dew on their foreheads and crossed themselves, then hid their hands inside their sleeves. Josephine watched their ducking, sliding glances, translated their whispers. It looked, if you happened to notice, as though they were getting out their prayer books because Mass was just about to begin, and showing them to each other, handling and admiring each other's missals, turning over the pages and pointing out the Gospel for the day.

So the transactions did not appear in the household accounts, as money spent on novels, and so Josephine's father did not know of them.

Reading made Josephine's insides turn over and over and brought juices surging into her mouth. She would burst out crying whenever she got to the end, whether this was happy or sad, because she had been thrown out of an enchanted world, the paper doors slamming shut behind her. She tried to read more slowly, to make the book last longer, but she was too greedy, that was a great part of the pleasure: reading as fast as you wanted and no one saying stop. If Beatrice noticed Josephine crying over a book, she would snatch it from her and send her off to bed. But she was usually so absorbed herself that she did not spot her daughter furtively wiping the tears from her eyes. She would be off in her own dream.

Books were their drugs, the magic carpets onto which they flung themselves in order to be borne away somewhere else, books lifted them up like powerful caressing hands and cradled them like mothers do, as though they were babies to be held and fed, they fell asleep, sated with reading, then woke again, into pages of words, unknown, beckoning, a new world, and started another book. All the books became one book, they streamed into each other, a channel of sparkling water which kept all of the garden green, in the midst of the encircling desert, and never ran dry.

The books were always there. Even when Josephine thought she'd finished them all, gobbled them all up, another would appear, mysteriously produced out of her mother's sleeve, then quickly tucked into the box and swaddled in coloured silk.

The room was warm. A fire crackled in the carved granite fireplace. A small brazier of glowing charcoal had been brought in to increase the heat, and onto this, from time to time, they would throw sprigs of dried lavender, for the pleasure of the pungent scent. Tapestries hung on the walls and helped muffle the draughts. Rugs covered the tiled floor. Close to the fire, Beatrice built a hill of cushions and bolsters, and here she lay with Josephine, reading. Josephine was close enough to hear her mother breathing. Beatrice smelled of lavender smoke and sweat and sandalwood. Josephine curled up nearby and sniffed her like spice.

Reading was her way into the world. It was how she imagined leaving home while she was still young. She tested out adventures through books only, for she knew nothing beyond the family, which was her house, enclosing her on four sides, the entire and only truth. White walls like sheets of paper, the rules of life written on them in invisible ink. Reading tore holes and slits in these paper walls and let her inspect another world.

She thought that books were true. The world they described was real. Men *were* perfect lovers. Their love *did* last for ever. She plunged into books to learn about this reality, to catch glimpses of it, while she waited impatiently for childhood to end and life to begin. Books were part of that marking time, for they let her forget that she existed, that she was flesh and blood bounded and finite, they let her float out of herself into a sort of golden cloud, spread, thinned, the book and the world were one and she was both and neither, she was not there, she was everywhere. If a log crashed in the grate and startled her into looking up she might find that a couple of hours had passed yet she had thought it a single second.

One evening, when Josephine's father was out, as usual, visiting friends, and she and her mother were reading, as usual, by the fire, Beatrice was called away to see to her youngest child who was teething and could not sleep. The nurse was in despair from the baby's grizzling and wailing, and implored her mistress to come. So Beatrice threw down her book, levered herself up from the floor, and went out. She was so pregnant that to balance herself she leaned backwards, and she walked with one hand on her waist.

Josephine finished her own book and wanted another. Beatrice did not return. So Josephine lifted out the tray of holy volumes from the chest and turned over the novels lying below it. There were several there wrapped in red silk that she thought she might dare to open and peep at. But suddenly the idea came to her to lift up the second tray and see what lay beneath that, if anything. Once or twice she had asked her mother what lay at the bottom of the chest, and Beatrice had replied: *nothing*. There is *nothing* down there.

The house was quiet. No one seemed to be coming. Josephine listened hard but all she could hear was the whisper and tinkle of the fire falling lower. She lifted out the tray of novels and set it on one side.

There were three books, each wrapped in yellow cloth embroidered with silver and gold thread, fastened up with a twisted silvery string, somewhat tarnished, that ended in a knot of tassels. She picked one up and tugged at the strings until they came loose, and unfolded the wrapper, which was so old that its creases were dark and cracked. Inside was a handwritten book, a thick scroll of paper wound onto a wooden stick. Like a rolling-pin, Josephine thought, but she had no time to examine it further for she heard a creak in the room above. She put everything back in a great hurry. When Beatrice came wearily into the room Josephine was banging at the crumbled ends of the logs with the poker, trying to arouse the twinkling mass of embers, like red stars, to throw up flames as well as sparks. Her face must have been red, for Beatrice gave her a sharp glance.

Her mother picked up *The Golden Legend*, and told Josephine to read a chapter aloud before bed. When Ferdinand came in, some minutes later, there they were, calm and dull, immersed in the life of a saint.

After that evening Beatrice kept the chest locked and took away the key.

Death was everywhere Josephine looked. A crucifix on the wall of every room reminded her of Christ's death on the cross. Her fault. Her sins nailed him up there. For this she deserved to burn in hell and probably would unless she kept a careful watch over herself every minute of the day. She hurt Christ twice: first, by being born at all, being born in a state of original sin and so forcing him to come down to earth and die painfully on the cross in order to save her, and secondly, she hurt him afresh by not being grateful enough.

She should have showed her gratitude by being good, but she did not. She quarrelled constantly with her younger sisters and brothers. She sulked when corrected. Sometimes she would lie on her bed weeping with hopeless rage.

Beatrice began slipping away into death when she was the same age as Christ. She was only thirty-three. Josephine was thirteen. She told herself that Beatrice was not really ill. She hid in her room. She began writing a novel, about knights performing marvellous feats of bravery in battles against the Faithless Ones. She showed bits of it to her cousin Magdalena, who was three years older than herself. Magdalena came increasingly to the house, and they grew very friendly.

Beatrice died. She was exhausted. She wore away, like cloth so thinned by use it can no longer be darned. She was a frayed hole. One day there was nothing there. She was gone.

The walls of the house collapsed. Whirlwinds and snow swept into the rooms. Ice piled up, blocking the doors and windows. Josephine was chilled and shivered. Her fur-lined cloak had been ripped off, and her skin too. She thought her entrails would fall out. How frail human beings were. Water and jelly and blood, cracked bones. She hardened her heart as fast as she could, tried to rebuild her walls, to clasp the roof like a hat, to gather her bedroom about her like a skirt. Inside she was very shaky. But she would not let anyone see. People were ghouls, peering at her sorrow, twisting knives of sympathy in her wounds. She retreated. She denied feeling anything. She stayed on the edges of family gatherings and spoke as little as possible. Chin in air.

Around herself she built armour. For skin she had a casing of metal. It held her in. Stopped her from spilling out. She brandished a shield and a lance. People shook their heads over how hard she had become. Only Magdalena understood, and talked to the real Josephine, not the metal one.

Magdalena had just become engaged. Josephine asked her why she wanted to get married, and her cousin shrugged and smiled. It was either that or become a nun. Can you see me as a nun? Magdalena asked. Josephine said: but marriage, that's the end, isn't it? You'll have to obey your husband all the time, sympathise with him all the time. Magdalena winked: oh, I'll find ways round it.

They lounged on their cushions on the floor of Josephine's bedroom, talking for hour after hour about whatever subject they chose. Conversation with her cousin was one of the strongest pleasures Josephine had ever experienced. An intoxication like reading. After these hours of talking, they would get up, stretch, stroll about the room, do each other's hair, practise dance steps. One day they crept into Beatrice's room and went through her clothes, which were still there. Josephine discovered that her mother's dresses fitted her. The clothes were an emptiness she stepped into, and it made her uneasy. She thought she might never want to wear them.

Magdalena helped her off with the dress she had tried on. It was the one Beatrice had often worn when she went to church. It was all parts and layers, tied and hooked together. The skirt undid and came off in one piece of thick, rustling orange satin. Then the bodice, orange and black velvet stripes, lifted away. The black velvet sleeves, attached to the bodice by tiny silver hooks, were slashed, so that you could pull through the fine white under-sleeves, puff them out, and display them. As Magdalena unfastened the right sleeve and shook it out before folding it to put it away, something fell out, tinkled to the floor. The key of the book-chest.

The chest stood there in its old place, a small carpet thrown over it, half concealing it, so that it looked like a stool to sit on while you tended the fire. Inside, the books lay in their trays as before. The two girls touched them all, unwrapping them, turning them over, opening them, looking inside. The books in coats of green silk turned out to be treatises on gardening, how to grow all the different herbs and what they were used for. Those covered in red were not novels, either, but medical works, with drawings of the bones that make up the human skeleton, and drawings of the insides of the body, all the tissues and organs very precisely shown. There were drawings of foetuses in the womb, tightly curled up, with large heads and hands like stars. Josephine put the book with this drawing into her pocket, then showed Magdalena what lay at the bottom of the chest. She tossed all the books in a heap on the floor, and lifted out the yellow-wrapped scrolls.

Magdalena was still and silent, examining them. She said at last: I *think* I know what these are, but if I tell you, you must keep it a secret. If your father knew they were here, he would have to destroy them. Let me take them away when I go in the morning. I'll hide them for you in my house, and then they'll be safe. They could easily be found if you left them here.

Magdalena dropped them into the deep pocket, like a bag, that hung on the inside of her sleeveless coat. She took two of the books on gardening as well. Josephine borrowed two of her mother's nightgowns for them to wear in bed that night, as a treat, and they went out of the room.

Magdalena often stayed the night. It meant they could go on talking as late as they chose, without anyone paying any attention. The nurse was too busy seeing to the younger children to bother much about them. And when they heard Ferdinand come in, and come upstairs, they extinguished their candle and lay quiet as two deer in the forest when the hunters go by.

That night, after hearing her father safely ascended to his room and his doors clapped shut, Josephine got up and relit the candle. She stood the candlestick on a dish on a pillow, where it could not get knocked over and do damage. Each of them put on one of Beatrice's nightgowns, carefully arranging the heavy falls of lace at neck and wrists. They pulled the bed curtains around them, so that they were in a warm tent of red hangings, and sat cross-legged, one at each end of the bed. They feasted on the sherry and sweets they had smuggled upstairs earlier. They got tipsy and forgot to keep their voices lowered, which was why they were so quickly discovered. Magdalena always made Josephine laugh so much that she was past caring whether the nurse stood outside eavesdropping or not.

They were looking at the book in the red silk jacket,

examining the picture of the woman with the foetus inside her. At the same time Magdalena was telling Josephine what she imagined might happen on her wedding night. She was describing that encounter while Josephine acted as the illustration to her words, gesturing with her hands and screwing up her face into an expression of rapture and exclaiming in a high squeaky voice. She was being the bride, inviting her invisible husband to approach her, wriggling her shoulders and lying back, panting, the part of the drama she found easiest to invent and which she enjoyed so much she repeated it over and over again. So when Ferdinand twitched open the bed curtains he was greeted by his eldest daughter lolling lasciviously on her pillows and summoning him with lewd gestures. She was wearing one of his wife's nightgowns and rolling her hips like a whore. She was drunk, half naked, and in possession of a filthy book. She was a wanton, like her wretched cousin. Her behaviour, in this private theatre behind the bedcurtains, shocked him so much that for some moments he could not speak.

Magdalena was bundled away, and Josephine forbidden ever to see her again. Ferdinand burned all of Beatrice's books that he could find, and the chest that had held them. He made Josephine feed the fire, handing the books to her one at a time. They took a long time to burn. Solid blocks of words, blackening, black, transformed into packets of feathery ash that finally fell apart, light black cinders, dancing black butterfly wings.

Josephine was despatched to boarding-school in a neighbouring city. A convent of nuns, very kind and very strict.

They had not heard of the scandal. Nobody had. It stayed a family secret, never mentioned by anyone. To the nuns it was routine that a young, motherless girl should be put into their care, to be supervised, controlled, chaperoned, and taught about God. Josephine stayed with them for three years.

The Life of Saint Petronilla

After the death, resurrection and ascension of Jesus, Saint Peter felt lonely and at a loss. So he used to invite the other apostles and disciples around of an evening, to reminisce about their days in the field with the Saviour, the miracles He had worked, the stories He had recounted, and the jokes He had told. Talking about old times cheered Peter up, and became the only thing that could console him for the absence of his Lord. He stepped up the number and frequency of his invitations, until his old friends were coming round to his house practically every night.

Saint Peter was of a naturally melancholy and tender-hearted disposition. After a few drinks and a few stories about the good old days of battling with the Pharisees and the moneylenders in the Temple and unbelievers in general, he would become so affected that he would start crying and find it hard to stop. He used up a great many handkerchiefs. Buckets of them, sopping and sodden with tears and snot, stood in the corner of every room.

Everywhere you went in the house you tripped over male guests chatting, telling jokes, shouting, interrupting each other, arguing about who had loved Jesus the most, going off on long impromptu monologues that had the others rolling on the floor and holding their sides in ecstasies of grief or mirth as the case might be, teasing one another, insulting one another, embracing one another drunkenly to vow eternal brotherhood, and swearing that only with each other could they find true friendship. At this point Peter would thump the table and call for more wine, which would be brought in by his daughter Petronilla.

In those days, men did not do housework, because they had more important things to be getting on with. It was one of Petronilla's jobs to collect up the buckets of her father's soaked handkerchiefs, boil, pound, rinse, wring, dry, and iron them every day. It was Petronilla who cleaned up in the morning after the late-night parties, who made up drunk and incapacitated guests a bed for the night and washed their sheets next day, who cooked the supper and provided trays of nibbles with the drinks.

– Such a good girl, my darling Petronilla, Saint Peter would say as she came in with another jug of wine or a bowl of olives: I don't know what I'd do without her.

And while Petronilla was in the room, all the apostles and disciples would be kind to her, enquiring courteously how she was and thanking her profusely for filling up their glasses and cooking them such delicious suppers, then after two minutes they would ignore her and start bantering merrily with each other again.

Petronilla furiously resented the way she was treated by her father and his friends, but, having been brought up to put the needs of others before her own, she seethed with anger only in private. She had no women friends she could grumble to, for she was so busy cooking and cleaning she rarely had time to leave the house. Other women in the village found her proud and touchy, preferring the company of men to their own, so they gave up trying to coax her out to women's get-togethers for a bit of a gossip and a laugh such as they themselves enjoyed. Having denied herself the opportunity to let off steam, and being incapable of standing up to her father, Petronilla fell ill of a fever. She kept to her bed, turned her face to the wall, moaned and trembled, and refused to speak.

When her father's friends arrived as usual that evening, they found a house overflowing with dirty crockery and glasses from the night before, tablecloths covered in crumbs and winestains, and nothing to eat or drink. The cupboard was bare, just as the house was in a mess, because no one had cleaned up and no one had been out to do the shopping. Buckets of wet, slimy handkerchiefs stood about because no one had been in to collect them up and take them away. Flies buzzed about. Ants ran across the floor.

The apostles and disciples were shocked. They felt acutely for Saint Peter having been let down so badly by his daughter. They felt sorry for him, and then cross and embarrassed at being sorry for the man who was now, after all, the head of the Church on earth. Sluttishness was not something they tolerated in their own wives and daughters. It indicated a failure of proper masculine authority and control. It was an affront to masculine dignity.

– You're the boss, old boy, they cried to Saint Peter: you can work a miracle if you want to. Go on, heal her, the little hussy.

– I'll leave her to suffer, thanks, Saint Peter retorted: she doesn't deserve to be cured. Let her stew in her own juice!

– Oho, mocked his friends: so you're not too sure of your powers, eh?

Two or three of them began to drift towards the door.

– Party's over, they grumbled: come on, chaps, let's go and find a drink somewhere else with someone who'll make us welcome!

Saint Peter panicked at the thought of all his friends leaving him amidst the domestic squalor, and never coming back. He could not bear the thought of staying alone, night after night, to weep for the days that were gone and would never return.

– I'll show you the power of the Lord! he bawled.

He ran from the room.

Five minutes he returned, holding his daughter by the hand. She was fully dressed, her face washed, her hair brushed, and her eyes demurely cast down as usual.

– There, boasted Saint Peter: is that a miracle or is that not!

Everyone applauded.

– Petronilla, commanded Saint Peter: clear up this mess,

fetch us something to drink and then make supper and hurry up about it.

— Yes, father, said Petronilla.

The apostles and disciples were highly amused.

— That's the way, they cried: show 'em who's boss! Poor old Petronilla, what a brute of a father, eh? Enough to make anyone ill!

And they rocked with laughter.

Petronilla piled the dirty glasses and crockery on a tray, whisked off the stained cloth, swept the floor, and removed the buckets of sodden handkerchiefs. She reappeared with a pitcher of wine and a plate of mixed hors d'oeuvres, and then vanished to prepare the supper. In no time at all she was back, bearing a huge platter of steaming fragrant couscous, scented with cardamom and coriander, topped with a rich sauce of kid stewed with tomatoes and garlic and onions and preserved lemons.

— Leave us now, darling, said her father: get an early night and catch up on your sleep. I don't want you getting ill again!

Petronilla blew her nose, smiled shyly, and departed.

The next morning she was ill again, and the next evening as before, her father had to go and perform a miracle to get her out of bed. Then, as before, she appeared before his friends, smiling and helpful, only too anxious to be the perfect unassuming hostess, to fill up their glasses and heap their plates high, before retiring and leaving them to their brilliant and sparkling conversation.

— Pretty girl, your daughter, said the apostles and disciples to Saint Peter: sweet face she's got, lovely girl isn't she, nice and quiet, lucky chap who gets her eh?

She had the trick of making each one feel, as she ran round the table with the salad bowl and the jug of vinaigrette, that he was the most intelligent and charming man in the world. She was a wonderful listener, for the two minutes that any of them cared to talk to her. She never spoke about herself, which they would have thought pushy and strident. They had no idea that her charm was the product of art, polished and practised. They believed her to be naturally simple, modest and delightful. They assumed that that was what women were like. At the same time they thought it a real shame that so few other women were as she was. A paragon. An example to her sex.

Her reputation for beauty, docility and housewifely excellence reached the ears of a local nobleman called Flaccus, who was looking for a wife. He approached Saint Peter and asked for his daughter's hand.

Petronilla, however, refused.

— I won't marry a pagan, she said: and in any case, I don't want to get married at all. I prefer to consecrate myself to God as a virgin. Men do not interest me. I prefer God.

The count came every day to court her. Petronilla took to her bed. She refused to speak, to eat or to drink. Very quickly she grew so thin that she was at the point of death.

— Make her well again, Flaccus begged Saint Peter: I've heard you can perform miracles, you can heal the sick, well, go on then, save your lovely little daughter from death, I implore you.

Saint Peter sighed.

– Very well then, he said: as a sign to a pagan of the power of the One True God I will perform a miracle and cure my daughter of her illness.

He stormed into Petronilla's bedroom. Flaccus followed him and hid just outside the door, so that he could see and hear what went on, for he was curious to know how the miracle was done.

Saint Peter stood over his cowering daughter and thundered at her.

"GET UP THIS MINUTE YOU LITTLE WHORE OR AS GOD IS MY WITNESS I WILL BEAT YOU SO HARD YOU WILL BE SORRY YOU WERE EVER BORN."

Petronilla got up and came out.

– All right, she said to Flaccus: I will marry you, but please go and find me some women who will accompany me to your house, for it is right and proper that I should not come to you alone.

Flaccus went off to the local village and collected together as many women as he could find. They were surprised to hear that Petronilla desired their company after all this time, for they were used to thinking of her as a man's woman, the sort who despised feminine interests and concerns, but because they were kindly women at heart they agreed to come and bear her company. In any case, they were so curious to find out what was going on that they found it impossible to stay away.

A large group of women therefore accompanied Petronilla to Flaccus' house, and set about with gusto preparing the wedding feast and party. This went on most of the night. The women sang, and played the guitar, and danced, and ate and drank, and Petronilla with them. Flaccus tried to keep up, but drank too much wine too quickly, and passed out, while the party went on all round him. Saint Peter had gone home early, depressed.

The party continued for a week, as was the custom. On the eighth day, Flaccus looked forward to life returning to normal, and to enjoying some peace and quiet alone with his wife. But to his dismay he found that his house remained full of women. They sat in the kitchen helping Petronilla prepare the dinner and chattering, they ran about helping with the housework, they lay on the roof drying their hair discussing childbirth and menstruation in such loud voices that he had immediately to go away again, they perched on the front step retailing the latest gossip from the village, they popped by at what seemed like all hours of the day or night to argue about religion and politics, they continually asked him searching questions about his most intimate feelings and experiences. He never saw his wife alone. She came to bed later than he did, and got up earlier.

In his desperation to be rid of these ubiquitous talkative women, he decided the only thing to do was to perform a miracle. He stalked into the kitchen one day, which was as usual full of steam and cooking smells and the cheerful, loud, gossipy presence of most of the women in the neighbourhood.

He could not get very far into the room, since it was so full of women, but he stood in the doorway and thundered, just as he had heard Saint Peter do.

"GET OUT OF MY HOUSE THIS MINUTE YOU WHORES OR AS THE GODS ARE MY WITNESSES I WILL HAVE YOU BEATEN SO HARD YOU WILL BE SORRY YOU WERE EVER BORN."

The women picked up their things and ran off. They vanished down the road, in the twinkling of an eye.

Flaccus strolled into the beautifully clean and neat dining-room and lay down on the couch reserved for the master of the house. He clapped his hands.

– Petronilla darling, he called: bring in some wine and hors d'oeuvres will you, and then see about making us some supper? And then who knows, if you're in luck, if you play your cards right, later on I'll give you a fuck you won't forget in a hurry!

The house was completely silent, he realised, because it was completely empty.

Flaccus took to going round to Saint Peter's of an evening. The two of them would drink wine, and eat bread and olives, and Saint Peter would tell Flaccus all about the old times. He cried less these days, because there was no one around to wash his handkerchiefs.

Petronilla died many years later, of old age, and her body was buried very neatly and tidily by her friends, as she would have wished.

THE STORY OF
JOSEPHINE

Josephine's one desire was to bury herself. To cover herself from head to toe in a black cloth, like the pall cast over a coffin. Never to speak. Sunlight hurt her, like people's eyes scraping at her skin. Her father's eyes branded her with red weals of shame. She hid from the sun. But her father's eyes were like those of God and could pierce the darkness in which she lived. He came to visit her on Sundays and spoke to her politely and kindly. He gave her the family news. She shrank away from him. She was not interested in his plans for her two sisters' possible marriages, her brothers' wishes to travel to the Far Country and make their fortunes there. She was a diseased lump of flesh which had been cut out of the body of the family and cast aside. She had no place in talk of the future. The only future that was real was the life after death. She would fry in the flames of hell for all eternity. She would be cooked alive, like the heretics who were burned in the water meadows outside the city walls, on the feast-day of Corpus Christi every June. Screams exploded from the heretics and filled the sky and forced themselves down your throat along with the smoke and the stench of roast human meat, but at least they died after a bit. In hell you did not die but went on suffering agony. She could not really imagine it, though she tried to. Her thoughts worried away at the pain. The heretics' shrieks were induced by torment and terror. They wanted to die. They embraced the fire, crying to it to be quick. They clutched it to themselves and used voices they had not used before, not even when under questioning by the Inspectors. The sounds were of surprise at fresh torture, at the intensity of the fire. The sounds they made were of dying and of longing to die so that the pain might stop. In hell it would go on and on. The remains of the heretics were buried in a mass grave within a loop of the river. But in hell you could not die.

She decided she would have to become a nun. To guard her soul from the waiting fiery pit she would have to spend her entire life in penance and mortification. It would be a kind of holding her breath, lest even by breathing she did something wicked. Damaged the air, stole goodness from it and gave back only poison. Corrupted others, by her existence. Her sin would have killed her mother if she'd been alive. It was better to put an end to herself, and so to have done with sinning. She would have to be crushed, like apples in a press. The only way to annihilate her evil self was to enter the convent.

Ferdinand had begun looking around for a suitable match for his beloved daughter. Someone of good family in the city, of pure blood of course, untainted by the tiniest trace of Faithlessness. The Faithless Ones had been either slaughtered or driven out and dispossessed, but it was suspected that some had survived, disguised as proper Catholics. If discovered, they were denounced, fined, and whipped through the city wearing yellow paper robes and caps. Ferdinand did not want such a one for a son-in-law. Like other Catholic fathers, he studied the family trees of his daughters' prospective suitors with fastidious care. Bad blood was a pollution. Only true Catholics were pure and therefore worthy of bedding his child. The idea of Josephine in the arms of a Faithless One made Ferdinand sick with disgust.

Josephine, learning of these plans for her future, left Ferdinand's house for good one morning in late December in her sixteenth year. She stole away like a thief, in secret, very early, before anyone else was up to see her go and ran to her father to tell tales.

The air smelled of frost. It was still dark. Her destination lay a little way outside the city walls, on the far side of the river, about a mile from the place where the heretics were burned and buried. Josephine walked to it by a roundabout route, to give herself the pleasure of following the course of the river as long as possible. In the open, it was wide and fast-flowing. Further inside the city, it became deeper, narrower. It ran between the backs of houses, under the frilled parapets of stone bridges. It lapped basement walls and vanished altogether for yards at a time in impenetrable tunnels. It spouted

out in pools and fountains in small piazzas and made a loop
around the little hill, almost an island, on which the cathedral was built. All over town you could hear the cathedral
bells very clearly, their unmusical clanging which Josephine
loved because it was the sound of her earliest memories,
lying in her cot and hearing the bells bang on the morning
air while she spread open her hands and caught palmfuls of
warmth.

She came, finally, to the arching stone bridge she had to
cross to get to the convent of the Incarnation, where she had
arranged to arrive at eight o'clock. The charm of standing on
the humped curve, the very centre of the bridge, was that
from here you could see the backs of things. She dawdled,
leaning her elbows on the cold stone balustrade, hands
folded under her chin, looking both ways, upstream then
down. Behind her now were the huddles of old houses leaning together above the dark water. Wind ruffled the top of
the river. Ducks squawked. A heron alighted on a boulder in
midstream. Turning, she watched lights come on in kitchens,
as casements slapped back. Greyness sharpened into oblongs
of gold. A hand set down a dish. She peered higher up, into
first storey rooms. Shutters opened, as though by themselves.
They creased and concertinaed. They folded back neatly out
of the way, like wings of hair being tidied on either side of a
face. Fingers tugged a catch, pushed the window open. She
saw the end of a bed, the brown frame, its curtains twisted
into a knot, a heap of billowy quilts. A man's torso, wrapped
in a blue gown. He was yawning. A woman in a white nightdress carried the quilts like a bundle of clouds in front of her

and threw them across the window-sill. They hung off it, drooping down like flags draped for a procession. Then the man and the woman vanished. Another door, lower down, opened a crack, and cats ran yowling.

Josephine shivered. She wanted breakfast. Dawn light crept over the river, silvery, severe. The breeze touched her cheeks with cold. She gripped the sides of her fur-lined cloak and wrapped it as tightly as she could about her body. She glanced down at her shoes. High-heeled, with pointed toes, most incongruous for this long walk through the city, but she had wanted to wear her favourite clothes. She turned and faced the river. She tipped into it her invisible sack of hot, troubling, spiked feelings. She weighed them in her hands then dropped them into the swirling waters below. Then she walked to the other side of the bridge. Ten minutes later she pulled at the iron bell-rope which hung by the convent's door. Behind her, in the depths of the city, the cathedral bells sounded their loud iron music. Eight o'clock. The big door swung open and she went in.

Josephine stayed here for the next twenty years. Like her childhood all over again. She was waiting for something to happen. While she waited she got to know the people and the place.

The site, here among the water meadows, was fertile and green, edged by willow trees on two sides. The convent buildings were ringed by orchards. Plantations of apricots, quinces, apples, plums and cherries. Vines flopped on wires trained against the garden walls. Vegetable plots patched the ground between the trees. Much of this produce was sold in the town markets, to bring in some income to the nuns. The poorer ones, with no dowries, existed on charity. Their porridge had to be got for them somehow.

Sandy paths ran round the gardens and linked them one to another. Here the young nuns walked on summer evenings, chattering to each other in the half hour allotted for useful recreation. They fetched earthenware pitchers of water from the well and tipped these over the plants. Josephine, in her early days, studied the orderly rows of courgettes and tomatoes and broad beans. She was supposed to become as obedient as they. Fruitful and neat. Keeping just the right distance from her companions. All weeds to be plucked out. She told herself: with the help of God's grace I can do it.

The convent itself was an old country house, formerly part of an estate that had been divided up and sold off. It was built around a courtyard, a two-storeyed structure thick-walled against winter frosts and summer heat. Visitors tugged the bell-pull at the gate, and were shown into the entrance hall, which was furnished with benches for them to sit on while they waited. The walls were hung with oil paintings on panels depicting the passion and death of Christ. The small square windows were covered with ornamental grilles. Carved chests, their lids open for the reception of gifts, stood near the door. A wrought-iron partition on one side gave on to the ante-room connected to the kitchens. You could buy cakes here, the nuns' speciality, a kind of golden macaroon shaped like a breast with a sugar nipple on top.

A corridor led out of the hall the other way towards the parlours. To Josephine these were only half-rooms, not real rooms at all. They opened directly off the red-tiled corridor, cramped cubicles with only three walls. A grille of black iron divided them in two. The nun entered from behind the grille and sat facing her visitor, placed on the opposite side. The visitor sat half in the corridor and half out. In winter small braziers of live coals were carried in to battle the draughts. Or you anticipated them and came wrapped in furs. In summer you sat in cool, welcome dimness, away from the scorching brightness of the sunlight outside.

The grille was not an imprisoning barrier. It was a symbol of the nun's choice to retire from the world and serve only God. Your hand could easily slip through its meshes to touch the cheek of a baby brought for your blessing or the fingers of a friend. The whole of your face could be viewed in one of its apertures, elegantly framed in twists of black metal. Sweets and pastries could be passed through, glasses of wine, cups of chocolate. When you leaned forwards you felt the coldness and hardness of the iron struts against your forehead and nose.

Her father's visits were like blows hammering the grille. He sat and wept, because his adored daughter was lost to him, or he ranted because she had entered without consulting him.

– I thought you loved me, he cried: you cold, hard-hearted girl. Is this how you repay me!

Josephine clasped the bars that separated them. She caressed them. She curled her fingers round them, testing their firmness.

Eventually her father accepted that her decision was irrevocable. He signed the necessary papers, and offered her a dowry. Josephine refused the money. The prioress forced her to accept it.

– I can't afford to take in any more poverty-stricken nuns, she scolded the new recruit: if you want to live here, you must be provided for.

Josephine knelt in front of her father. He put his hand through the grille and she kissed it in token of her filial gratitude. That was the last time they ever touched each other.

After that, when he came to see her, he talked to her of the love of God and reproached her only with his eyes. Josephine clamped a lid on anything truthful she might have said. She murmured pretty nothings and could see how much she bored him. Her hands flew up and down in her lap. She giggled and simpered and prattled like the child of ten she had once been. Any other words she might have spoken shrivelled up. They withered up and died.

She drove him away. He came to see her less often, hurt and puzzled by her silliness which put such a distance between them. He left her alone. He sent her curt messages about the health of her sisters and brothers, the progress of his business affairs, the birth of children to distant cousins. Josephine rarely wrote back because she had nothing to say.

A summons to chat to a visitor in the parlour might come at any time, but in between these disturbances Josephine found, at first, that she was at peace.

Her favourite place was the courtyard, which had been

turned into a cloister when the house was converted into a convent for nuns. A vaulted stone arcade, open on the inner side, surrounded a small garden divided into four squares, with a well in the centre, tied together by gravel paths edged with low hedges of box. Inside these four pockets of garden grew four bay trees. Around the well, pots of flowers clustered together, flanked by stone tubs of clipped privet. It was a place to walk and day-dream, taking pleasure in the strong sweet smell of box, the clash of vivid green and dusty green, the redness of the terracotta pots against the sharp grey and blue of the gravel. Sun and shadow, darkness and light. The rasp of crickets and the cooing of pigeons and the creak of the winch handle when Josephine helped the cook wind up a bucket of cool water from the deep well. It was a place where you could be silent, sitting very still in the heat of the afternoon, unremarked by anyone, so quiet that the lizards darted close and ran over your feet.

Sometimes Josephine trudged back and forth watering the flowers. Sometimes she trimmed the hedges, enjoying the click click of the shears as sprigs fell away, snipped, from the long blades that opened and shut like a dancer's legs. Sometimes she got down on hands and knees to weed the gravel. Nobody bothered much about what she did, as long as she turned up in chapel on time and did not cause trouble. The rules summoned you this way and that, from bed to prayer to refectory to prayer again, but in between she found little parcels of minutes and seconds she took for herself, once she realised that no one noticed her love of reading and of solitude. She found hiding-places where for half an

hour at a time she could be by herself and think her own
thoughts, while the other nuns flew about together in little
flocks laughing and talking, very friendly and childlike and
gay. She lay in the long grass behind the beehives, or sat on
an upturned bucket in the woodshed, or behind the door in
the dairy.

Nobody minded her. She was just one nun among many.
She was supposed to conform, on the surface at least, and
what went on underneath was her own affair.

Certain rituals and gestures had to be learned. The
pattern-book of etiquette was exactly like that of the world
outside, complex and severe, perhaps even more so. You had
to bow low to the older nuns and stand back against the
walls when they went by. You had to address them in codes
of humility and pleading. And so on and so forth.

Really what it was all about, Josephine realised quite
quickly, was learning how to survive, with the least pain and
discomfort to yourself that you could manage, in a small
city of women. A good nun was a refined, courteous, ladylike
being, sweet, docile, meek and mild, and as such, no trouble
to anyone.

She did try to do more than simply tolerate the life. She
struggled for years to get the hang of how she was supposed
to become holy. She wanted to be holy. Also she did not. She
wanted her old self to die. Also she wanted to remain
Josephine.

She was supposed to become pliant, she could see that,
she was supposed to become unremarkably part of the community of nuns, a willow twig weaving itself into the massed

hurdle, osier compliantly becoming part of a basket. But Josephine was more like a whippy hawthorn branch a gardener tries to plait into a hedge. She kept flying up and snapping back. Scratching. The training process was for life. Until you had hardened into place and could not be prised loose without breaking. She was determined to stick it out. Fifty years of self-denial might save her from having to go to hell.

Some acts of mortification were easier than others. In this convent you had a choice. You could skate by on the easy route, depriving yourself of things you did not really care about while consoling yourself for the sadness of your life with all the little luxuries you could afford. A pierced metal box of hot bricks to support your feet in church in winter, a wool-stuffed hassock to kneel on, a copious supply of clean underclothes. Josephine compromised, like everyone else. Her education in childhood had taught her to forgo, in the interests of feminine deportment, the pleasures of running up and down stairs, shouting, putting her feet on the table, and so on. So she was already well practised in physical self-restraint. But she saw that her upbringing had similarly inculcated the need for privacy. Accordingly, she gave that up. Her father sent plenty of money for her keep, so that she could have afforded to live as the rich nuns did, in her own suite of rooms, with a servant to cook and clean for her. But she chose instead to live in the common dormitory, where night after night she lay sleepless, listening to sniffs, farts, snores, creaking beds, cries from the depths of nightmares. It was a penance she imposed on herself. Eventually, she got used to it, and learned to sleep through the racket which had ceased to bother her. So she felt it was not a penance any more at all. She discovered, instead, that daily life in the community was difficult enough. You did not need to add extra punishment.

It was the seemingly small things that bothered her the most. They caught on her skin and irritated her like splinters she could not dig out. She thought she had accepted obedience as a discipline necessary to organising a large group of people, but she resented not being able to choose what time to go to bed, or what kind of recreation to enjoy. She continued to mind acutely not being able to sit down and pick up a book whenever she wanted to. Her half-hours snatched for reading felt like deprivations rather than pleasures. Similarly, poverty she thought she could easily accept, as a form of freedom, a welcome lack of anxiety about material possessions, but poverty of the imagination she silently raged against. Even a poor person may possess two spoons, she thought, and have the small delight of choosing one over the other, each morning, to stir her coffee with. Josephine disliked being discouraged from exploring what she liked: this blue cup, with a wide frilled loop of handle, over that brown one, which is chipped.

— Exercising discrimination in this way, one of the older nuns said reproachfully to Josephine at breakfast one morning: noticing the cup you drink from and whether it pleases you or not, creates a barrier in you against God.

— Choosing this particular spoon, Josephine asked: because it is thin and long, with a nicely pointed shallow bowl, will put God off?

73

– Nothing created has any value, said the other nun: only God has value and he is a spirit.

This was the thinking among the poorer nuns, at least. The rich ones praised the virtue of holy poverty while enjoying dressing in lawn and silk, drinking chocolate poured from silver pots into silver bowls and whisked to a froth with whip-sticks carved from cherry and olive wood, and giving their leftover food to the little dogs they kept as pets. Josephine wondered: so which secret artist made the cloister garden and how did that person get away with having created beauty? The answer, she discovered, was that the garden was permissible because it linked the chapel to the house, and was a symbol of the power and artistry of the Creator. Similarly, the quantities of gold and silver used to dress the chapel were a measure of the nuns' wish to honour God. The more gilding and draperies, the better. The more hours they put in making lace to edge the altar-cloths, the worthier of God they showed themselves.

Chastity was the one vow Josephine had no trouble with. She felt she was giving up nothing in not having children. When she tried to think about why, a smothering darkness descended, a cloud in which she hid. She shrugged, and stopped wondering about it. She had plenty of outlets for her affections. She sang and danced for her companions at recreation, made up stories for them, wrote charming little verses to celebrate their feast-days. She was much in demand for impromptu evening entertainments, and this suited her. Sister Maria and her other new friends needed her. Therefore they must love her.

Every month, like all the others, or more frequently if she felt the need, she had to make her confession. The confessional was the ear of God, silted up with the knowledge of human weakness, clotted with the wax of human disgrace. You whispered your faults into this ear, and begged for forgiveness. Back came the voice of God's representative, giving you absolution and penance. The confessional was at the back of the chapel, a bulge in the wall. You stooped to enter it, creeping through the tiny entrance, then closed the latch of the wooden door behind you. You hunched on a three-legged stool and leaned forwards, pressing your mouth close to the black mesh that separated you from Father Peter, the convent chaplain.

Month after month Josephine accused herself of spiritual laziness, of being lukewarm in the religious life, of not wholeheartedly living the Rule, of failing repeatedly to measure up to the ideal. She grew bored with this litany, which did not change, as she grew bored with Father Peter's advice, which, equally, never varied.

– Just be a good nun, he counselled her: just obey the Rule. That's all that God expects of you. He doesn't expect heroic deeds, my dear daughter.

– Why not? Josephine wanted to ask.

She thought she knew the answer. Heroic deeds might be more fun, and could be applauded by an audience, while the essence of her life here was concealment, obscurity, humility. It was what she had chosen, hadn't she? Therefore she shouldn't complain. She should not mind the smell of damp which oozed out of the stone wall at her side, Father Peter's sour breath. The martyrs, whose stories she had so admired as a child, had contended with different smells: the stink of lions released into the hot sun of the arena, the scent of fresh blood, of wounds and death. What was the smell of the executioner's axe, of vats of boiling oil? What was the smell of courage? All she knew was the smell of ennui.

Josephine had believed, when she entered, that she was performing an extraordinary act. Leaping into the unknown; giving herself totally to God and no one else; abandoning herself to God's love. She had committed herself, taken an irrevocable step. She had flung herself into the abyss. Yet she was finding, with a shock, that life in the convent was much like life at home, life at boarding school. Other people told you what to do and how to behave and your time was not your own. Her life here was not one of great and glorious adventure, of splendid renunciation. With pain she recognised its ordinariness and dullness, and with shame she acknowledged how bored she was.

One Saturday afternoon, some ten years after her entry into the religious life, she knelt as usual, after her confession, at the altar rails, reciting the decades of the rosary that Father Peter had given her to say as her penance. In her heart she shouted out to God: so where are you? Are you here at all? Am I looking for you in the wrong place?

In the middle of the following night she woke up to find a Presence standing next to her bed. He was waiting for her to notice him. He was attending her, still and patient, as though he would have stood there for ever without making a sound, until she deigned to wake up and notice him. His gentle arrival burned into her dreams and she tumbled out of them, back into the dormitory thick with snoring nuns. She opened her eyes to a blaze of light. He was the light. It was his radiance that had woken her, as though it were music, snow striking crystals. He stood inside a glory, a brilliance which came from him and composed him and spread out in dazzling rays. His face was tenderness itself. When he bent over her she was enveloped in his kindness and compassion. He was so beautiful that she hardly dared to look at him.

– Daughter, he commanded her: tell me who I am.

His tones were so soft, his smile so sweet, his eyes so full of love, that Josephine could not be afraid.

She said: your Majesty, you are the Lord Jesus Christ. Tell me what to do and how to serve you here in this place.

Then he took her in his arms, and laid her close to his heart, so that she thought she would faint for joy.

He said: you are my beloved daughter. Stay with me, daughter, don't leave me, stay with me for ever and be utterly mine.

After that he came to her nearly every night, visits which continued for several years, and which, when dutifully reported to Father Peter in the confessional, laid Josephine open to the accusation of lying, vanity, presumption, heresy, and spiritual pride.

Nothing Father Peter could say or do stopped the visions. Josephine was ordered to deluge the figure of Christ with holy water or to throw books at him, for he was most certainly the devil come to tempt her onto the dangerous path of thinking herself Illuminated and not in need of the wisdom of priests. She was ordered to turn away from him and shout 'Begone foul fiend'.

Christ laughed, and enveloped her in his light. He would not go away. He said to Josephine: you need a confessor who will understand you and be your friend. Ask the prioress to let you confess to someone else. It is your right to make that request, under the constitutions of the Order.

The prioress complied with Josephine's demand, as she was bound to do, even though she heartily disliked this departure from normal custom and routine. She distrusted Josephine as a trouble-maker and showed her a severe face.

– You need someone to take your soul in hand and curb your tendencies to self-indulgence, she remarked: I recommend you to consult Father Lucian. He has a reputation for being impossible to fool.

That was how Josephine came to meet Lucian, the man who would become her close friend and play such an important part in her life. She had already heard of him, of course. He was well known for his learning and had written several books much praised by other scholars. He lived with forty other monks in a monastery in town, and took his turn with them saying mass and preaching in the monastery church. He was familiar with the ways nuns sought to relieve the monotony of their humdrum existence. The swooning, the tears, the hysterical fits, the sighing and blushing, the girlish raptures in front of holy pictures, the visions, the excessive self-imposed penances to make themselves the object of others' admiration. None of them ever thought up anything new.

– I feel sorry for you, he said to Josephine on the first occasion of listening to her confession: your life here must be exceedingly dull. But at least you have an imagination and can use it to liven things up.

They embarked on a discussion of whether Josephine had seen Christ with the eyes of her intellect, the eyes of her soul, the eyes of her heart, or none of these. It was a kind of classification in which Lucian was expert, and it kept them going for quite some time.

THE LIFE OF SAINT
THECLA

Thecla began a love affair with Thamyris. He was unhappily married to a woman who was so beautiful that she spent most of her time caring for her beauty so that it should never fade. She disliked sex, Thamyris said, because it was messy and sticky and made her sweat and go red in the face. As soon as lovemaking was over, he said, she leapt up and washed herself. Nor did she want babies, because these would ruin her figure. Each time she suspected she was pregnant she drank perfume to make herself miscarry. He knew this because the slaves who tended her spied on her and told him.

He had married his wife because she was so beautiful. All the men in the city had wanted to possess her, but he was young and handsome and well born and so he won her. At parties he watched other men admiring her still, exquisite face, her high round breasts and narrow waist, her swishing, imperious walk, her black silk hair.

Thecla also watched Thamyris' wife, and recognised the power of her pure beauty, which made you want to kneel in front of her and pay homage as though she were a goddess, far removed from ordinary women. Thecla was able to persuade herself that Thamyris' wife did not care about her husband having an affair. If she didn't want him in bed herself she could hardly complain that he went elsewhere.

When she was honest with herself, which happened extremely rarely, Thecla admitted that there was a pleasure to be had in taking a married man from his beautiful wife. This remained a secret, shameful joy, which she confessed to no one.

Another source of delight was the discretion that was expected of Thamyris, who held a government post. Thecla, who worked as a scribe in the governor's legal department, recording the progress of lawsuits, dropped her eyes when Thamyris walked past her department's doorway or came in on some pretext. She tried to be as cool and indifferent as a stone in a pond. But she could not stop herself from shivering with delight, blushing, and breaking out into perspiration. She would bend over her work at these moments and hope no one noticed. Thamyris, to prolong their game, would come up to her and address her. He would ask the meaning of a particular legal term, in front of the other scribes. She forced herself to seem composed, not to smile, to look at his feet and nowhere else.

They snatched time and places for making love which

heightened the danger and the excitement. On the beach at night, in the archive of the government palace, in an anteroom at an official reception in Thamyris' own house while his wife was out visiting friends. Thecla lay in her rival's bed and triumphed. She had broken in, like a burglar. She was an interloper in the other's place, in this silk tent they drew around themselves to increase their intimacy and from which they shut out the rest of the world. The slaves were discreet, Thamyris explained, and loyal to him rather than to his wife because he treated them well, was kind to them, and never made unreasonable demands. Thecla understood that he had had many lovers. She was just the most recent in a long line. But she did not mind. This meant she was free. She had walked in. She could walk out again, once she grew bored.

For the moment she was not bored. She revelled in the pleasure Thamyris gave her in bed. It was new to her. Her previous lovers had groaned over her, puffing and panting and labouring to make her come. Sex was a task they had to perform well, and if she, Thecla, did not also perform well, to prove what good lovers they were, then she had let them down. They required her orgasm as a trophy. They notched her up, as another success. Except that they could not, because Thecla could not come. This upset the men, who tended to give up after a few goes and try elsewhere. They told Thecla she had a problem and departed in a huff.

Thecla knew herself to be frigid. It was a terrible word, like a blow, like a vice clamping her limbs, she was trapped by the word, unable to move, it told her to give up wanting pleasure, all was hopeless, she was not a real woman, there was nothing that could be done. That is what frigid meant. Somehow or other the orgasm eluded her. She would feel excited, she would want to fuck, the man would enter her and pump away, and then her feelings would inexorably and gradually lessen, until finally she felt nothing at all, while above her the man panted and cried out and came and slumped down on top of her and fell asleep.

Thamyris told her that it was she, Thecla, whom he desired and loved. Thecla specifically and no one else. This was a new experience. To feel singled out and chosen, rather than to assume she was being fucked because she was available, because she would do, because one woman was much like another when all was said and done, particularly in these free and easy days when women behaved like men and took lovers openly and were not ashamed to admit they did so.

Thamyris was a skilful lover who wanted to please a woman and knew how to.

– Don't rush, he said to Thecla: let's take our time.

She found this frightening. A man wanting to linger, to stroke her all over, to spend time kissing and caressing. She still couldn't let herself come with him, though she did enjoy herself.

It was so hot. To lie naked on a wide low bed in a stolen afternoon in a hired room down a side alley, that was the only possible thing to do. Skin on skin, moist, the sweat slipping between them, smelling of the wine they had just drunk, his perfume of juniper berries, the odour of sex which rose up like steam from their tangled arms and legs.

They gave each other presents. Collars of white jasmine

fastened with tassels of orange silk. Slices of red watermelon
pocked with black pips, curved like a fleshy red grin. Sticks
of carnation-scented grease they rubbed over each other.
Alone together in their back-street room they could be naked
all the time. Thecla felt whole. Clothed in her skin. A complete being, rather than a hole men poked their cocks into.
She preened and strutted for Thamyris, she lay on the bed in
poses both comic and erotic, displaying herself and laughing
at the same time, she strolled about munching mango or
papaya waiting for him to come and lick the juices off. He
padded about, and she watched him. She knew him all over,
as though they wore each other like coats, they could nuzzle
and tease, they could be fierce and bite, often they lay head
to tail sucking each other.

Thamyris stroked her cunt with gentle and expert fingers.
They lay on their sides to fuck, so that he could go on
touching her as he moved in and out, and it was this com-
bination that finally made her come, the fact that she was
lying in his marital bed with him, the fact that he made love
to her with cock and fingers together, touching her exactly
as she wanted to be touched, the fact that he took his time
and waited for her, the fact that he kept to a steady rhythm
so that she could relax. It was rather like a baby might feel,
she thought, being swung and cradled and rocked and fed
and knowing that the arms that held you would not let you
fall.

He made her laugh when he told her that in order to stop
himself coming too quickly he thought about doing his
accounts, or calculating his tax debts, or watching gymnastics

in the public stadium. He did this for Thecla. He concentrated on her pleasure. He gave to her steadily and without
stinting. And she let him, she felt that this eager, skilled lovemaking was indeed for her, his gift to her, and she took it.
She luxuriated in it.

It became so easy to come with him that she even grew a
little bored, lying in bed making love with the certainty of
coming, so comfortable, then they would turn over and sleep
a little on the hot sheets they threw off because only nakedness was supportable. And sometimes Thamyris was bored
too, so they tried new positions. Lying half off the bed upside
down twisted about rocking and levering and pulling.

She was content to go on like that for ever. To be the
mistress was enthralling, because it was forbidden, because
there was the danger of being found out, because it was not
supposed to last but did, because she could see Thamyris
only at specific times when he could get away from his work
or his wife to be with her and so she could live the rest of her
life for herself. She could see her friends, read, go dancing, sit
up late talking. It suited her that he could not make too
many demands on her. She remained free. She could be off
at a moment's notice.

People noted the change in her. She paraded her new
sense of herself. In her lunch hour she strolled in the ministry
gardens wearing a short, sleeveless red linen dress and high
heeled shoes, scarlet lipstick on her full, wide mouth. She
swung her hips to bed music as she walked and the little boys
whistled after her. Her colleagues in the office nodded at
one another.

From time to time Thamyris muttered about marriage.
Thecla felt panic-stricken. She laughed at him.

– I'm not going to be a *wife*.

What she was going to be was a poet. In her free time she
had begun writing poems. She worked on them in the early
mornings, when it was cool, before it was time to jump into
a rickshaw and go to work. She showed the poems to
Thamyris one day. He read them. He smiled and shrugged.

– Much too complicated and difficult, darling. That's not
real poetry. Women aren't born to be poets, love. They're
born to be mothers.

Thecla showed him no more poems, but she went on
writing them. Thamyris was more tender to her than ever.

– You'll look so beautiful when you're pregnant, he
murmured to her one hot afternoon.

She pushed him away and got off the bed.

– I'm not going to have children. Never never never.

He came after her.

– Marry me. I'll get a divorce, then we could get married.
We could have a family.

She ran down the outside staircase into the hot street,
buried herself amidst the fruit stalls, banana fritter vendors,
shoe shine boys, dissolved into the thronging crowds, the
dust underfoot, the shimmering sweat that outlined the
bodies pressing against hers, the stripes of neon light blinking
above the open fronted shops. A barrel organ played. Cars
hooted continually. It calmed and soothed her nerves to be
here. She roamed the alleyways of the market area all afternoon. She bought herself a new pink silk vest and a flowered

gold and pink sarong. She went to have her hair washed, her toenails painted.

A crowd had gathered around a preacher on a soap box. As they listened they ate peanuts and threw the shells onto the ground where dogs crunched them underfoot. Thecla drew near and hovered in a doorway.

The preacher was a short sturdy man with dark hair, small burning eyes, and an arrogant manner. He spoke with passion about nothing that Thecla could understand, except that it concerned a new God not like the old gods she had grown up with. She began to grow bored and would have begun to drift away from the fringes of the crowd where she stood except that she noticed that she had caught the preacher's eye. She pretended not to have noticed, while lifting her chin and turning aside a little so that he could admire the line of her throat and her profile. She saw the preacher's wife watching her too, a plump woman standing meekly behind the soap-box looking bewildered at the noisy jostling crowd.

The oration was over. The preacher's wife pushed through the departing people holding a little bag and begging for money. Thecla stared at the little dark man who balanced on his toes in front of her, a compact coiled-up bunch of energy. He was like a clenched fist.

— I am Paul, he told her: you are in need of salvation and I have come to teach you how to find it. Listen to my words, be converted, see the light, and you have a chance of being saved.

— I'd like to learn more, Thecla said since there are some

points in what you were saying just now that I don't understand at all.

She was looking at the curly black hairs on his brown forearms, the shape of his lean body under his workman's clothes. The preacher's wife was making her way back towards them.

– We can't talk here, Paul said: why don't you meet me later, over there, and we'll talk more?

He jerked his bearded chin at the wine shop to one side of them, where the proprietor was lighting and hanging up the coloured paper lanterns that advertised his trade.

Late at night it was still very hot. Sweat made you feel close to the person you sat and sweated with. The sanded floor of the wine shop was littered with chicken bones, scrunched up pieces of tossed paper people had used to hold their chicken portions with, old cigarette butts. Music wailed from the radio. Somewhere behind them, past two or three rows of wooden houses, flowed the river, brown and wide and deep, stilted houses on its banks, past the warehouses stacked with tea and rolls of silk and barrels of spices it went, to the far away sea. The mosquitoes whined about their ears. Paul smoked cigarette after cigarette. They drank local whisky mixed with mineral water, they drank beer. Paul talked to Thecla about God. He moved from here on to telling her about his childhood. He made up the story of his life for her and gave it to her, a parcel of words he put in her lap. Thecla listened. She asked questions, she challenged him from time to time, she tossed her head and disagreed, she flattered him, with her bright eyes and amused look, her soft lips shaping themselves around a comment, her cocked head and alert flirtatious listening. He told her she was the most intelligent woman he had ever met. Astonishing in one so young. His wife, he conveyed, was loyal and devoted, but not an intellectual.

Strings of little twinkling coloured lights dipped and swayed on the open shopfronts across the unpaved street where men squatted smoking opium pipes, playing cards, tossing fortune sticks. Paul threw his last cigarette stub onto the ground.

– I've got some more cigarettes in my room, Thecla said: come with me and fetch them, if you like.

She waited. He got up.

– I must go, he said: my wife will be wondering where I am.

They stared at each other. Shadows moved on the shabby plastered wall beside them. A dog howled from a nearby shack. Paul's eyes were dark as the river, glittering.

Every day after that she went to hear him preach in different parts of the city. He spoke with such authority, such certainty, such passion and such complexity that she was captured. She gave way, she bowed down before him, she was completely taken in by his arguments – except his opinions of women. Women played no part in his scheme of revolutionary religion. They were followers of holy male leaders and that was that.

At night Thecla met Paul in bars and they talked and fought. Tipsy on whisky they tried to convert each other. She preached women's need to struggle for their freedom. He preached male reason and rationality and thought. Women, he thought, were soft, easily damaged, prone to neurosis and hysteria, over-emotional. They were, he suggested with glinting eyes, sexually rapacious, all-devouring.

Battle was joined. On Paul's terms. Thecla proved to him that she was not like other women. She was better than they were, she was as good as any man, and she was also, wasn't she, desirable and sexy and beautiful. How could he resist her?

His wife was meek and fair haired, as soft and plump as a pudding. Thecla was kind to her when they met, in order to hide what she was up to, what quarry she stalked. Paul's wife smelled of vanilla. Her round face was gentle and unlined. She wore long gathered skirts in pale yellow and pale blue, she wore cheesecloth blouses with crocheted yokes that curved over her full bosom. Thecla was sharp and angular with long arms and legs. She wore tiny mini dresses to show off her figure, and she had a habit of lying on the floor, when the three of them occasionally had supper together, with arched hips and thighs elegantly crossed. She was stupid. She believed she was invincible. She was hunting Paul and she believed she had every right to do so. For his wife she felt such envy she could hardly bear to face it. She wished to be cruel to her, as though the other had somehow hurt and damaged her. Some deep womanly qualities she must have, if Paul had once loved and married her. Very well then, Thecla would prove herself once and for all the better woman of the two. No mercy towards a rival.

Paul was the master. Her master. On her knees before him she fought with him and flaunted herself, she ran between the poles of his carriage, he jerked on her reins, she curvetted and pranced. She spoke his language. When she continued to insist that women were equal to men in every way she heard her voice go up into a register of screeches, of eldritch howling, of such terror of madness, of such foreboding, of such red ballooning rage, that she stopped short, gulped down her whisky, hastened further towards tipsiness.

Thamyris returned from a trip away and found Thecla distant, irritable. His caresses felt all wrong. She thought about his wife, who was ill with some nameless complaint, and listened to Thamyris proposing marriage to her again. Unease rose up in her throat, sharp and sour bile.

She suggested that they separate for a time, so that she could think seriously about his offer of marriage.

He had brought back presents for her. A necklace of coral, a tortoiseshell comb, a mirror framed in tiny pearly shells. He was so pleased with his thoughtfulness, so eager for her to like his presents and praise him for his sensitivity, that she wanted to yell at him. She drew sharply on her cigarette, wrapped her arm across her waist. When he had gone she swept the presents into an old cardboard shoebox and put it under the bed, along with his love letters and all the dried flowers and trinkets he had given her over the past year. Then she prepared for Paul's visit.

She swept the floor. She drew down the white linen blinds, lit the lamp in the corner, put clean sheets on the bed, shook up a heap of floor cushions, prepared an opium pipe. She lit joss sticks scented with cedar and pine. She lit white candles. On small bamboo trays she laid out pickles, salted almonds, slices of fried mango. She cooked a fish curry flavoured with lemon grass and coriander, spiked with chilli and ginger, soothed with coconut milk, and set it aside for later reheating. She put out bottles of beer, a bottle of whisky, packets of cigarettes. She stood in her big copper basin to wash herself, tipping scoops of water over her head. Then she put on her pink silk vest, her pink and gold sarong, made up her eyes, dabbed citronella along the window-sills to discourage the mosquitoes and sat down to wait.

Thamyris had taught her not to rush, how to linger. And so, when Paul arrived, she took her time. She did not want to frighten him away.

They talked for several hours, lounging on the straw mats on the clean, cool floor. Drinking and smoking, nibbling the salty nuts and bits, drinking some more. They ate the fish curry, served on leaves, and the prawns Paul brought with him, so hot with chilli you blinked and sweated as you bit into them. They ate tiny fish cakes from the street stall just outside, dunked into vinegary sauce and tasting both sweet and sour, they ate deep fried bean curd. They ate mangoes. Thecla ate hers with her fingers, for the pleasure of licking them afterwards while Paul watched. They smoked a pipe of opium together.

– Of course, he reproved her: to a revolutionary intellectual, food is not important.

She lay on the floor at his feet, propped on one elbow. They drank more beer and whisky. Eventually Thecla got up and danced. It was the only language she had to tell him how much she wanted him. Words meant the dialectic, the discussion of God and politics. They could not be used to admit desire. He was the one in authority, the man with power, and he would not have permitted it. He frowned upon it. But he could not stop Thecla dancing. Slowly and dreamily to the sway of the opium inside her.

Then they were on the bed together, clothes thrown off and flung to the floor, Paul was on top of her looking down at her while she looked back at him. They did not speak. She rushed towards him, no taking her time, no long caressing, no chosen position or careful technique, and she came as she didn't know she could from the strength of looking into his eyes and desiring and fucking and being out of control.

She lay next to him exultant, joyful. He threw his arm across his face and muttered that it had all been a bit much.

Thecla took his hand. She told him she loved him, she wanted to be his companion, to travel and work with him, to care for him.

Paul smiled wearily. He kissed her, put his clothes back on, and departed.

The following evening, when they met in a café, he told Thecla that although his marriage had broken down irretrievably a long time ago, it was only now that he felt able to leave his wife. The woman he was planning to live with from now on was a disciple Thecla had not yet met. She was a very sweet, peaceful, feminine soul, Paul said, not strong and independent like Thecla. She needed a man to care for her and to protect her. She was tiny and physically fragile. Internally, she was so delicately made that it was easy to hurt her while making love, so that they had to be very cautious, very gentle. He cherished her. She was the woman he had chosen to be with.

Paul left the café. Thecla sat on. She felt she was a giantess ten foot tall. She must not move or she might break. She was gross and huge. She was aggressive and unlovable. She was an insatiable monster who terrified men and threatened to devour them. And she was very tiny at the same time, a flea squashed under Paul's foot, he was the voice of God thundering to his creature the universe, and she lay silent and speechless while he trampled on her. There was something terribly wrong with her but she didn't know what it was. Only he could tell her what it was because he knew everything and was all-powerful. But he could not tell her because he had gone away leaving her with nothing. He had removed himself. She was nothing.

Thamyris came to see her to try and persuade her to change her mind and marry him. Thecla frightened them both by standing in the corner and weeping in a terrified stammering way.

– I can't marry you, she repeated: I mustn't, I can't. I think I'm ill.

When he tried to take her hands she shouted at him.

– You're so hard and bitter, darling, he told her: you should let yourself have babies one day, it will mellow you.

He smiled at her tenderly, as a brother might, and went away.

Thecla fled that country. She escaped from its flat burning plains, its red and gold temples, its polished gods, its hot winds perfumed with ginger. She ran away leaving no address and seeking none. She wandered until her money gave out.

She was homeless. She was exhausted. On a harsh coastline jutting out like a lip, lonely and windswept, she found a cave. For the next twenty years it sheltered her. Icicles fringed the entrance, cold jagged teeth. The floor was of sand covered by ice, hard and ridged, scoured and swept by occasional winter high tides. Thecla slept on a rock. Snow drifted into the cave and carpeted the ice and made Thecla a white covering. She clung on, like a chilled limpet. She did not know what else to do.

She died in the ice of the cave, frozen solid inside it. The ice closed round her and held her bones.

THE STORY OF
JOSEPHINE

Christ not only visited Josephine nightly in her cell but gave her a child to love and bring up as her own. It was common practice, of course, for small girls to be raised in convents, but to Josephine the arrival of Isabel was a miracle.

In later life, Isabel could remember very little of her early childhood. Who was Isabel then? She didn't know. Someone fed and washed her. A pair of hands set her down on a dusty path, her fingers were raised and held, she tottered then walked. Her nose was level with flowers soft as skin. Sweet, strong perfume. Insects as big as boats that whirred and thrummed. Brilliant colours hot as sunshine. She learned the names: pink, orange, red. The exquisite breath of the flowers hid the stench of rotting meat, spoke warnings that banged Isabel's heart till she cried and the hands swooped down and swung her through the warm damp air.

She heard the grown-ups say: oh, children don't notice and can't remember and won't know, Isabel is not aware of what goes on.

But Isabel thought, years later, that children do understand. In their own way. Even if they do not know what they know. At that age it is part of them, hair and blood and fingertips. The knowledge of children stays buried inside them so that it cannot upset the adults who take care of them. Adults are fragile and must be protected by children from pain. To be an adult means having forgotten the pain of childhood and also its bliss. If you remember these things you cannot grow up.

Isabel's life began a second time. She was six. Her mother was dead of fever in the Far Country, and the new baby too, and so her father came back to his homeland on a visit and brought Isabel to live with his sister Josephine.

– You were part of a cargo of oranges and cocoa and silver, Josephine told Isabel, tickling her cheek with one finger: you arrived at my door, my precious, with a basket of gourds and a sack of red chillies.

Isabel never tired of hearing those stories of Josephine's, of her early life in her aunt's house. She clamoured for them over and over again. Josephine gave her a past. Josephine's memory held her, she was the hammock in which Isabel hung suspended and rocked to and fro. A rope bridge, delicate as spiders' webs, stretched over a deep chasm of forgetting in which, if you dropped into it, you would die. Josephine told Isabel how she arrived from overseas dressed like a doll to show off the wealth her father had won from the pagans he killed or seized as slaves: emerald rings on every finger and emerald necklaces wound around her throat, a green velvet dress so stiff with yards of gathers and gold embroidery that she could not walk but had to be carried, a black velvet cap stuck with long green plumes ripped from parrots. Josephine took these clothes off Isabel and put them away. She sewed her a tiny habit like her own, a brown dress in which Isabel could race around and get dirty, no coif but a black scarf to hold her hair back and stop it falling into her eyes. Isabel had long, black, curly hair. At night she sat between Josephine's knees and had it brushed then twisted into a plait. She was old enough to do it for herself but she refused. She liked the feel of her aunt's fingers patting and tugging at tangles, smoothing her down. The touch of the comb on the back of her neck made her shiver all over with delight. It was a taming process. Josephine raked the crackling mane, fiery and resistant as grass you gather up in the meadow, and talked.

– You used to have bad dreams, she told Isabel: from which you woke crying for your nurse. You cried so much, at first, in those early months here, that I moved out of the common dormitory and got us a room of our own. So that you could cry as loudly as you liked, my roly-poly, my little bear, my furry caterpillar, my duck, my honey child, my darling girl.

Isabel's father left her at the Incarnation and went back to the Far Country, intent on fighting the pagans and making money, as before. Isabel could imagine his face by looking at Josephine's, blurring them together. The family likeness was very strong. Both had big dark eyes, deepset, above strong cheekbones, full mouths, curly black hair. Josephine never cut off all her hair as some nuns do. She wore it short, because that was convenient and healthy under a close-fitting coif, but she did not shave her head bald. She even grew her hair a little, at Isabel's insistence, to give her niece the plea- sure of combing it. She washed her hair twice a week, and Isabel's too. She was particular about keeping clean. Some of the nuns thought that lice and bedbugs and unwashed armpits brought you closer to God but not Josephine. She dumped her niece in the bath every night and scrubbed her. Then they brushed and arranged each other's hair.

It was easy for Isabel to live with her. She made it possible for a small girl to run about and not be lonely or bored. The convent life was relaxed and happy-go-lucky. For Isabel it was like having an army of aunts, most of whom played with and spoiled her, and the ones who didn't, like Sister Maria, who was too ascetic to play, she just stayed away from. There were no dangerous people or places. A child could wander anywhere and be safe. Isabel quickly grew used to being left by herself when Josephine vanished into the chapel with the others several times a day to say the Office. She played with the dolls Josephine had made her out of clothes pegs, or climbed trees, or went to watch the cows being milked in the shed next to the dairy, depending on the season and the time of day. Josephine taught her to read and write, to sing, dance and sew. Both of them began longing to leave the convent at about the same time.

*

Josephine forced herself to stay at the Incarnation for over twenty years, until dissatisfaction cracked her open and she felt forced to change her life.

The main problem with that house was that there were too many people living in it. A hundred and fifty nuns, plus the rich ones' servants, and the occasional paying guests the convent took in to make ends meet. You cannot find peace and quiet in a house you share with so many people, most of whom seem to thump up and down stairs all day long or who fly about the corridors clack clack clack in their high-heeled boots in and out of the parlours slamming the doors and shrieking to each other for things they've forgotten, much too lazy to enter a room to find someone, so yelling for her from fifty yards away. They all played music. Wherever you went there was a group of sisters practising the lute or the guitar, the drum or the tambourine, or trying out some new harmony, some new setting for a motet. Or they danced, stamping out new steps, somehow always in a room just above your head. Elephants doing the flamenco and the polka. The ceilings shook. They had no notion of silence, of course. They chattered and gossiped and sang, caterwauling and squeaking, all day long. If you didn't join in they thought you were a snob forever in a huff despising them and they would bang past your chair in the library or the dining-room extra loudly, upsetting your book or your plate, just to show they didn't care.

Then there was the parlour. Anyone who wanted, anyone at all, at any hour of the day more or less, could come and pay the nuns visits in the parlour, and the sisters had to drop everything and present themselves when asked for, it was not only considered good manners but part of their vocation, to be available to guests at all times. Convent-hopping was a fashionable diversion for pious ladies and gentlemen looking for safe flirtations. These spoilt darlings and gallants got bored very quickly. It amused them to while away their afternoons with a group of demure nuns hanging onto their every word, being oh so charming, making small talk hour after hour. Nuns were a nice change, a form of refreshment, a different kind of sticky cake, an alternative to the usual glass of mint tea. The nuns were supposed to provide the visitors with edifying conversation and holy thoughts which they could not be expected to procure for themselves, being too busy and too worldly, but all that these smartly dressed people really wanted was an audience. Josephine and her companions had to be polite, never to show temper or indeed boredom, but to sit there hands folded twiddling their thumbs smiling and smiling just as nice nuns should and chitter-chatter about the life of the soul but far more often, if the truth be told, about the conspiracies and intrigues of the inhabitants of the city, their squabbles and reconciliations. Delicious morsels of tittle-tattle were pecked up and brought to the nuns piping-hot, and their role was to make the speakers feel so important, so clever and wise, to throw the ball back unobtrusively, in short to be perfect hostesses. Ah, they were skilful, those nuns. They were courtesans. They sent their visitors away delighted with their performance. They were experts at faking pleasure.

Satisfied visitors donated money to the convent which

meant that the inmates could eat. The nuns sang for their supper and if they did not sing there was no supper.

Josephine said to the prioress: couldn't we work? Couldn't we earn our own living somehow? Surely any sort of manual labour would be less degrading than this coaxing cash and bequests out of our patrons?

The prioress was scandalised.

– But you ladies are of good birth!

This meant that their genteel hands, let alone their refined sensibilities, were not to be soiled by physical labour.

– Embroidering priests' vestments by the hour isn't work, I suppose, Josephine said: since we're not paid for it.

Nor, as she knew very well, was spending days on her knees forced to pray for patrons' souls. Anything you did for the church was done out of duty and obedience otherwise known as love.

The convent was not, of course, a proper convent at all, but a dumping-ground for spinsters. Girls considered to have no chance of getting married, because they were too poor, or were perceived as ugly, or considered to be spoiled goods, were put away by their families into the Incarnation. It was a junk cupboard full of surplus women who had certainly not chosen to live there, who did not prefer the company of women to that of men, who had had no say in their destiny. There was nowhere else for them to go but this crowded hostel where the rules kept them childish and denied them any responsibility. There was nowhere else that single women were allowed to live. They had to be put away. They were refuse, rubbish, and when they looked at each other that is what they saw: they were not valued highly; they were not valued at all.

Yes of course there were some holy nuns in that place, with genuine vocations. One or two. Their existence shamed Josephine into buckling down, accepting reality, trying to make the best of things with some dignity. But most of the time, like the others, she hung about in the parlours chatting and flirting with admirers and nibbling the sweets they brought in order to try and dull her awareness of the wasted life she was leading, that she would lead until death.

Is this all? she wanted to scream.

She had brought pen, paper and ink with her to the convent. Remembering how much she had enjoyed writing formerly, she tried to go on with it again. She was encouraged to scribble little playlets for the others to perform on feast-days at recreations. Also pretty verses and songs. All these were approved of, as long as they were sufficiently pious and sweet. Letters were permitted, because she could always include a paragraph or two wheedling friends and family for money, so that benefited the convent too. But other kinds of writing were frowned upon. In any case, in that noisy and hectic place, there was rarely sufficient peace for her to collect her thoughts and see what they were. Just occasionally she wrote quick notes that were for herself alone. *Sister Maria conceals her anger under a high girlish voice, and the angrier she is, the more soprano and twittering her speech. The prioress pinches her fat lower lip between forefinger and thumb when she is perplexed. She was a hair-twiddler when young. She is constantly reaching up to twiddle a lock of hair and looking disconcerted to encounter a veil instead. The two workmen who came to mend the chapel roof referred to us as holy hens. Are all nuns called that or do we squawk and cackle more than most? One of them was smoking a small cigar. He tapped the ash into his coat pocket, very neatly. I saw him from the kitchen window, when he was sitting against the wall in the yard, eating his midday meal. He had the cigar to finish. I wish I could try a cigar.*

What she wished most of the time was that she could be a hermit in the desert, one of those desert saints who never had to receive visitors when they didn't want to and were left alone, surly and silent, to get on with their work, praying or writing or whatever it might be. They could insist on their right to solitude in large doses. They sat on pillars to meditate and avoided all obligations to their communities. They never had to be charming to anyone, let alone even polite. They could be completely selfish and pursue their aims with utter ruthlessness. They did not have to smile and pretend to be grateful for being patronised. They could be invisible. Forgotten about. Nobody looking at them, checking and criticising. Nobody judging them on how pleasing, elegant and feminine they were. Nobody pitying them for their unmade-up faces and merely serviceable clothes. Desert saints, Josephine conjectured, leaped about barefoot, clad in goatskins for ease and coolness. Nobody ever required a desert saint to spend hours in a cramped and stuffy parlour tittering and simpering. If you were a hermit you hid yourself in the wilderness and could not be found by all the visitors in the world who came looking.

Silence and solitude, your sole food; rich as butter, honey-sweet.

Josephine's visions of Christ faded, dissolved, went away. Partly, she thought, it was the noise in the convent. Partly it seemed to be because Lucian, though he listened to her with sympathy, behaved exactly like Father Peter in making her recount her raptures in great detail. He could not allow her simply to experience them. He had to analyse them, to see whether they were dangerous. By now, town gossip about the Incarnation nun prone to ecstatic night-time meetings with a man in gold claiming to be Christ had reached the Inspectors' ears. Christ smiled reproachfully at Josephine and disappeared. Before falling asleep she still recited her set prayers but nothing extra. At night, now, in her room, she listened to Isabel's peaceful breathing and jerked down notes for the story of her life that both Peter and Lucian insisted she must write.

— You don't want to become the subject of an Inspection, Lucian warned her through the confessional grille: you must forestall them. You must clear yourself of the suspicion of heresy before someone denounces you.

To be inspected meant to be questioned inside the Inspectors' own prison. The questioning was done with machines specially invented for the purpose. The speech of the machines consisted mostly of metal barbs, hooks and prods. The Tease, for example, was a hinged cage, which, as it closed upon your face, advanced metal arrows towards your eyeballs. The Cajoler, as it embraced you, sent one spike piercing your vagina and another your rectum. The

Tickler was a flail that shredded the flesh of your back or breasts. The Persuader was a vice that gripped your skull and crushed it. Sooner rather than later, if you were sensible, you screamed *Yes.* Then it was up to the Inspectors, sitting in their specially summoned court, to decide upon your punishment. Those convicted of serious heresy and therefore necessarily sentenced to death, were displayed to the faithful in frightening theatrical ceremonies, paraded through the city in processions, and then burned at the stake. If they were lucky, someone cut their throats for them first, otherwise they were disembowelled alive while still burning.

Peter and Lucian described all this to Josephine, whom they cared about and wished to protect.

She scratched along, page after page. A tale of youthful arrogance and foolishness followed by contrition and renewed dedication to being a dutiful daughter of the Church. She mentioned the visions of Christ as briefly as possible. This looked like prudence and modesty but was not. It was angry sorrow at their going. The visions had been hers at first; for her alone. She should have kept them a secret and told no one. In the hands of priests and Inspectors they were destroyed. The visions had created their own privacy, a shining curtain she drew around herself and was enclosed by. She had destroyed that by talking about them, giving them away. She had prized them highly yet had let them slip from her hands.

Anger made her breathless, and curt. Fear made her clumsy. She could take little pleasure in the writing of her book. The prioress, who would only have been half-sorry to see Josephine given the good whipping she believed she deserved, approved of the younger woman's painfilled efforts. Writing should be a discipline, not something you enjoyed and got puffed up about. Once the book was approved, after a delay of several years, while it was read by one Inspector after another, the prioress relented towards Josephine. The *Life* was given to the new novices when they entered. It was considered an exemplary text. Josephine, seeing her conceal-ments and dissembling pronounced virtuous, felt she was being well punished for her cowardice. She was bitterly mor-tified, but could not allow herself to show it. That would only have put her back into danger.

The years slid past. Isabel was transformed from a skinny monkey who leaped at Josephine's neck and clasped her close into a girl with clear golden-brown skin and black eyes like apple pips. She took note of the clothes worn by female vis-itors to the convent and made herself dramatic dresses like theirs out of her old ones cut up and stitched together. She wore these patchworks proud as a duchess, stepping along with neck stretched and fingertips extended for imaginary courtiers to kiss. Sometimes she turned back into a tomboy and swung from the gutters and tried to ride the convent goat. There was an invisible line marked on the ground, as though for a skipping game, and she hopped and swung happily to and fro across it, without getting stuck on either side. She still had plenty of time left, before she was sucked into her future and fixed for life. She still felt free.

A letter from one of her married sisters brought Josephine the news of her father's illness. While she was fretting to and fro about whether or not to ask permission to visit him, a second letter, following quickly upon the heels of the first, announced his death. He died of diseases of old age. A stroke and a heart attack. He was buried in the family vault in the city burying-ground.

The family house in the city was sold. Josephine's elder brother, the heir, was in need of money, and wanted to build his own house, to display his modern taste and all his trophies brought from the Far Country, the silver and ebony and jewels. Also, he wanted a smaller house, with less room for guests and the sort of relatives who were for ever turning up needing somewhere to stay. In his smart home there would be no room for unmarried aunts and cousins. They would have to shift for themselves, as Josephine had done.

A door onto the past clanged shut. Ferdinand had been sixty. Josephine was over forty now. A grown-up woman. She had learned to endure, to write elegant begging letters and other deceptive texts, to take care of a child, to be diplomatic and discreet. Underneath stirred the old Josephine, curious, full of longings. Who she was might be disguised under a habit but it had not changed since she was a girl. She wept, remembering how closely she had once approached her father, tugging at the hem of his coat and stretching up her arms, sitting on his knee and burrowing her hands through the opening of his shirt, undoing his laces in order to get at his warm skin and tickle him; laying her head against his breast to try and hear his heart beat, steady as the church bells calling out the quarter hours, repeating the summons to love your father, love him, love him. His hands

were so big they clasped her head like a bonnet, covered her
ears like muffs against winter cold. His beard and moustache were very soft. Her fingers plunged among his curls.
Clambering up him, held in his arms, she had tested the
world, which for a long time had been a safe place out of
which you did not fall.

She saw that he had been the foundation of her life here.
She had ended up in this place as a result of loving him. He
had loomed in the distance, her cathedral. He'd been her
horizon. On the day of his funeral she walked round and
round the cloister trying to take in this new sense of the
world without him, no right way up any more, no edges.
That design was gone. He'd been her architect, but now all
the doors and windows of her soul blew open and banged in
the gale.

She cried as you have to when someone dies. To mark
their going, their absence. As though they're a tree torn out
of your earth. You have to cry, to acknowledge that, the
wrench of loss, the gaping hole inside. Also she cried for
sorrow, that she had not known him better. Stuck in her
own trouble, she had seen Ferdinand only as a wall against
which she beat her fists. She wished he could become her
father again. She wished she could have known him better.

Her father's soul had lived inside Josephine. Now in his
dying he had collected himself together, he had taken back
his soul, he had gathered it up and departed. She was frightened by how large and empty she felt. Grief came rushing
into her with the force of a flash flood, surging into the
empty spaces inside so fast she feared she would drown.

It was winter. Snow fitted itself onto the peaks of the distant mountains, the gardens shrank to clumps of rigid black sticks, the paths wore a sheen of ice. December padded past like the shadow of a wolf. The solstice shut down like a candle snuffer. The light dwindled, a glimmer of yellow at midday. Josephine felt she was unable to nurse it, she did not know how to cup it between her hands, keep it alive. She let it go out. She was a failure as a daughter, a failure at loving. Her light was extinguished and would not return. For her the Christmas celebrations were meaningless. The turn of the year was a twist of the screw, down into further darkness. She gazed at the porcelain image of the God-baby lying on glossy straw in the crib in chapel, under swags of gilded holly and fir, flanked by pots of red persimmons and miniature lemon trees, and knew that God had not come to her and could not help her.

Josephine, swimming in darkness, was forced to recognise that she was in a state of crisis. Promptly, therefore, she lost her vocation.

She had been plucking up her courage to do so for twenty years and at last she managed it. One January day, at around noon, her vocation vanished. The experience was not dramatic but banal. That was what made it convincing.

She was dawdling about just outside the refectory, feeling bored, smelling the all too familiar and sickening smell of burnt rice, shivering, and looking out of the window at the sodden garden, and realising that this was all she could expect for the rest of her life. Also, she was very hungry, and longing for something good to eat. But nothing was ever going to change. Here she was and here she must stay, give or take a brief trip or two to visit one or other of her married sisters should they ever invite her. The most exciting thing that could ever happen to her would be that the rice for dinner would be burned. Or that it would not be burned.

January. The hopeless month, when vitality is at its lowest, when the light is dull and misty and grey, when mud clogs your feet, when the world disappears behind fogs, when wetness soaks the ground like misery, and the trees are bare and bleak, and nothing is stirring, and life seems to be flickering out.

January is the month for dying, when you give up, unable to believe that long days and light evenings will ever return. January: month of depression. If I were a root, Josephine thought, I could just quietly establish myself underground, lie dormant, wait for spring. But if you were a nun you had to get up and set to, stitching altar-cloths and albs, whether you felt inspired and capable or not. That was discipline. Performing tasks set you by someone else, that never ended, that were always renewed. The reams of sewing folded around her mouth and nose like heavy January clouds.

Belief in her vocation to live as a nun at the Incarnation had fallen off her like a dress she stepped out of and kicked to one side. Belief in God Himself was the problem now, like a petticoat she was not sure whether or not to discard. If God were a petticoat, better to let go. If God was, He was more than clothing. She abandoned the petticoat along with the dress. Without them she did feel naked. But also much lighter. That feeling of space inside returned. Like a huge underground cavern whose existence you sense but whose depths you have not yet entered and are frightened of but longing to explore. Who was she if not a smooth gliding nun with a stuck-on smile?

Next morning, at Mass, she did not go to holy communion with all the others. There was something menacing about the white disc of bread, the gold chalice of wine. Rays shot out of them and shouted. She crouched low in her stall to avoid their force.

– This bread is my body. This wine is my blood.

Those words were true. Were they? If they were true, another statement might be true too. What statement? Fear loomed, a grey cliff, and blocked language out.

THE LIFE OF SAINT CHRISTINE

At the age of fifteen Christine started behaving very oddly. No one could understand it. She skulked in her bedroom, reading trashy novels which made her cry, and writing poetry. She combed her hair forwards over her face and glowered from behind this lank curtain shining with grease. She ripped off her nails down to the quick. She ate too many sugary biscuits and put on a lot of weight. She hardly spoke, but preferred to communicate in grunts.

– She used to be such a happy, attractive child, her mother complained to her father: what's wrong with her?

– Leave her alone, he advised: it's just a phase she's going through. She'll grow out of it.

Her mother had other things to worry about, for her health was bad. She suffered from headaches and depression. She took to her bed. This was a refreshment. She side-lined herself. She sought peace and quiet. She didn't want to have to worry about her daughter. She could do nothing for her. Christine frightened her. Her eyes burned, as though she were mad. She lurched about in an ungainly way, swinging her bulk from side to side like a clumsy cow. She would burst into tears for no reason and slam out of the room. She could not bear being teased but snarled at people. She hung about close to her mother's sickbed, fiddling with things. She dropped bottles of medicine and broke them and had to be sent out. Her mother sighed.

– She's no daughter of mine. I don't know where she gets it from.

She told Christine to run off and play: go outside, get some fresh air. Go and see to your father. See what he wants and look after him. I feel so ill, I must rest. I must not be disturbed.

Christine was taken with a seizure that was so severe her limbs went cold and rigid. She fell into what seemed the stupor of death. Her face turned greenish-white, her hands curled into convulsive fists.

– She's just doing it to get attention, the doctor told Christine's parents: there's only one way to stop her tricks. She's playing dead. So give her a funeral and bury her.

Christine's mother was too ill to get up for the funeral but her father and her two sisters went.

The open coffin was placed in the church. There lay the fat, ugly girl with her greasy hair and chewed fingernails. Her frilly white shroud, trimmed with lace, looked all wrong.

The requiem Mass began. They reached the *Agnus Dei.*

The prayer before Holy Communion. Lord, I am not worthy that Thou shouldst enter under my roof, but say only the word, and my soul shall be healed.

Christine sat up in the coffin and opened her eyes. She opened her mouth too, but no sound came out.

What happened next was witnessed by everyone in the church. Christine flapped her hands and flew. She soared upwards and landed on one of the timbers of the roof. She perched there, her arms wrapped around a beam and her feet dangling high above everyone's heads. She peeped down at their astonished, upturned faces.

– Come down immediately, d'you hear? the priest shouted: or I'll let you have what for!

– I can't come down, Christine screeched: all those people down there smell so terrible, I can't stand it. The smell of human bodies makes me ill.

Her father coaxed her down.

– I promise you, he said: if you'll only come back down to earth and come home with us like a good girl, you can have a room of your own where you can be private and where you won't have to smell any human bodies. None of us will come near you. All right?

– All right, Christine said.

She flew down, her lumpy body graceful as a swan's, her shroud flaring out like white wings. She circled the church twice then made a neat landing on the altar-rail.

– You were just doing it to get attention, her sisters scolded her: you show-off.

Attention was certainly what she got. People flocked to

the house to see the barmy hysterical girl who had flown up
to the roof during her own requiem Mass when she was supposed to be dead. The visitors pretended to be kindly guests
but they were tourists of the grotesque. They were ghouls.
They forced their way into Christine's bedroom and stared
at her and touched her. Some pinched her, to see whether
she was in a stupor. Some jabbed pins into her, to try and
provoke another seizure.

Christine made frequent attempts at escape. Holding her
nose against what she cried was the unbearable stench of
human bodies she flew onto a branch of the apple tree in the
garden. She lay in the stream and let the water cover her head
like a veil. She hid in the chicken coop. She said her prayers
standing on one of the sharpened tops of the palings of the
garden fence, or else lay on the ground curled up into a tight
ball.

– What have I done to deserve such a daughter? lamented
her mother: either she's gone mad or else she's possessed by
the devil. She's lost to me for ever in any case.

While her mother's tears flowed, her father's patience
snapped. He approached the doctor and asked to have
Christine confined. For her own safety, he explained: they
must catch her, and, this time, put her away for good. For he
was fed up with spending half his time chasing his wild
daughter and rescuing her from whatever trouble she was in.
Sooner or later she would hurt herself really badly. For her
own protection, she should be put somewhere where she
could not damage herself.

The doctor agreed.

– It's all an attempt to get attention, he explained: so if you shut her up where no one can see her she'll soon come to her senses. That's what you do with toddlers in a tantrum. That's what we'll do with Christine.

Christine was standing on the window-sill outside her mother's room, perching on one leg like a stork and scratching at the windowpane with her fingernails. They trapped her by opening the window from the inside and beckoning her towards the sickbed where her mother lay fast asleep. They caught her in a net and dragged her from the house.

Through the town they carried her, like a prize fish to be put on show in the marketplace. Inside the net she kicked and fought, she scratched and spat, but to no avail. Out of the centre of town they went, and into the suburbs. The asylum that they had found for Christine was on the very edge of town. A tall, sturdy tower. Not at all an unpleasant place.

Christine was to live here from now on with her eleven companions, girls of about her own age who were all as mad as she was, and had been similarly deposited there until such time as they recovered. Christine was in her early twenties by this time. She was of an age to be married, and indeed that was probably, said the doctor, what was wrong with her: that she wasn't. But he had hopes that she could be cured, even though when you mentioned the word marriage in her hearing she screeched and flew up to the ceiling.

The tower was locked and barred, so that no one from the outside could get in, and no one from the inside could get out. The doctor kept the key.

The tower had twelve windows, one for each girl. Three windows on each of the four floors. The windows glared at the world outside, grumbling at it to keep its distance. Like unblinking eyes which kept constant surveillance.

Raw red brick with stucco decoration, that was the tower. The front door had been sealed up with breeze block and cement. The white iron lace of the porch was rusty, the panes of its little roof cracked or missing. Nettles choked what had been the front path.

Each of the mad girls wore a single handcuff which was tethered by a long chain to a pillar in the centre of the kitchen. The chains were long enough to let them get about, up and down the spiralling staircase and in and out of each other's rooms. Sometimes they performed a crazy dance around the pillar, as though it were a maypole, and then had to untangle themselves, stepping backwards through the dance, undoing the knots and plaits the chains had formed. This calmed them. It was their ritual, for those times when they felt anxious and panicky. Sometimes Christine let herself fly in this dance, rising to ceiling height and wrapping her chain round and round the pillar, feeling the tug and pull of chain and handcuff, pitting herself against them. At other times she lay on the old sofa in the kitchen, drowsy from smoking the dope she grew in her window-box, and could not be sure whether she had just dreamed being able to fly.

She got on well with her eleven companions. Their removal from the world and their detachment from its ways gave them a certain interior freedom. They shared the house-work and cooking. They lived simply, from necessity, but they were inventive. They kept all their clothes in one vast wardrobe and held them in common, so that each morning the pleasure of deciding what to wear could be multiplied eleven-fold. Christine got into trouble when she tried to put on clothes too small for her and split their seams beyond repair. She screeched, flew up to the ceiling and sulked. There was a black velvet coat with silver frogging she coveted, that she could not fit into. A cocktail sheath in green lamé with pencil straps, that would not do up on her. She consoled herself with an organza balldress she wore with workmen's boots, a quilted flying-suit she wore with diamanté high heels. She was playing. Games for middle-class misfits. Their poverty, for example, was not real. It was picturesque. It was monitored by the doctor. Dressing-up was another drug, to comfort them. For what? For being mad, she supposed. You did not get shut up unless you were mad. The mocking voices in her head sang to her: mad bad sad, mad bad sad.

One morning her parents appeared on the far side of the gate separating what had once been the front garden from the road. They rested their hands on the rotten top of the gate and creaked it to and fro. Christine poked her head out of her high window.

– Light of my eyes, pleaded her mother: my darling, please hurry up and get well and come home soon. You've been mad for quite long enough. Come home now. I know you. You're just pretending to be ill. We'll say no more about it. Just behave, and come home. Why can't you be like the others? Why do you have to be so extreme? Why do you have to choose to go and live like this, in such dirt and mess, with all these mad women, oh it breaks my heart, why do you have to hurt me so much, why can't you be normal and ordinary, you do it on purpose to make me suffer, you are so ungrateful, when I think of all we've done for you and this is how you repay us, I really do think you must have gone mad, you are a wicked girl to hurt me so, you are mad, you must be, to want to live like this, you wicked, wicked girl.

– Oh, but I like living here, Christine said.

To her the tower had become a tower of rock crystal, of ivory, that was studded with pearls, whose roof was of jasper and emerald. It enclosed her like the garden in the *Song of Songs*, she lived at the heart of the mystic rose, she was the fountain sealed up, the secret spring that did not flow. These visions proved how mad she was so she kept her mouth shut.

– I'm perfectly happy, she added.

– Flesh of my flesh, shouted her father: stop behaving like a little idiot. You little slut. Stop pretending to be ill. Come home and help your mother.

– Flesh of your flesh, am I? Christine shouted down to him: then take it back!

And so saying she bit off her tongue, spat it into her hand, and threw it out of the window. It struck her father in the eye and temporarily blinded him.

Her parents fled in horror. Christine banged the window shut. She made a poultice, of nettles and herbs, for the raw red stump in her mouth. Opium eased the pain. She felt much safer now that she could not talk. There were words she was now incapable of uttering. That was that.

She got on with her life, such as it was. At night, when her eleven companions were in bed, she would lie on a mattress under the window and watch the stars. She burned cones of incense and drank wine. Some nights there were thunderstorms, purple and black, the sky streaked and ripped by lightning.

It was an intensely hot summer, the heat crackling and palpable. Snakes writhed in from the garden through the cracks in the walls and the gaps under the eaves. They basked on the window-sills. They were grass-snakes, harmless, but long and strong. They could climb walls, slither across the ceilings, and swim in the bath. Christine tamed them and taught them tricks. It helped to pass the time. At first they bit her when she picked them up, but then she learned to grasp them firmly as they thrashed and wriggled, to soothe them, to make them feel safe. The snakes responded. Within weeks they had grown so used to her that they would twine themselves around her neck and limbs like plaits of brown jewels. At night, when the girls danced in the kitchen, the snakes danced with them.

Summer in that dusty, sun-baked suburb was endless and hot. Yearnings grew in the girls to leave the tower and go to the sea, to dive down into cold blue-green water and dart in and out of coral and waving, brilliant weed. Christine dreamed of drowning in the sea with a millstone tied around her neck, of dying among the fish that streaked past in flashes of scarlet and yellow and black. She dreamed of being reborn, of rising out of the sea and being rocked in a boat like a baby in a cradle. The other girls dreamed similar dreams. They all wanted to be let out. But the doctor was on extended leave, and all their parents on holiday. There was no one to check their mental health and release them. They would have to wait until the autumn.

In late summer, the fair and the circus came to town. The local people held a fête to celebrate. Decorated floats were taken in procession up and down the streets, the bands played, the children marched and played whistles, the older ones twirled batons and danced. There were donkey races and fancy dress parades and beauty contests.

The fête procession passed by the tower. There was no one to tell the organisers not to allow this, that it might be unwise, for all the doctors were on holiday. So Christine and her eleven friends dressed up in their gaudiest finery and sat at their windows to watch.

The floats were smothered in paper roses in sugar pink and lime green, hung with silver streamers. Each one was a tiny moving stage for a theatrical spectacle. On one, there was an auction of women, sold to men passing in the crowd. On a second, three bearded ladies in pink satin slips lathered their chins and shaved. On a third, a mermaid and a seal performed in a tank. Acrobats tumbled and re-formed into human pyramids. Divas sang arias. A corps de ballet of men in frilly tutus acted the sylphides from *Giselle*. Top-hatted musicians burst out of cello cases.

What was by day a milk-float, but was now an untenanted choir dais, came to a halt under the tower window. The driver was hot and fed up. His cargo of gospel-singing Girl Guides had failed to show. He lit a cigarette, opened a can of beer, and looked casually out of his cramped little cab up at the tower.

Twelve girls stared back down at him. One girl framed in each window. The driver wolf-whistled, shrugged, beckoned, spread his arms wide. The girls nodded. The driver folded his arms, leaned back against the padded head-rest of his seat. He waited. Nothing happened. He wound down the window of the cab and flicked his cigarette butt onto the pavement.

– Come on then, darlings, he yelled: if you're coming. I haven't got all day.

The girls vanished from view.

Inside the dresser drawer in the kitchen they kept a sharp knife for cutting up butcher's meat. Christine tested the blade on her thumb and watched the blood jerk along the line of red.

So we're all agreed? she gestured to her companions.

They nodded.

– We're all agreed.

Each girl held out her left hand. Each one wore, on her wrist, the tight handcuff to which was attached the long chain whose other end was fixed to the pillar in the middle of the room. Christine cut off the others' left hands one by one, letting the severed and bleeding chunks drop to the floor, the cuff and chain with them. They left these in a gory heap for the doctor to find on his return from holiday.

The snakes knotted themselves together to make a ladder from the window down to the garden. One by one the girls slithered down. Girls and snakes leaped onto the back of the lorry. The driver roared them away into town.

One of the most charming and bizarre events at the summer fête that year was the performance by the semi-handless maidens and the dancing snakes. When the fête was over, and the fair and circus drove away, Christine and her friends went with them.

Christine discovered that she could no longer fly. She seemed to have forgotten how. Try as she might she could no longer rise from the ground as she had before. When she concentrated, and stilled herself, and willed herself to rise into the air, her arms rose up and her shoulder blades and her hands and feet, and she danced, and the snakes danced with her. This way she earned enough money to live on. She danced at weddings, births, and funerals, she shook up the spirits and jiggled them about, then poured out violence, caged in contortions, in tightly controlled steps and gestures, for her audience to use as they wished. When she had saved up enough money, she went to a jeweller and got him to make her a silver hand, a silver tongue.

Silver-tongued, silver-handed Christine. The people who flocked to watch her shuddered with pleasure at the perversity of a mutilated woman dancing, languorous and cool, in the embrace of a snake. She became more and more in demand. She worked the nightclubs and the bars and the café-theatres as well as the family parties.

Being on the road, a different gig in a different city every night, was exhausting. She died, worn out, at the age of forty, and her eleven friends and all the snakes danced her to her grave.

THE STORY OF
JOSEPHINE

Josephine began dreaming of another house and trying to find it. She kept dreaming of founding a different house.

This imaginary other house seemed utterly real. She went on continually searching. It existed somewhere, she was certain. If only she could find the way to get to it. Each time, in a dream, she found another house, she thought that this time she had discovered *the* house, the one she had been wanting all these years, for so long.

It was always somewhere else. Just in front of her. Invisible. Beckoning. It seemed to Josephine that if she could find it she would be able to stop the restless wandering of her heart. She would be able to be still. But she did not know exactly where this other house was. She could not see it in daylight.

At night the walls of the room she was sleeping in dissolved and she entered that other house. Which she discovered had indeed been there all the time. But she had simply not understood that and so had not known, either, how to cross over into it. She found that the other house had been near to her, all these years. Extremely close. Just a hand's touch away.

All she wanted was to be there. To live in that house and not to have to leave it. The place on the planet where she was meant to be, that was what it felt like. Her bit of earth. Her feet planted on her spot.

The real house. The living house. It existed. She could get to it. It was not phantasmagorical, shining like a soap bubble then bursting when you touched it. All her life, without knowing it, she had longed for it, and now she would discover the way there.

She practised saying it: my house. This house is mine.

But not this one. *That* one.

How to reach it? She had no map and needed to draw one. As the first step on the unknown road she started writing a second book. She'd spent twenty years as an apprentice. It was time, surely, to make something with what she'd learned.

She discovered she had been practising the arts of insincerity, superficiality and fakery all too well. Posing as a good nun, she had smoothed and polished a pleasing surface of nice prose which now disgusted her. She collected up all her pretty little playlets and verses and stuffed them into the kitchen range. She held them down with the poker and rejoiced as they burned then collapsed to flakes of black ash. Something hot and urgent leaped inside her at the same time, as though she too were being consumed, as though she had thrown herself into the furnace along with all her insipid scribblings and was being hollowed out by the fire. She was being made ready. As though she were a dancer, limbering up. Bending and stretching to prepare her muscles, to get a performance into shape.

She forgot the raised round lid of the stove in her hand, the seethe of red flames she bent over, the weight of the poker she stabbed into them. She was on an outing with Beatrice. Long ago, leaped back into the present, was now, she was six years old or so, and it was midsummer. Noon. A great festival. Patches of that day were clouded over, a white fur folded around knives, but one moment escaped and shimmered in the hot sun.

Green grass underfoot, at one end of the water meadows. Groups of people making their way in one direction. A bustle, here, of men putting up booths and stalls, nailing wood into place, shouting and banging. What was it? The circus? The fair? For some reason, Josephine was both bored and afraid. Her mother, belly bulging out under her skirt, walked slowly. Her hand was sticky.

– Oh look, Josephine said.

It was the fat lady she saw, in that burning and sullen space of day, the fat lady walking the wire she had slung between two waggons loaded with firewood. Just a few feet off the ground. Silly enough, you could say she was: not even attempting the high wire. She was her own little sideshow. Not asking for money. Just wobbling and practising. People glanced at her as they streamed past, making their way towards a platform some way off, at the far side of the meadow, but Josephine and Beatrice stayed to take a look. The child sensed a reluctance in her mother's gait. She tugged on the hand that towed her steadily along, and halted their progress. Beatrice let go. She blotted her sweating face on her handkerchief and pulled her white lace shawl over her head, as far forwards as she could, to keep the sun out of her dazzled eyes.

The fat lady started out along her curve of rope. Daintily, gaily, she tittuped forwards, her wand balanced in both hands, herself so round, so far from wandlike, her head cocked on one side and each foot, in turn, arching and pointing then gripping the wire.

She was a ridiculous and touching figure. Josephine loved her. She cried, watching. At the courage of the fat lady to be herself, a person in disguise, wearing her padded skin-coloured costume of make-believe. Voluptuous flesh made of wadding, pink bolsters rolled up over thighs and hips, obese pink nakedness carried so lightly, with such nonchalance. Big blue eyes, a red wig, a gold figleaf stitched between her legs. And Josephine cried also at the fat lady's courage to be more than herself, not held back by fear or gravity, twirling herself so delicately out into dangerous space, swivelling there, then concentrating, gathering herself together, poised and plump, summoning all her skill, placing one foot in front of the other to curl around the arc of the rope, edge her floppy bulk along.

Beatrice secured Josephine's hand again, telling her not to cry, pulling her away. The fat lady got inside Josephine. She was the first artist in her life. She was important.

– A mountebank, Beatrice said impatiently: representing sinful humanity struggling against temptation, trying not to fall off the rope of righteousness into the pit of iniquity.

Beatrice dragged Josephine off, before this happened. Josephine screamed, and dug her heels into the grass. She wanted the show never to end. She wanted to stay there for ever, caught up with the fat lady in a dance of air, eternally rehearsing her pirouette like an angel on a pin.

Now, in the convent kitchen, Josephine was crying some more, because she was the fat lady but could not do her turn, she had lost her bravery, her taste for tricks, and everyone would jeer at her as she fell off her wire, splat! onto the unforgiving ground. It was only what she deserved. She had set herself up as a nun with ambitions, foolishly she had fancied that she could write books, and indeed her pretensions had to be punished, it was only right that she should be shown up for the sham she was.

She had lost all faith in her vocation as a nun, and now she had lost her skill at writing too, which was the only talent, besides being a hypocrite, that she had considered she possessed. Her desire to write had vanished along with her desire to serve God. Her bright, shining desire which drew her onwards like a lone star in the dark night. Now she teetered in the glare of spotlights with an audience giggling and pointing, waiting for her to lose her nerve and fall. To crash. To limp off while the watchers mocked.

When she was younger, writing her first book, it had been much easier. She held her wand lightly, balancing her lack of confidence, her inexperience, with her determination to succeed, to weave an illusion that would have the Inspectors foxed, so arrogant, so full of hope was she, she would thumb her nose at them and twirl in wily sentences and they would be taken in. They would have to admire her, she would make them sit up and take the right sort of notice. Look at me look at me look at me!

Whereas all she had done in fact, fool of a woman bowing and scraping and currying favour, was precisely and exactly to live up to their expectations. She had danced their prescribed dance and performed their set gestures, had sung their recommended song, and received their polite applause. Their graciously given approval. They had given her permission to carry on writing sweet little books they heartily despised. Josephine stood in the kitchen and snivelled with shame. She wanted to say sorry but she did not know whom to address.

All these thoughts she was supposed to report to Lucian, who had remained her confessor all these years. He had read the first draft of the *Life* she had composed for the Inspectors to read, had criticised it and suggested alterations, had encouraged her to finish it. Their relationship was a professional one. A kind of friendship. When you work with someone, Josephine discovered, on something that matters passionately to both of you, you start to love them. That's in the nature of things. You both give yourselves to the work, and you love each other for doing so and for what you share: that commitment. However, since she had not given herself fully to the book she had written, and since Lucian had encouraged her to be subtle and discreet, in short to lie,

Josephine knew that he and she were not fully open with each other. Their friendship was held back within reserves. This was reasonable, she felt, for in so far as she was a nun and he a priest, her thoughts were not her own anyway. She had to show them to him, in simple and childlike language, and wait for his approval or his blame. He was her teacher. Her soul was a book for him to read and it was up to her to make sure the story was fluent, agreeable and comprehensible. But this new story wasn't. It was incoherent and disturbed, with a confused beginning, a messy middle, and no end in view. She floundered about in its telling and used language he had never heard from her before, more hasty, more honest.

– I did want to become a saint, she blurted out to him: a great saint. But I failed. I'm just a mediocre woman, just another mediocre sinner. And now I've discovered I haven't the gift for writing either. I'm mediocre at that too. I'm a failure. I'm a hypocrite and a fake and a coward and a fraud. I'm so bloody gifted at pretending everything is all right when it's not. I fool everybody. I fooled the Inspectors with that lying autobiography. I fooled myself that it didn't matter that I was unhappy. I'm just a silly woman of forty who's good for nothing now I've lost even the tiny skill I thought I once had.

– When I was younger, Lucian said: and so much more confident, I was entranced by praying. I soared upwards on wings. But now I'm older, I find God through doubt as much as through belief. We search for him in the darkness. I'm full of doubts. That's what faith means.

Josephine leaned forwards. She braced her spread fingers against the confessional's grille.

– I don't believe you, she said: you're like a bareback rider, utterly nonchalant astride your steed, trotting or galloping or flying over jumps as you please. You believe in yourself and what you're doing. You don't have any trouble writing your books, you just dance and spin and hurl yourself through the hoop, out onto the trapeze. You don't see yourself as a fraud. You don't feel flimsy and empty inside. You're in control. Of yourself and what you write.

– It is certainly true, Lucian said: that I know I have a secure place in the world. I enjoy what the world offers me. I accept it. I don't feel anxious about it.

– Exactly, cried Josephine: you flex your muscles and make jokes and gallop freely in the wind. That is certainly the impression you give. Of being completely confident and in control.

There was a pause. Josephine felt the darkness split as Lucian smiled.

– Perhaps you idealise men? he suggested: perhaps you envy us?

Josephine choked on the bile that rose up her throat and spilled into her mouth, sour and hot, a savage fluid she spat out as words.

– You dare to say that, you, sitting there so calmly and telling me what I feel, when you're the one with all the power, all the authority, all the freedom –

She was spluttering, like a volcano that wanted to explode, shower him with red lava and watch him writhe then die.

– I'm struggling to tell you something I don't know how to say, she shouted at him through the grille: I don't know why I bother when you're so stupid, my words always vanish when I'm in here, this set-up always makes me feel so small and so silly. And then you have the cheek to tell me I idealise men. You've got all the power and I've got nothing.

– Why do you think you've got nothing? Lucian said: I don't think that.

Josephine cried in silence. Hot tears flooded down her face and leaked into her mouth, bitter and salt.

– Let's go and talk somewhere else, Lucian said: it's impossible in here, you are quite right.

They emerged into the chapel. Josephine was relieved to see that it was empty. There was no one gleefully peeking to note that her eyes were red or that she was standing in the aisle looking at Lucian, whose face she had never seen close up in all the years of sitting in that stuffy black cupboard talking to him. She thought: I'm never going in there again, that's it, over and finished.

She examined what had been a voice and now had a face and legs. How could he have sat in that box, being so tall? He must have had his legs folded up under his chin. Black eyes, silver-grey hair, beaky nose, weatherbeaten skin. He saw a short, plumpish woman with large dark eyes, a full mouth, thick dark eyebrows..

They surveyed each other, nodded.

Josephine said: I'm supposed to go and hang out the washing now. Why don't you come and help me? Nobody will object. The garden's not part of the enclosure.

She felt free to make this request because she had lost her vocation and possibly her faith as well. Also, speaking to him outside the confessional she owed him less respect.

They collected the big hamper of wet washing that stood ready outside the laundry door, and carried it between them into the apple orchard. The washing lines were strung between the trees. You needed two people to hang the sheets out, they were so heavy. It was a wild windy day. The sheets flapped and crackled, they billowed and snapped. Josephine and Lucian flung them up over the line, one clasping the hems to hold them fast while the other pegged them firmly down. The sheets whipped and cracked taut as sails on a boat, and Josephine wanted to be on one, sailing away as fast as she could from this place. That was her answer. She had it from the weather and the washing, before she or Lucian had said a word. They tamed the sheets between them, one by one, slapping them over the line and bringing their sides down to hang evenly, laughing and struggling with the wind, and Josephine's veil and habit rushed from side to side with a gale inside them and she remembered how she had thought of her vocation and God as a dress and petticoat to be cast off. Now the wind was taking them from her again.

What the wind gave back to her in exchange was another piece of memory. She looked at the jerking clothes-line and remembered the fat lady inching along. She remembered the Corpus Christi festival. Many sideshows. Men in costumes on high stilts, dancing bears, fire-eaters. Little theatres mounted on carts. All these had a religious significance, which Beatrice had explained. The lures and wiles of the

world and the devil, from which Christ rescued us with his
own body. Over and over he rescues us with his body, in
Holy Communion at Mass. Corpus Christi. The body of
Christ. Also it was a celebration of the fact that the souls of
the heretics were going to heaven after their bodies had been
burned. The townspeople stood in rows in the meadow and
watched the heretics, dressed in green gowns and green paper
hoods, with their sins written on their breasts in black letters,
march up, flanked by soldiers. Corpus Christi was for the
heretics too.

All morning, Josephine could remember it now, the
people of the city stood in the great square outside the cathedral, listening to the denunciations. The priests stood on a
high stage and read them out in thin reedy voices. Latin
words that were frightening because you did not understand
them. The sun struck down, God's mailed fist knocking the
unrighteous to the ground. Smell of fear and sweat, and children's piss when their mothers held them over the gutters.
The choir sang, high and shrill. Some people fainted in the
heat. Hour after hour it went on, and the people had to
stand still and listen, it was required of them by Holy
Mother Church. Not to attend was to displease the
Inspectors and bring suspicion on yourself.

At noon came the fire in the sky that blotted out everything except the screaming. The priests and the choir led the
procession, with the heretics surrounded by soldiers. The
townspeople straggled after them. People were anxious not
to miss getting a good place. Through the meadows they
went, past the acrobats and actors putting up their stalls and

practising their performances, to where the pyres were stacked ready, by the river.

Josephine saw clearly what happened, at first, for she was set on Ferdinand's shoulders in the front part of the crowd. He gripped her feet and she put her hands on either side of his head, stroking his soft curls. She watched the heretics, in their green garments, led to the stakes and roped to them. Bales of brushwood were piled waist high around them.

The brushwood came from one of the waggons to which the fat lady had tied her practice line. The flames danced and teetered and wobbled just as she had, they stretched out their arms and flapped them and screamed and Josephine joined in the screaming because she saw the fat lady had been consumed by the fire.

Beatrice hoisted her off Ferdinand's shoulders and laid her on the grass. Josephine roared. She bit earth and stems and their bitterness choked her. The world was red, ballooning in her ears, searing her throat. Red claws, scraping and scratching. Red eyes of a wild beast leaping on her to devour her, tear her to ribbons, sink its fangs into her soft flesh. Through it all she heard the cries, those newly invented bursts of sound, of astonishment that there should be so much pain in the world.

She sat down against an apple tree, her back braced by its rough bark. She felt sick. But if she closed her eyes she saw visions of hell.

She said to Lucian: my whole life so far has been governed by fear and lying. I realise that now. I became a nun for the wrong reasons. I wanted to be a saint, but not because I loved God. I was frightened of dying and going to hell. I didn't love God. I feared him.

Lucian lowered himself to sit next to her on the grass. It was like watching an insect collapse elegantly on sticklike folding legs.

– You'll have to start all over again, he said: that's all.

Josephine fished in her pocket for a handkerchief. With it came small twists of paper which scattered themselves between grass blades. The wind picked them up and whirled them away.

– It was just the same with writing, she said: I was always trying to please other people. You, for a start. Father Peter. The Inspectors.

She trumpeted into the handkerchief then mopped her eyes. Lucian didn't look at her. He was giving her time to recover. He plaited grass stalks and chewed the ends while Josephine sighed, wept some more, blew her nose again, yawned. She felt she was making a most unholy racket but she couldn't help it. Inside her, something hard and ridged had melted, gone runny. Now it flowed out of her, snot and tears.

– I think you need a change of scene, Lucian said: why don't you go away for a while? Why don't you go and stay with friends, your cousin Magdalena for example?

THE LIFE OF SAINT AGNES

Of course Agnes was a virgin. She was only twelve years old, after all. Still, in that country where girls matured at ten, you had to think about marrying them off while they were still very young. You couldn't be too careful. For in those far-off days a girl had to be kept pure, for the sake of her future husband, who must not be sold damaged goods. He had to know that his sons were his, in order to pass his property on to them. Not to some other man's bastard.

– But Agnes is still a child, the gods be thanked. Much too young to be thinking about boys. Let her stick to her dolls, her pet lamb, her caged finches, her games of tossing jacks and counting cherry stones.

So said her father, who doted on his only child and regarded her as the epitome of perfect innocence. Now he beamed and kissed her as she tickled him under the chin with a yellow orchid, patted the bristles darkening his sun-reddened skin.

He pushed her off his knee. He puffed out his chest, his dark eyes sparkling as he watched his pretty daughter jump about with her lamb, teasing and coaxing it to make her father smile. He stroked his thick black moustache, chopped like a brush above his red lips.

Agnes' mother said nothing. She wiped her hot face on her sleeve. At eight o'clock in the evening the heat had thickened like milk gone off. It settled on the pale green plastered houses of the little town, implacable as crusts of curd, cracked and sour, at the bottom of a jug. The dog, an ill-kempt heap of fur and fleas, lay crumpled at the foot of the courtyard wall. The stones gave back the warmth they had stored during the day, fiery as an oven. Lizards panted in the crevices of the gate posts. Crickets rasped in the almond orchard on the far side of the house.

Agnes' mother squatted on the parched earth under the fig tree in the corner of the yard, with Agnes snared between her knees. She grasped her daughter's long yellow hair, divided it into tails flowing through her cupped palm. She brushed it out, down, below Agnes' waist, crackling gold as a thicket of gorse. Only on marrying did the women of that country cut their hair. They sheared off a foot or so, to signify their altered estate. But virgins like Agnes wore their hair long, a resplendent sign. Agnes' hair was her mother's pride and joy. Her treasure, which she guarded as jealously as any miser his heap of shining coins. She tended it as though it were a rare flower, a cherished animal. She washed it, oiled it, curled it and stroked it. She gloated over it and called it her precious, her darling.

Now she combed it. She parted it into nine strands then deftly plaited these in threes, her fingers pulling then weaving. She tamed the wild and wavy hair into silky braids which she kept from escaping with knots of red ribbon. All these neat tails of obedient yellow she then wound round each other on the top of Agnes' head, fastening them there with long pins she drove in like nails.

She did this not for vanity but for compassion, to lift the hot burden of hair off her daughter's neck and shoulders. Her own brown mane was soaked and dark with perspiration. She wore it, as did all the virtuous married women of the town, in a coiled chignon, with a thick fringe in front.

Agnes sighed with relief. She felt much cooler now that her hair perched on top of her skull like a hat. Also she felt more grown-up. She rose to her feet and paced about the courtyard in a new way, holding her head high, balancing her tightly braided and precarious yellow crown, stretching her neck up and out, letting her arms and hands float.

Her father watched her. Outside the courtyard gate life went on as usual, cruel and violent. Death caught people easily, tripped them up, coshed them, hauled them off. But here, at home, Agnes' father could close his doors against accident and disease. The tame finches chirruped in their cage, and Agnes' pet lamb, tethered to the fig tree by a long red ribbon, staggered to and fro and bleated, and his wife and daughter were happy and good and protected from harm.

After supper Agnes' mother lugged their rolled-up mattresses to the roof and spread them out under the ceiling of stars. Up here you caught a breath of passing wind. The faint breeze brought with it a ripple of music from the bar in town, mixed with laughter, the hum of voices. The snatch of song lured you, it danced inside your ears, it revived you. It suggested pools of golden lamplight, the fragrance of pipe smoke, the chinking of small glasses of tea or wine.

Agnes was wrapped in white muslin veils against the mosquitoes which swerved about. She sat up under her canopy of starry sky to receive her father's goodnight kiss. He trod, whistling, down the stone steps, shut the gate behind him and strode off to the bar. Agnes' mother pulled her covers over her face and slept. Agnes lay awake, staring up at the stars and listening to the music which drifted towards her, full of gaiety, as though it were noon not night. The strumming rhythms, the soft insistent drumbeat, summoned her. Get up and join in. Come on girl. Shake your hips, shift your shoulders, *dance.*

Blundering home by the light of the moon, his stomach jiggling with wine, Agnes' father sang to himself as he swayed along. He was enjoying the peace and beauty of the night and his freedom to coast through it, in and out of shadows, undisturbed by a single soul. This was one of his favourite transitions, coming home alone after a party, moving from the hot intoxication and chatter of a night out towards the welcome of his own bed and his wife's face turned towards his on the pillow.

Lifting his eyes to the darkness under the trees to feel

their moist breath on his face, he spotted a slender white figure dawdling along the road in front of him. A ghost? A burglar? No, it was one of the tarts from the bar, idling suggestively, with breasts thrust out and head thrown back. Doing a half dance, weaving from side to side, tipsy, inviting. He smiled. Saucy piece she was, wiggling her arse at him like that. Good legs, what he could see of them.

He caught up with her just outside his house. He seized her in his arms and fondled her, slipping one hand inside her clothes and hauling up her skirts with the other. Her head was bare. She smelled of wine and sex and smoke. She was his daughter. Her veil hung off her shoulders, her hair had half fallen down out of its plaits, her eyes were dreamy, dazed.

He put the lamb's leash on her and tied her to the fig tree for the night, then climbed up to bed. His wife snored. Agnes tumbled onto the dusty ground and slept.

In the morning she sat cross-legged, her back against the fig tree, holding her pet lamb in her lap, while her father shouted at her.

— I wasn't doing anything wrong, she insisted: I was listening to the music in the bar, that's all. I stood outside, round the back, where it was dark. Then I looked in through the window. Nobody saw me. Nobody knew I was there.

She sulked. She pouted. She played with the lamb.

— I saw you in there dancing, she said: with those girls. Those two in red satin petticoats with cropped hair. Those bad girls who work in the brothel.

She scowled.

142

– What's it like, then, going with a prostitute? What's the difference?

– I'll teach you to go out alone at night, yelled her father: I'll show you, you little slut. Going out to meet men and behaving like a whore, you're no daughter of mine.

He turned to his wife.

– Strip her naked.

His wife said nothing. She obeyed. She hauled Agnes to her feet and tore off her clothes.

Agnes raised her hands to her head. She pulled at the ribbons that confined the plaits on her hair in some kind of order. She shook her head, to unravel the plaits. Her hair fell down to her feet. It enveloped her, a shining, rippling curtain of gold. It covered her head like a hood, it lay over her shoulders like a cloak, it clothed her, every inch, like a splendid dress. She made a window by parting the thick blonde tresses with her hands. Her little face peered out.

– Cut all her hair off, her father ordered his wife.

His wife said nothing. She obeyed. She pushed Agnes to her knees, picked up handfuls of the bright hair and sawed at the soft strands with her kitchen knife. She tugged and hacked. Long hanks, glossy as silk, fell at her feet.

Agnes was left with a rough yellow fur sticking up all over her head. She leaned down, collected up all the thick lengths of her cut hair, and held on to them.

– Throw her out into the street, commanded Agnes' father: let her go and live in the brothel, that's where she belongs.

His wife said nothing. She obeyed. She untied the red

143

ribbon fastening Agnes to the fig tree, marched her over to the gate, pushed her through it, hurling the ribbon, the lamb and the cage of finches after her, so that nothing should remain in the house to remind her of the departed girl. She bolted the gate behind her daughter, and returned to stand next to her husband. Both of them burst into loud weeping. Now they had no daughter. Now they were wretched indeed.

Agnes stood in the street. Though it was still early morning, the sun was already high and hot. She felt its warmth move over her bare skin in light caresses. Like wearing a dress of air. Then, as she began to walk into town, she became clothed in sweat which flowed over her as though she were swimming. She wore a coat and trousers of sweat, gloves and sandals of sweat, bracelets of sweat on her ankles and wrists. Her head, shorn of its heavy yellow hair, felt cool. She held it high and stepped briskly along, the cage of finches swinging from one hand and the lamb's leash looped through the fingers of the other.

No one was yet about. So far she had the day to herself. The promise of more heat, shimmering and molten, poured from the bowl of the sky. The pungent and aromatic scents of herbs and flowers drifted to her from over high walls. She lost herself in the twisting alleyways.

She entered a narrow street with closed, blank façades on either side. Balconies jutted out on either side and almost met overhead. Half-way along, a door stood propped open. A red and white striped pole stuck out. A few paving-stones set in the dust in front made a tiny yard, separated off from the street proper by a couple of painted wooden stools and a

charcoal brazier. An old man was just letting down a flap of
blue cotton to procure a triangle of black shadow, a patch of
coolness. In the darkness behind him, an old woman wielded
a twig broom. She was sweeping what appeared to be a mess
of hair and nail clippings over the sill. She didn't stoop over
the broom. She worked it dexterously with her wiry arms,
whisking the pile of mess into a heap just in front of Agnes.

The old man blinked at the nude girl.

— Well, he said: that's not a bad way to keep cool!

The old woman cocked her head on one side.

— Neat idea, your hairstyle, but you need a trim. Why not
pop inside and I'll do it for you?

The lamb trotted up and bleated. The old couple burst
out laughing. Its coat was as tightly curled as the fleece
covering Agnes' cunt.

— I'm looking for a room, Agnes said: do you know
anyone round here who could rent me a room?

She wished she could drown in the black mouth of their
doorway. She longed to be inside. Out of the heat.
Somewhere dark and cool where she could lie down on a
mattress and sleep. She was hungry, too. She wanted her
breakfast.

Their gaze swarmed over her, as though they were tailors
measuring her for a suit of clothes. With their shrewd and
kindly eyes, they dressed her. They put a blanket of understanding round her naked shoulders.

— We've got a room to rent at the back of the shop, the old
man said: you can have it if you like. But how will you pay
for it?

It felt exhausting, standing outside in the hot street which was as bare as she was. She was desperate to eat and drink, to lie down. To hide. She looked at the little wooden stools. She imagined the customers sitting on them, drinking mint tea while they waited their turn. Watching the life of the street go by. Then one by one they vanished inside. The interior of the shop smelled of sweet hair-oils and perfumes. The old man would shave them, the old woman would wash and trim their hair and give them a manicure.

Agnes held out the cage of finches. She pointed to the lamb.

– I'll give you these, to start with. And then perhaps I could work in the shop?

The old man lit the brazier. The old woman brought out a black iron skillet. Agnes, stylish in a skirt and shawl of tablecloths, fried up little cakes of mashed beans and made green tea. They ate and drank together, sitting on the little wooden stools. Then Agnes washed up, and went inside for a sleep. That evening, in the cool of the day, when the town woke up from its long siesta, she started her new life as a hairdresser's assistant.

The old woman tidied up Agnes' hair. She gave her a chic, sophisticated crewcut, that stuck up in tiny points on top. She showed her how to find her way around a make-up box, and taught her to paint her eyes with coloured pastes and shiny kohl. She gave her an old red satin petticoat to wear, a pair of slippers made of red feathers. She hung the cage of finches in the shop doorway, where they could twitter at passers-by, and attract new customers with their song, and she tied the lamb to the red and white striped pole. It became everybody's pet. The customers played with it as they lounged on their painted wooden stools and waited to be shaved.

From time to time Agnes would appear from indoors, lean against the door post, glance up and down the street, then vanish again. A glimpse of her was unpredictable. She was not easy to catch sight of. More and more men were attracted in for shaves, haircuts and manicures. Girls who looked like Agnes, with cropped heads and skimpy red satin clothes, were not to be seen outside the brothel, or, occasionally, the bar. So the men flocked in to the barber's shop to get a good look at the new hairdresser's help, and business flourished.

Word quickly spread among the local women that a skin-head beauty, hardly more than a child, had appeared in town. They came to visit her, at first in twos and threes, then in gangs of five or six. The women mopped their red faces, wiped their sweaty hands on their skirts, and drew near to Agnes. They gazed at her enviously. She looked as cool and fresh as well water.

One by one the women squeezed past Agnes in the shop doorway, sat down in the back room, and had all their hair cut off. They emerged, one by one, with much nervous giggling, running their fingers over their bare napes and through their crowns of soft spikes, and delightedly exclaiming at how much lighter and happier they felt.

The fashion for very short hair swept through the town. Old and young, matrons and virgins, all got rid of their long locks.

The other craze that year was for red satin petticoats, the sort of elegant yet practical gear worn by the girls working in the local brothel.

Now all the women in the town were dressed alike. You could no longer distinguish a good woman from a bad one. You could no longer be sure whether the group of women hanging around the butcher's shop in the evening with their children, laughing and gossiping, was a bunch of virtuous wives or a bunch of tarts.

With all the cut-off hair that she carefully swept up every evening after her last customer had departed, the old woman made wigs. She lent them out to women who needed to don them to persuade their husbands to make love in the day-time. But most of the women raced around much of the time bald and cool and cheerful.

When the old couple died, Agnes took over the barber's shop. She found that she liked working in the nude, on especially hot days, when, in the darkness of the back of the shop, there was no one but the customer to see. When she herself died, at an advanced age, she was buried wrapped not in a shroud but in the long flowing tresses of her golden hair.

THE STORY OF
JOSEPHINE

It was common for nuns to leave the Incarnation for short or long periods, to help out relatives or patrons in need of their services and supposedly edify them by pious example. The prioress encouraged this practice as much as possible. Fewer nuns together in the house at any one time meant fewer mouths to feed. Nuns visiting friends could beg for alms and endowments. At the very least, they could wheedle for gifts and return with donated baskets of food. Josephine easily obtained permission to go.

– Six weeks to begin with, said the prioress: and longer if you are asked to extend your stay.

Josephine wrote a letter to Magdalena, forwarding it care of one of her married sisters, who knew their cousin's address. She packed a small bag, mended and pressed her clothes, and waited to be off.

The reply arrived by return. Magdalena invited Josephine to come immediately. She sent her affectionate greetings and looked forward to their reunion after so many years' separation. She was a widow now, with plenty of room for guests, for her three daughters were married and gone from the house.

Josephine went to find Isabel. Her niece was sitting on a bench outside the kitchen, making herself a necklace out of pastry beads, baked then painted. She was threading them on to a length of cord, stabbing its glossy tip through the holes, concentrating, the end of her tongue caught between her teeth.

Josephine sat down beside her, interrupting Isabel's painstaking creation. She held her niece's hand in her own and explained that she had to go away for a while by herself.

She asked: will you be all right here without me for a bit?

Isabel plucked her hand back and twisted out of Josephine's attempted embrace. Her mouth thinned. She put her chin up and tossed her hand over her long curls. She said in her quickest and coolest voice that of course she would be all right. Then she swept her beads into the front of her skirt, holding it bunched like a pocket, stood and looked at Josephine's face for a second, and scrambled away. When it was time to bid each other goodbye, she made sure the farewell was in front of the prioress and a group of the older nuns, so that their behaviour had to be restrained and decorous. She kissed the air in front of Josephine's cheeks, then strolled off, hands twitching her skirts so that they swished from side to side. She vanished back inside the gateway and Josephine stepped into the street.

The city she walked through, to get to Magdalena's house, was not exactly the same as the one she remembered, the one she had left, and yet she knew it well. She reasoned with herself that it was bound to have changed since last she saw it twenty-odd years before and yet she found she could make her way along its zigzagging inner corridors, across its tightly packed little squares, through its dark tunnels, without difficulty. What a charm there was in that freedom of going where she wished, as her feet led her or as memory or her heart suggested. She strolled and lingered. Churches in plenty, hidden inside circular courtyards, their white domes glistening like heaps of sugar, doves strutting on the white cobbles in front of them. The fronts of palaces, bleak and forbidding to the outsider, rearing up to forbid you to enter, yet their doors, propped half open, letting you glimpse greenery and fountains as you went by, and arcades running along to keep the sun or rain off as you went from shop to shop.

She went through the meadows and vegetable gardens just outside the city walls and walked to and fro for a little in the grove of walnut and sweet chestnut trees that shaded them. She crossed the river on the white stone bridge and followed the winding highroad further into town before branching off it and plunging in between the closely packed houses and towers of the district where she had grown up. She passed the house where she had lived before, now painted and restored by its new owners, the walls plastered a burnt orange. Through an open window in the second storey she glimpsed a woman she had once known, talking to two others, but she did not call or wave. The enchantment she was in depended on wandering further on, not stopping too long or talking. She was in no hurry. The whole day lay before her like the city, opened out like a fan. She could thread back and forth in it as she chose.

She roamed those streets she half knew, discovering them afresh, finding out what she'd almost forgotten, how one joined the other, how one neighbourhood was related to another, what lay waiting just round the corner: a carving in a niche high up, a white statue of a satyr pausing against a dark green privet hedge, a cat asleep on a hot window-sill.

She entered an inviting arch, cut from thick black shadow, and found herself going along a narrow brick alleyway, the walls so high on either side they almost shut out the light of the sun, but vines and other creepers grew on the red walls, their great leaves swept past and sprawled on the paved brick underfoot. This passage, which Josephine did not think she had ever been down before, twisted and turned abruptly, and seemed to run into the very heart of the city. She stepped along it, half afraid of how dark it was, half enjoying the dazzling dance of shadows shot through with lances of light, needles probing black and white lace, then she turned a corner and saw the blaze of sun marking the end. She came out into a pleasant court with a covered well at its centre, and on the far side of this she saw Magdalena waiting for her on the steps of her house.

Her cousin grasped her by the elbows. They kissed each other.

— You haven't changed a bit, Magdalena said.

– Nor have you, Josephine said.

This was true. The girls they were gazed at one another. Their gestures were the same as they had always been. Their old ways of talking quickly came back to them, their old slang and codes and nicknames. The passage of over twenty years had given them both some crowsfeet around the eyes, some lines on the neck, the loss of the perfect bloom and freshness of youth. But this didn't matter. The girls who had been fast friends could recognise each other. They had not gone away or been replaced. Looking older, Josephine realised, was the least important thing. It was simply to be expected. The many minute alterations in skin and hair somehow made Magdalena even more like the person she truly embodied – as well as the girl she still was, the woman she had become. She was not less beautiful now than when she had been very young. Her beauty had altered and deepened. It expressed her. She was beautiful because she was Magdalena. Josephine loved her. She had never stopped loving her. The only new thing in twenty years was that now she could admit it again. She breathed in her cousin like air, she opened to her, she felt herself expand. Watching Magdalena talk, with flashing eyes, mobile and playful mouth, free gestures, she was reminded of swallows, their darting and sure flight, their wheeling and curving and pirouetting. Magdalena had that confidence. She had practised her flying. She was airborne still. While Josephine had lain upon the ground and huddled in fear.

She was propped in a carved wooden chair padded with cushions. She leaned back against their softness. She tilted her glass and let the yellow wine slip, cold and dewy, down her throat.

The room in which they were sitting was the room where Magdalena spent most of her time when she was indoors, reading, or talking to her friends, or eating dinner with her guests. It was on the ground floor, at the back of the house, panelled in silvery-grey oak, and warmed by a large fire. It opened on to the garden behind. A strip of terrace, set with strictly clipped yew and box bushes in earthenware pots, gave on to a flight of stone steps and a screen of chestnut trees. You could not see into the garden from the house, which was its charm. You had to go into it, to discover it. To find out what it was like you had to become part of it. It drew you into itself. You got lost in it. You were just part of the living green.

Magdalena took Josephine into the garden. Cramped between high brick walls in the heart of the city, it was narrow and long. It felt large, full of endless possibilities. It was very calm. You felt at peace as soon as you stepped into it. In summer heat you were soothed by looking at green arches of jasmine and honeysuckle and white roses. Standing underneath them you felt cool. Sunlight flickered, broken up by the green leaves, over grey-white gravel, rows of terra-cotta pots that marked the edges of the paths, the brilliant lime green of orange blossom bushes, their vivid colour all the more refreshing against the dark green of the box and privet and ivy behind them. The colours were all at your feet, the flowers in the pots. Dots and splashes of pink, lavender, mauve. Some of the pots were brownish-grey, others were dark orange, with chipped lips that showed rose, burnt crimson, blackened scarlet. Now, at the end of winter, the colours were black and grey, the glossy darkness of evergreen.

The garden was in parts, separated by hedges, connected by archways and tunnels. A collection of tiny rooms. There was a kitchen garden tight with winter spinach, carrots and cut-down herbs covered with straw. There was a fountain whose water came from the river that ran underground here. There was a well. Magdalena had dug channels all through the garden, to make irrigation easier. She sent sparkling water streaming through these tiny river beds, so that even at the height of the dry season the garden stayed green. It was a technique handed down from the Faithless Ones who had been driven out, or burned, like the heretics, as though they were poisonous weeds.

– But I still grow their medicinal plants, Magdalena told Josephine: look.

They were at the far end of the garden, where it petered out into wasteland and scrub, separated from a thicket of nettles and brambles by a wicker fence. Magdalena grasped a section of fence, a wicker hurdle which though bulky was light and obviously easy to lift. She dumped it on one side and walked into the nettles, sliding through them on a tiny narrow path she had cut, a secret way in you could not see before diving into it. Brambles and hairy stalks and bearded nettle blooms towered over them on either side. It was like the parting of a Green Sea. At the heart of the wilderness was a neat patch of herbs, each one a plant that was now forbidden to be grown. Faithless medicine had been banned, along with Faithless religion and science and poetry. But Magdalena, like others in the city, having learned something of these ancient arts of gardening and medicine, kept them secretly alive. If she were found out by the Inspectors, she would be convicted of occult practices and burned. But in fact, she told her cousin, shrugging, though the Inspectors made regular visits to her house, they suspected her of something quite different, the kind of sin they punished merely with fines and heavy taxes.

– I amuse myself, Magdalena said: that's quite unforgivable.

They sat by the fire in the big downstairs room, drinking more wine and eating anchovy-stuffed olives and salted roast almonds, pieces of fried cheese speared on toothpicks. Then Magdalena cooked supper. Partridges roasted on a spit over the fire, the birds cooking while the two women talked, each one occasionally putting out a hand to turn the handle of the spit. The sputter of fat fell onto the fire, which leaped and hissed. Magdalena cooked mushrooms and rice in a big blackened frying pan she jiggled in one hand while waving a wineglass in another. After supper they wrapped themselves in double thicknesses of furs against the startling and brilliant cold of the February night, and stood deep inside the garden to gaze at the constellations of stars in the black sky. Together they put some shine and shape on the last twenty years. Then Josephine slept on a feather bed in a small square room on the second storey, in a quiet threaded through by the cool fluting of owls.

On the following evening, when the guests arrived,

Josephine began to understand how Magdalena supported herself, and why the Inspectors panted, sniffing, around her house, to spy mischief and fine her for it.

Magdalena, a widow who owned her own house, but had no income, for all her husband's money had gone to give her daughters dowries and get them married, now earned her living by holding a salon. She threw parties, and charged her guests a moderate fee for supper, dancing and music, conversation, and games. She lent Josephine a yellow satin dress, some pearl earrings, some yellow high-heeled shoes laced with silver ribbons, and insisted she join in.

After a few nights of this, Josephine saw that her cousin's succession of parties was not born simply from financial necessity but functioned to keep all her suitors at bay. Since everyone in the city thought that a beautiful middle-aged widow, with a fine house and garden, would be wasted if she were not married off once more, a never-ending stream of male visitors duly turned up at her house. Men of all ages, urged on by their families to try for this agreeable acquisition. Night after night, Magdalena set them to playing games.

They did not seem to mind a bit. This endless courtship, which was renewed from night to night, seemed to suit them. Perhaps, like their hostess, they were in no particular hurry for it to end. And so, in the meantime, in the intervals of formal dalliance and compliment-turning and the offering of bunches of hothouse narcissi and hyacinths tied up with streamers of pink ribbon, they courteously joined in the conversation, and in whatever game was proposed. In turn, they suggested what the company might like to play next. Josephine was discovering that conversation in this house was curing her of dullness, confusion and grief. Similarly, conversation appeared to cure the visiting gentlemen of an excess of desire. The elegant turning of sentences seemed quite to drive away all impatience and lust. One after the other they succumbed to Magdalena and transformed themselves into her devoted friends.

A code of etiquette determined the conduct of the guests involved in each game.

– It's simple, Magdalena explained to Josephine: anyone, at any time, can say stop, and this must instantly be obeyed. Trusting that, you can go as far as you dare, and farther still, knowing that you can release yourself at any time, and that your partner will scrupulously respect that.

Costumes and props were kept in a big cupboard in the entrance hall. At midnight, they all met in the downstairs room for wine and a late supper. The games rarely kept them all in the same room all evening. It was amusing comparing notes over chicken tarts and shrimp patties, or, of course, keeping quiet and guarding your secrets for yourself.

Sometimes they played picquet, or cheat, or cribbage. Sometimes they drew the chairs into a great half-circle around the fire and simply talked. Guests who could make others laugh were greatly prized. Guests who could turn their experiences into funny stories. Sometimes a book was produced, and they read to each other, or recited poems, or sang. Sometimes they pushed the chairs back to the walls and danced, clasping each other in hot, scented arms, twirling very fast in a waltz or throwing each other to and fro in a tango.

It all depended on their mood, on what had caught their fancy during the day just passed. They dreamed up their games according to whim, the fish thrashing in the nets of their imaginations. A lot of it was silly and childish but nobody minded.

One of the games involved all the women seating themselves on chairs lined up in a row behind a large white sheet suspended from one of the beams in the ceiling. Each woman removed one of her stockings, then allowed her naked foot and ankle to be seen by the men standing on the other side. The men inspected the row of arched feet that wiggled and pointed as their owners laughed and talked behind the white screen. If the men guessed whose foot was whose, they kept it to themselves. Each man chose the foot he liked, and then kept a date with the woman it belonged to. They partnered each other for the next hour or two, inventing, between them, the amusement they would share.

The game could be reversed. With triangular apertures slit in the white cotton, the men in their turn sat in a row. Only this time it was noses that poked through. You selected a companion on the basis of adoring his nose. It could be quite surprising to find whose nose belonged to whom. A nose, stripped of the face that gave it meaning, changed character. Many of the men, who had secretly worried about their noses not being long, beautiful or otherwise pleasing enough, were charmed to discover that these organs alone could attract delightful women to want to slip away into darkened rooms with them, there to while away the hours with all manner of subtle and inventive linguistic and physical tricks. The next day, walking through town on business, the men carried their noses high and stroked them, smilingly, as they went along.

When the evening's entertainment involved putting on a play, you could choose to be an actor or a watcher. And again, in the course of the night, you could take turns to be first one, then the other. Some of the plays required no watchers at all, if the actors were just two, and satisfied that they could perform both parts equally well. There were some plays that gained from being done privately.

You might choose a scene or two from a famous tragedy, or comedy, from one of the playwrights whose works could be found in Magdalena's well-stocked library. Or you might prefer to make up your own piece of theatre, inventing the action as you went along, relying on hints and clues thrown out by the others sharing the stage.

Almost anything was possible in the quest for amusement and pleasure. If desire for release were strongly present, the evening's performances could not fail. And if you were not in the mood for theatre, there were plenty of other diversions. Some of Magdalena's most frequent and ardent guests never did anything else besides loll on the sofa reading novels. One man liked to sit in the pantry testing different sorts of marmalade. Another preferred Magdalena's closet. He would tidy her glove drawer for her, hour after hour. A third liked to try on her dresses and to parade them for the assembled company, one after the other. A fourth preferred to stay outside all evening, reclining high in the branches of a tree.

The Inspectors assumed Magdalena was running a straightforward brothel. They exacted the usual bribes, rake-offs and taxes, then left the house alone. The guests were discreet about each night's events. The parties continued undisturbed. At the end of the evening Magdalena took a guest to bed, or slept alone, depending on how she felt.

Lucian arrived one night. Josephine saw him come in and doff his wide-brimmed black hat. He was in black coat and breeches, his thick grey-black hair tied back by a black ribbon. He looked around with sharp blue eyes while he shook out the lace at his wrists. He was a tall, heron-like figure. He was a priest and yet he did not look like one. She was standing at the back of the entrance hall. She turned round and fled.

She ran downstairs to the kitchen, slid through it past toppling towers of dirty plates, and gained the garden via the back door. There, she ran as fast as she could, plunging into the trees. As usual, she found herself lost in a very short while, in a part of the garden she was certain she had never explored before.

Moonlight poured down, whitening hedges and trees, its brilliance making everything at once bright as day and utterly unearthly. The gravel Josephine crunched over was composed of pearls. The stems of bushes were silver twists. All the leaves glittered, and all the flowers had opened their enormous eyes. The night was very still, birds and animals all fled and hidden. Moonlight fell down like snow, hushing the world. Her feet trod onto grass stiffened by frost. The high, crumbling brick wall at her side supported apple and pear trees, pleached along it. Their leaves twinkled like jewels. There was a white fountain at the end of the alley, a long plume of water folding into itself, the spray cascading like diamonds. Josephine reached the fountain, and sat down on its stone rim. She watched Lucian walk towards her, two wine glasses in his hand and the neck of a bottle of wine sticking out of his pocket.

They drank the wine, which tasted as silver-chilly as moonlight, and talked. One thing Lucian told her astounded Josephine. He pointed to the high wall just behind them and said: that's the wall of your convent. Those tree tops you can just see are the trees of the nuns' apple orchard. He laughed at Josephine's astonished disbelief, saying: you obviously went a very long way round to get to Magdalena's house. And of course that was true.

Later on, they went in to supper, and later still, Josephine showed Lucian the cupboard, very well stocked, from which guests desiring to stay the night could choose a nightgown.

THE LIFE OF SAINT
THAIS

Thais became known as The Sinner. This was a name she gave herself, because she committed such wicked deeds.

By day she was the daughter of a respectable couple in the suburbs of the city. She was kept close and never allowed out alone, guarded from all encounters with young men until such time as she should be given in marriage. Sex was never mentioned in front of her, so that she should be kept pure. It was hinted at, sometimes, in roundabout terms.

– Men are a bad lot, I'm afraid, said her father: rapacious, violent, no respecters of women. Never trust a man. He'll only take advantage of you.

Thais threaded her arms around her father's neck. She rubbed her smooth cheek against his bristly one, she inhaled his smell of earth, grass, sweat and beer.

– Not you, though, my darling Papa, she would reply:
you're the best man in the whole world.

She pinched his earlobes and kissed his nose, Papa her
hero, her handsome papa, whom she worshipped, whom
she adored.

At night, in her room, she sat cross-legged on her bed,
pleating the coverlet of yellow silk between her fingers, listening to the hum and clatter of the city beyond the bolted
and shuttered windows. Gangs of young men roamed the
neighbourhood in the early hours, looking for fun.
Sometimes they fought each other with clubs or knives.
Thais, hearing footsteps, a cry, would jump up and stand
barefoot on the tiled floor, straining to work out what was
going on. Brawling, yelps and groans, shouted insults. A
sudden silence would come, startling as a knock on the ribs,
a moment that stretched out and wrapped itself around a
body slumped to the ground like a bag of sand. Then the
sound of feet thudding away into the distance.

In the mornings, when Thais' mother took her bunch of
keys and unlocked the heavy street door, stepping out with
her basket to go to the market and buy bread, she would discover blood spattered across the pavement, long smears of
blood marking where a body had been dragged away. The
splashes of blood were crimson stars. They darkened as they
dried. The sun bleached them, the rain washed them, until
they were no longer recognisable as blood and did not need
to be noticed or discussed. Thais' mother protected her
daughter from the bloodshed by never referring to it. There
were certain words she never uttered. The doors of the house

she kept locked at all times, and the doors of the heart, the lips and the tongue. She exclaimed in horror at what went on in the outside world, then compressed her lips. Silence, like a bit, forced itself down on her tongue.

Thais' father worked in the government counting-house. He sat on a tall stool at a sloping desk, adding up columns of figures for the state. He ran his fingers over the red, blue and green beads of his abacus, flicking them up and down the wires on which they were strung. Like playing a harp. The tinkle of money. In his free time he went hunting with his friends and a pack of small yellow dogs. Depending on the season, he killed rabbits, hares, pigeons, thrushes, quail, wild ducks, boars and deer. He came home with a bag of warm, bloodied corpses, with coats of feathers, or fur, and he hung the dead animals up in the back kitchen in neat rows. Warm gamey stench in there, rich, rotting. Sometimes he went off on these hunting trips at the weekend. Sometimes for weeks at a time.

He adored his daughter as he adored his wife. This lady he kept on a pedestal, particularly while he was away from home, but his daughter he played with whenever he was around, throwing her up and down in his arms and tickling her until she screamed with delight, carrying her around on his shoulders or his back. He got down on all fours and pretended to be a lion, he stood her on his feet and clasped her hands and danced with her, he was the trunk of the palm tree up which she clambered.

Now that she was growing up, however, he tried to discourage these games, thinking they were no longer suitable.

He held Thais off when she leaned against him, he pushed her away when she planted herself in his lap and demanded a cuddle. Sooner or later, though, smiling and laughing, he would be forced to give way, and his daughter would nestle against him, her arms round him and her head on his shoulder. Sometimes she would dart sly looks at her mother, seated opposite, sewing. She would toss her head at her, as if to say: I've won!

When her father came home at night, Thais would rush to greet him, to be the one to embrace him first. She served his supper, she sat by him while he ate, she poured his wine.

– You are my king, papa, she assured him.

– Poppet, he replied: you're my princess.

– Your *queen*, she corrected him.

Thais did not notice her lack of liberty, for in her mind she was free. She passed the days reading and day-dreaming. In the afternoons, when the rest of the household slept, she lolled on her bed making up stories in her head, or she dressed up in her mother's cast-offs and enacted dramas to an invisible audience.

At night she led her secret life. All the doors and casements of the house magically opened and she soared out, able to go wherever she wished.

One night she dreamed of a lover whose face she could not see. She dreamed of dancing with him in a dark marvellous room whose walls were soft and black as shadows, merging into the night sky. She dreamed of riding with him on a carousel of beds in that night-time room, on a four-poster that rocked, reared and sank, that pranced like one of the gilded wooden horses on the whirling roundabout at the fair. Now the poles supporting the canopy were tall slender white feathers, snowy as goose quills, and the bed was a plump goose who ploughed the air with Thais and her lover high above the city. The wings of the goose fanned open wider, yawned and split as an arrow buried itself in her breast and she plunged and tossed, and fell, fell through layer after layer of clouds, letting slip her cargo of lovers onto the bed in Thais' room, its fat and silky pillows and goosedown quilts.

Thais lost her lover then, because her mother was calling her to get up, little one, and come and have breakfast, and the dream melted away like the mist and spray hovering across a waterfall. In the light of day Thais couldn't hold it back. It vanished under her fingers, invisible ink, like writing in lemon juice, she had forgotten how to read. It slipped off her like a fabulous dress her mother had lent her and now snatched back.

At breakfast the talk was all of the party at the government palace, to which they had been invited and to which Thais' parents were to go. Thais begged very hard to be allowed to accompany them. She leaned against her father and stroked his face, she coaxed him with pretty endearments. She peeped at him through her downcast eyelashes and played with the rings on his fingers until he snatched his hand away and said yes, she could come.

Thais danced off to her bedroom.

– Take good care of her, mind, her father said to her mother: don't let her out of your sight. In that rabble, who knows what kind of people will be there that we'll have to mix with.

He was off out hunting. If he got home late, they were to go on to the party, and he would meet them there.

Thais' mother wore a dress of black satin overlaid with black and silver sequins. She wrapped her shoulders in a stole of black gauze dotted with silver stars. She smeared blue paste on her eyelids and painted her mouth bright red. She tied up her hair with a wreath of silver vine leaves and hung silver loops in her ears.

Thais would have liked just such a costly and alluring outfit. Her mother, however, insisted she wear a gown and veil of white silk, as becoming to her age and station. Young girls did not wear black sequins, and that was that. She allowed her a single strand of pearls, and she let her dab scent onto her neck and wrists.

Thais scowled and sulked. She looked with contempt at the wrinkles creeping around her mother's eyes and mouth, the lines on her neck, the coarse skin on her forearms. What a waste for her mother to get all dressed up like that, when she was old, with no beauty left. Whereas she, Thais, was bursting with youth and freshness and only needed beautiful and expensive clothes to set her off. She knew she was pretty, for her father told her so constantly. Her father was her mirror. She held him in both hands, at arm's length, and pirouetted in front of him. She twisted this way and that, she preened and languished. And he gave her back herself, adult and powerful and possessed of the capacity to charm and bewitch him. She could never let go of him nor he of her.

Without him looking at her she did not exist. Her eyes sparkled in order to catch the reflection in his, she put her hands on her slender waist and arched her neck to call out the doting admiration in his face. When she walked into the room it was her father's gaze she immediately searched for, for he brought her alive. She lived in him. He framed and shaped her. His approval let her twirl and leap and brim with gaiety. When he did not look at her she dwindled and shrank and felt wretched. He was her secret of eternal youth. She gave him her own youth and in return he made her feel that she would never grow old. He cradled her in his longing eyes, he tweaked her this way and that, like a strand of hair to be smoothed into place, he corrected her words and her tone of voice. In return, she had his love.

That was her reward. He loved her, Thais, more than any other father in the world loved any other daughter. And quite right too. She was the most beautiful, the cleverest, the most gifted, she knew exactly how to please him and what to say. She paid him the best compliments anyone could. She was a delightful companion. She was never boring. Her adoration made him feel large, splendid, capable of anything.

Thais was fighting her way out of childhood. Going to the party, getting dressed up, was the egg of her mother's house cracking open. She slid into the world. She committed herself to the steep marble steps leading up to the palace, the echoing entrance hall. Her feet rapped on rosy stone. Her mother let go of her hand in the ante-room and Thais slipped away from her, to dawdle in the doorway and wait

169

for her father to arrive. In between them Thais tried on new selves.

Safely walled in by women adjusting their veils and tweaking their jewelled collars into place, Thais let drop her wrappings of white. They fell to the floor. She kicked them behind her, walked swiftly forward, abandoning them to be trodden on by the crush of bodies pressing forward to the mirror. In a moment she was free of the powdering perspiring crowd, gliding between them unnoticed, and away to breathe the fresher air, untainted by so much perfume and hot flesh, of the rooms beyond.

The dress which had been concealed under her floating layers of white was of yellow silk, cut from her bedcovers and pinned and ruched around her with diamanté clasps from her dressing-up box. A tube of sunflower yellow that skimmed her shape, outlined it. Scooped down below her collar-bones, then twisted on the shoulders into two yellow knots. Sleeveless, to show off her arms. Cut low, to show off her breasts. As tight around the hips as was compatible with walking. She had made herself a stole from the same silk, which she trailed from one hand.

She paced along the corridors hung with gold draperies festooned with gold tasselled cords and bunches of pink and yellow tiger-lilies, pausing every time she came to one of the mirrors to check that her beauty was lasting not dissolving. Then she moved on again, slowly enough to catch the admiration of passers-by, quickly enough to catch sight of herself in the next mirror before she ceased to exist. The mirrors played ball with her, tossing her from one to the next. They were her stepping-stones. They were ice-floes, broken-up bits of glacier floating down a river, and she had to leap lightly between them in order not to drown.

She reached the end of the corridor, where there were no more mirrors, only an archway ahead, with a flight of steps, leading down towards what she thought must be the garden, and a doorway beside her, curtained in hide, two flaming torches thrust into the bracket beside it.

From inside the room she could just hear the sound of laughter. A man laughing. Her father's laugh. She would have recognised it anywhere. She put out a hand, swept aside the brown skin curtain, and plunged into a cave of blackness.

The dark wrapped her like bedcovers. It was the room of her dream, walls soft and shadowy as moth's wings, dissolving into the night sky. At the same time it was an underwater darkness shot through with currents that swirled her into the centre of the room, where the bed was. Just as it had been in her night-time vision, only now everything was reversed. The sheets and pillows were of black satin, the quilt of black goose feathers downy and soft, and the poles supporting the black velvet canopy, sewn with sequins, were sturdy black quills.

Hands that she could not see grasped her waist and pulled her down. An invisible mouth brushed hers, whispered to her to shush.

– Papa? said Thais: is that you?

In the black mirror of the bedhead, ebony polished to a deep black sheen, she thought she saw him. But she could not be sure. It was a fine game, the best ever, to hold still under the caress of the hands that searched her face, her neck and shoulders, to feel his mouth print kisses on hers, to pretend to squirm at the touch of his bristly cheek.

– My little one, he murmured: my little girl.

He was sleek and supple as a great black cat. He smelled of the night, of the outside, the harsh sweet smells of earth and grasses, as though he had been hunting. Thais was his captive bird, pretending to flutter, uttering little cries, happily imprisoned in his net.

He was gone. She sat up, dazed. It had been a dream, out of which she had just woken. Into another dark room in another dream.

Now he was there. His breathing presence. The lover whose face she could not see. This time, however, as he seized and caught her, she was sure. Her hands recognised the fur on his chest and belly and forearms.

– Papa, she said: I know it's you.

She sniffed and stroked and licked him. She lay down, pulling him with her. In that thick, warm darkness in which she could see nothing, not the shape of his face. Their two bodies played in the black night of the bed, the room.

So was this what her mother experienced? Thais wondered: was this what her mother had wanted to keep all for herself and never let her daughter find out about? Was this what her mother had forbidden her daughter ever to try?

How could you describe it? You could not. It was the most blissful experience it was possible to have. You could not find words to say how deep and sweet this pleasure was. A warm, intense, golden explosion inside which threatened to destroy you, it was so close to pain at one point, it was so violently good, it drove so strongly. A burning, melting sweetness that pierced you then wrung you out. A slow shock that dissolved the bones, heated you in a furnace, turned flesh to water that flowed.

She pressed her knees and thighs together to try and keep the feeling, to possess it fully. But the wave that had swept up and through her ebbed away. She stretched out, arms and legs arched as far as they would go, clenching and unclenching her muscles, back in her skin, the outlines of the body. Back to being herself, with a name, a face, clothes that she must put back on.

She was waiting for the dream to end, to fall out of the box of night onto the soft quilts and pillows of her bed at home. But the dream had shed her and gone off, it abandoned her where she lay, and she could not find her way home again. She could not wake up. The dream had deposited her at the bottom of a deep well; she floundered in oily black water. Her bobbing white face in the darkness, the round mirror of water, was the one you see when you lift the well cover and peer down, down, down. She could not get out unaided, and no one came to rescue her.

The sides of the well, brick overgrown with mosses and weeds, were slimy against her face. Her hands beat the surface of the water but found nothing to hold on to. The stone lid of the well clanged shut, sealing her in, blotting her out from the face of day looking down at her. A black halo of light that merged into the black pipe of water. She floundered at the bottom.

Once or twice the lid of the well was heaved aside and she saw daylight far above her. Her mother's face peered down at her, frightened and white. Her mother was speechless. No sound came from the round O of her mouth. In any case she was too far away from Thais to hear. She could not see her daughter who trod water so far below her, who was part of the darkness now, utterly lost to her. The lid of the well thudded back into place. Eternal night once more, in which Thais swam. This evil, stinking hole was where she lived for the next twenty years. She was shut up inside it. Nobody knew she was there.

That was the punishment Thais endured for her great sin. She was so wicked she could not live in the world like other people. She had forfeited any rights to love or happiness. She had betrayed her mother. She was utterly lost. Demons leaned over the lip of the well from time to time and shouted this at her. They prodded her with pitchforks so that she gulped dirty water and nearly drowned. They sneered at her. Then they too went away and left her alone.

Eventually she died there, at the bottom of the well, and in time her flesh and bones rotted and disintegrated and became part of the filthy water.

THE STORY OF
JOSEPHINE

Josephine stayed with Magdalena for over a year. The prioress of the Incarnation, harassed by bills and creditors, who had gladly given her permission to absent herself for six weeks, was relieved that the discontented and antisocial younger woman would be out of the way for much longer than that. One less hungry mouth to feed and one less difficult soul to worry about. Josephine went back regularly to visit Isabel, who was now fifteen years old and should not have been left to fend for herself in that house of wellmeaning but careless women, who spoiled her one day and neglected her the next. Josephine, watching her niece sulk and flounce, was ashamed of herself.

– Come and live with me at Magdalena's house, she suggested: you'd like that, wouldn't you?

Isabel shrugged.

– I don't care. If you want.

Isabel duly arrived. She had taken her child's dress of green velvet that she had worn when she arrived nine years before to stay with Josephine, had ripped out its many yards of material, and sewn herself a new skirt and waistcoat. Round her neck and on her wrists and fingers she wore her emeralds, and stuck through her chignon, like an arrow, was a green feather.

– You'll have to keep an eye on that one, Magdalena warned: she wants to run wild, I can see.

Josephine laughed.

– Unlike me, I suppose. And you too, my dear.

– We're older, Magdalena retorted: Isabel has no idea about anything.

Josephine's life started off again. It had to. She was well over forty, but she was hardly finished yet. She had left behind her one kind of existence. She had put it away, placed it on one side, as you relinquish certain books, pictures, clothes you no longer need. You give them up and give them away.

The change was serious, but it was easy. She had simply walked out of one house and into another. The difficulty had lain in making up her mind to go. Looking back, she marvelled at how long it had taken her to recognise her need to alter her life. Time to put a spurt on, she felt now. Get cracking. Seize this second chance and use it. Some sort of stepping-stone.

The stay at Magdalena's was temporary. A breathing space. It gave her time to collect herself, wonder what she should do next. Here she had time to herself, in which she could do as she pleased. After the regimen of bells, timed duties, at the Incarnation, this was extraordinary self-indulgence. Once more she shared a room with Isabel. They each had a wooden table and chair, a bed tented in white drifts of mosquito netting, a green damask cushion. The ceiling was painted blue, with a star on the boss in its centre, and the walls were decorated with a frieze of unicorns, sphinxes, mermaids and angels. In the evenings, Josephine laced herself into her lowcut dress of yellow satin, dusted on powder and rouge, concealed her short hair under close loops of pearls, and went to work in the salon downstairs. She acted as Magdalena's assistant, an additional hostess, supplying chat, flirtation, jokes. This way, she felt she contributed towards the board and lodging of Isabel and herself, as well as having a good time. Sometimes Lucian turned up, and sometimes he did not. Their conversation, during his absences, was carried on by letter.

Isabel danced in and out among the guests, who petted and cosseted her. She tested herself on the men, a little girl one moment, a languishing nymph the next. She acted the child, perched on some admirer's knee, pouting prettily, pulling his beard and demanding barley sugar, then played the honeypot, swaying forwards, all bosom, with fluttering eyelashes and mincing steps. Josephine watched her and thought: well, she could always get married, if she wanted to. But Isabel tossed her head and insisted no, the thought of marriage bored and revolted her, she was going to live with Josephine always. For the moment, anyway, she was pleased to be out of the Incarnation, content to be with her aunt.

The guests departed in the early hours. In the daytime, Josephine got up late. She drank a cup of coffee or of chocolate, very deliberately selecting the cup and spoon of her choice and relishing this. The wide, shallow cup of thin porcelain, painted with a wreath of scarlet poppies, or the taller, narrower one, a dark blue glaze scattered with yellow dots. The plain tin spoon with a dented bowl, or the engraved silver one. She ate a croissant, or some sweet brioche, or a slice of bread and butter, depending on her mood, on what she craved to taste. Often she breakfasted with Magdalena, sitting on the end of her bed and talking over the happenings of the night before. Or if she had tip-toed downstairs to join Lucian on one of the wide sofas in front of the fireplace, where he slept when he stayed the night, she would share breakfast with him outside in the garden, sitting under the jasmine-draped pergola and scattering crumbs for the birds. Josephine hid her nocturnal expeditions from Isabel. She believed herself to be very discreet. Her niece slept late in the mornings, and, by the time she struggled bleary-eyed from bed, Lucian was long gone.

Now that spring had arrived, the garden broke open with life, with fresh green. The grass grew so quickly you could stand and watch it sprout. The honeysuckle and clematis hurled themselves up their supports, putting out new tendrils every day, clambering towards the light. The vines exploded, as though they were ropes suddenly pulled, shaking out flags, flares of bright green. The garden swarmed with urgent leaves.

Josephine became a gardener. She hoed and mulched and weeded. She scythed the grass, tied in the long swaying branches of flowering creeper, raked the gravel and watered the bushes in their pots. She discovered this was work she loved. The earth was a green body, and she was allowed to enter into a relationship with it. She was a baby again, climbing all over her mother, tenderly and aggressively tweaking her earlobes and pulling her hair, licking her neck and rolling in her lap, and she was also the mother, supervising this riot of green that had sprung up and needed patient, constant attention. She had to attend to it carefully, day after day, alert and ready, springing to nip and shear unruly or damaged parts, finding the balance between unrestrained development and over-severe shaping. You could be as curious and inquisitive as you liked, when you were a gardener, peering into the yellow hearts of blossoms, inspecting the undersides of leaves. You could be strict, chopping back stems to encourage thicker growth or deadheading flowering bushes past their best. You could idle about, sniffing and stroking your favourite plants, admiring the ardent and elegant bees swerving from bloom to bloom. Every day, there were changes to be noticed. A sprout of old man's beard in the hedge, which you discovered was a wild form of clematis. Strange dark yellow poppies arrived from nowhere and blooming at the back of a flowerbed. Wands of willow that you'd stuck in to support the sweetpeas suddenly rooting and bursting into leaf, a living fence. Josephine was happy, digging and planting, lugging cans of water from the well, pricking out seedlings, pruning. She marvelled at the energy with which everything wanted to grow. She sent water streaming through the garden and felt it respond, a thirsty animal drinking eagerly and then stretching itself, flexing its green muscles under its green skin. She coaxed jasmine and morning glory up ladders of sticks and watched with delight as they flowered.

In the afternoons she stayed in her room and read, or wrote in her notebook, or simply sat still and did nothing, before helping Magdalena with the preparations for the evening ahead. Sometimes she went out for walks around the city. Long, aimless walks, in which she let instinct lead her, wandering back and forth across the river, strolling through the arcaded market square littered with straw and vegetable peelings, stripped-off leaves and withered stalks, or weaving new routes through back streets. Sometimes Isabel accompanied her, but more often she came out alone, leaving her niece to complete the lessons they looked over together in the late afternoons. It was the hottest and quietest time of day. Most people slept. Josephine vagabonded undisturbed. She enjoyed the way that the city, emptied of its hurrying crowds, showed its bones, its austere and elegant angles and curves. She enjoyed, equally, the way it came back to life, like a great animal sleepily rousing itself, opening one eye, lashing its tail. Music started up. Voices called out and clamoured.

One afternoon, in need of a rest and a sit-down to ease her aching feet after a lengthy stroll, she entered a dark gothic doorway and found herself inside the cathedral. She sank into a pew and eased off her red leather shoes, using her toes as shoe-horns. She touched her fingers gently to her heels, whose burning skin was fast puckering into blisters, and winced. Why she had chosen to go out in new, tight-fitting, high-heeled shoes she could not imagine, unless it was in order to arrive here in this calm interior, a domed darkness fragrant with cold, heavy incense, an invisible organ sending low, sweet notes at her like gold darts. The bare soles of her feet met the marble floor. The chill jerked her eyes wider open and she began to take stock of where she was.

She had not been inside the cathedral for over twenty years. Here was her childhood preserved, like golden apricots in brandy that could wait in a dark cupboard until you opened the door suddenly and found it. Like an insect caught in amber, it was there, physical, touchable. Like a fossil, it had not changed. It inhabited a different timescale. It went on existing, while she grew up and grew away, and now she had returned and entered it and could hold it between her hands. The choking perfume of frankincense and myrrh, of lilies and dust, the splash of holy water dropped on her face by Beatrice's fingertips, the cool black-ness, the plaintive pealing of organ music, the warmth of women's bodies crushed together near the baptismal font, the rustle of their sleeves. Treble and flute, long golden rods of song that reached for her, the sound of heaven she called it as a child, it entered you and swelled you up like a cloud and you wanted to rise into the air, float to God. The smell of heaven too. Cold, and deep, intense as a wound, the breath of hothouse flowers and spice and dust, her mother's rose and vanilla sweat. God was there, God shaped the cathedral which sprang outwards as the body of God, a great heart beating in darkness, a rounded interior in which you curled up, carried by God, the arms of God holding you close, an embrace in which you soared and leaped and played. God was not Father, not Lord and King. God was blackness, darkness, sweetness, limited to no one shape but part of everything. In the cathedral you could let go into God, that was why people loved going there, it was a safe place in which to release their longing, let it flood out and meet God. You dissolved and became part of God. Prayer simply meant letting that happen. The experience of love shattered you, like a nail driving in to send splinters flying. Gold in the crucible beaten and transformed. The human substance irradiated and on fire. God both soft and fierce, destroying you then letting you fly, God flooding through you so fast and violently you thought you were dying.

Josephine had forgotten that. Now she remembered. She had lost that God. God had condensed down to teacher and judge chasing her into the convent, threatening her with hellfire. She had not found the God of her childhood in the nuns' chapel at the Incarnation with its brilliantly-lit choir slung with gleaming lamps, its gaudy plaster and gilt decoration, its shrill-voiced choir, its ornate silver altar vessels, its hideous and lifelike crucifix whose Christ drew your eyes with his nailed body arched and twisted in agony, his gaping wounds encrusted with scarlet blood. You abandoned me, he always seemed to be saying: wicked daughter, you abandoned me. So that she did not have to look at him, Josephine had taken to praying with her head buried in her hands, a pose which drew criticism upon her. The gesture of a show-off.

Josephine had not entered a church during her stay with Magdalena. She had felt no need to attend Mass or say her Office. But here, in the cathedral, on this particular afternoon, she could sit loosely and breathe in the enormous quiet. It surrounded and bent over her. It scooped her up into itself, a vast emptiness that was full of God. Quiet reverberated with her breathing, the pulse of her blood. The dimness in which she sat was a blackness dusted with gold, glittering with tiny points of gold, very fine, a gold mist veiling the darkness. Sweetness arrived and entered her. She felt what she had not felt since childhood, that shiver across her shoulder-blades, which increased, then built rapidly, a molten intensity which poured through her until she felt she would rise into the air. The force ebbed a little, swept up and down her spine once more. She trembled all over, clutching the back of the pew in front of her with both hands. Then the power that had visited her gathered itself up, stopped shaking her, and rolled off somewhere else. She felt as though she had been struck by lightning.

Tears fell down her face. She wiped them off with the back of her hand. She yawned. She was exhausted, as though she had been wrung tight, like a cloth. Yet she was very light too, saturated with joy. She reached down for her shoes, and picked them up. On the way out, she lit a candle at the altar of Our Lady of Solitude. She left her shoes there, and went out barefoot.

The heat dropped onto her as she came out of the small

padded leather door cut in the great wooden one and let it thud softly to behind her. The square was deserted in the burning, still afternoon. The streets were white and empty. She moved over dust and gravel, over sun-warmed cobbles and paving-stones, carefully, testing them with the soles of her feet, springy air under her arches, which took her weight, reconnected her to the ground at every step, as heels and toes met earth.

The city swung and murmured around her as she paced through it. Bees droned above bougainvillea flopping over walls, behind which hammocks creaked in loggias. Fountains splashed in squares. The air smelled of olive oil, oranges, spilled wine. Dogs sprawled in gutters. Inside the black doorways of bars, men hunched over drink and cards, or slept, collapsed, face down, on tables. Behind her, the cathedral bells began to toll.

She reached Magdalena's house, and went into the garden. The gravel of the paths was sharp, and struck at the tender skin already sore from the tight shoes, the unprotected walk home. She trod over to a strip of turf where walking was easy, soft grass springing back, fresh green cushions. She followed this narrow path through a white wooden gate, and discovered, behind a rose trellis, a tumbledown hut. She unbolted the door, propped it open, and went in.

The earth floor was scattered with glossy golden straw. The walls were whitewashed. A wooden bucket lay overturned on its side in one corner. Josephine set it the wrong way up and sat on it. Through the open doorway came the rasp of crickets hidden in the slope of dazzling green grass.

The light was inside the grass. Blades and stems swayed, heavy with light. Swallows dived past. A woodpecker knocked at the trunk of a tree.

– The old pig-sty? Magdalena said that evening: of course you can use it. Nobody goes there any more. We haven't kept pigs since my husband died, so the smell should have vanished by now, I hope.

Josephine swept out the straw and pulled down the cob-webs. She carried in the table and chair she used in the bedroom she shared with Isabel. She took in pen, ink and paper, her green damask cushion, and an old lace tablecloth which she hung across the doorway. The lace screen kept the flies out but let in the light. It swayed in the slightest breeze, sending shifting, complicated patterns of sun and shadow that danced on the floor and fell on Josephine's shoulders like a veil. She had a proper, three-legged stool for sitting on now when she wanted to prop herself against the doorframe, loop back the curtain and just stare mindlessly at the outside. In the bucket she kept a bottle of water, a few books, a knife, and her lunch wrapped up in a handkerchief.

That was the summer when aunt and niece started having secrets from each other. If Josephine was not sharing Lucian's makeshift bed in the salon downstairs, she often slept in her hut on a pile of borrowed cushions. So that if Isabel felt free to invite young men she fancied the look of, after one of Magdalena's evening parties, to spend the night with her upstairs, Josephine was none the wiser.

Josephine was hunting for something, she did not know exactly what. She sent a note to Lucian, trying to describe the discoveries she wanted to sniff out, and asked him to send her books from the university library, all the books he could borrow that might be useful to her.

Lucian wrote back: the university library does not lend out its books, and anyway, all the books you want are in Latin, Greek, Arabic and Hebrew. They are also all on the forbidden list, and kept hidden in the vice-chancellor's office lest the Inspectors discover their existence and burn them.

Josephine wrote back: so please go and read them yourself, then come back and tell me what they say.

With Lucian's help, Josephine nosed through poetry, philosophy, medicine, cookery, astronomy, mathematics, gardening, science, biology and chemistry, and theology. She tried to pass on to Isabel some of what she was learning, for she regretted that her niece's education, like her own, should be so limited. She taught her by posing questions to which she did not know the answers. What, exactly, is a body? What is life? Death? Time? Matter? God? Ignorance was a bearable state, she discovered, which involved being imperfect, not being in control all the time, feeling more or less powerless and helpless. This process of education, she found out, was not an advance into synthesised knowledge but into humility. In the universities, she was certain, dwelt professors and scholars who had access to the right books, to the brilliance and wisdom of each other's conversation. They were further ahead on the road to enlightenment than she. Without their privileges, she persevered. She found she enjoyed speculation, that it did not matter whether or not Lucian told her she was right.

Most of the time, indeed, he insisted he did not know. He said that most wise men were in that condition most of the time. Josephine did not completely believe him but she felt comforted.

Not-knowing laid you open to receiving knowledge. That seemed to be the point of it. Once you admitted your lack, your emptiness, the waters of thought rushed in and filled you to the brim, overflowing. Conversations with Lucian, with Magdalena, and with Isabel, were Josephine's food. When you embarked on a conversation you could not be sure where you were heading nor where you would end up. That was the whole point. You were free to gallop in a certain direction, to be seduced aside, down a side alley, and find you had reached somewhere new. A fertile place which nourished you, and released you into the next adventure of talking. You could have these conversations with books, or with people. The only condition was that you be in a state of love and desire; aggressive sharp desire and soft yielding desire, both at once. You took and were taken. You led and you followed. It was just the same making love. A good conversation was as good as making love. Making love well was as good as making conversation. Making good conversation made you want to make love.

This was different from the talking that went on in Magdalena's salon, which was formalised, ritualised, kept within bounds. Josephine discovered she enjoyed both. Flirting, playing an agreed game, using words to perform an agreeable and witty quadrille, with the steps well known in advance to both sides, and ending nowhere dangerous, but in bows and flourishes and compliments; and the other sort, wilder and more difficult and frightening, to be invented on the spur of the moment, step matched to opposite step, gesture invented to match opposite gesture or combat it. More naked and raw, this kind of talking, it made you vulnerable, it exposed you, you could only do it with people you trusted, it was a serious game. She needed both sorts, as she also needed long hours of silence and solitude, every day. For reading and writing; for praying. At other times she wanted to make love with Lucian for hour upon hour, urgent and redfaced and shouting, until she was spent and fell asleep.

Magdalena, one day, produced the three yellow-wrapped scrolls that she had taken, all those years ago, from Beatrice's sandalwood chest.

– I couldn't understand them, she explained: so I put them away. I'd forgotten all about them. You should have them. They're yours.

Josephine carried them to her hut, and placed them on the table. She undid them one by one. The ancient coverings fell away from her hands and she remembered Magdalena and herself playing, girls full of curiosity pulling up their skirts to display themselves to each other. Some darkened room, with a wide stone ledge set under the window. Warm sun on her skin. Knees bent and pulled apart while Magdalena peered. Oh you *woman*, her cousin had shrieked and they had convulsed in laughter. The smell of herself, like fresh curds. She liked it, in those days before she learned she shouldn't. Inside, she had something particular that meant she was a woman. She wasn't sure what it was but she was proud of it. Then she'd learned to feel disgusted with herself. Foul, evil-smelling, like a heap of carrion attracting gross, buzzing flies. Yet a long time ago, there had been innocence and gaiety, the comfort of bodies, living inside herself without giving it a second thought, she had not been ashamed at all, she remembered that now. She stared at the scrolls.

They were written in what she could recognise, from Lucian's teaching, as the script of the Faithless Ones. Elegant and cryptic pen strokes. A closed code. They had been annotated, in the vernacular, by an enthusiastic reader, whose excited and fiery comments spattered the margins of the text. The black loops and dashes of this person's hand were unmistakable. The writing was that of Beatrice.

The crystal cave, she had written: the secret stair, the house under the sea, the green fire inside the blue-flowering sage, the seraphim in the golden cloud, the melting glacier, the dark heart, the arrows of flame, the emerald gate.

She had also frequently written and underlined the words *yes* and *why*.

Josephine puzzled over these scraps. Like bits of poetry shaved off and allowed to fall, little curled-up rolls, on the workshop floor. She murmured the words over and over to herself, until they ceased to make sense, turned drowsy and hypnotic as a chanted prayer. She forgot who and where she was. She had no edges, no outline, she flowed out and merged with table, chair, open door, sunlight.

The earth spoke to her. What the earth said was untranslatable. It was a language Josephine was drawn into. She collapsed and fell in, as though the earth had parted and revealed a great yawning split, reddish brown, as when the earth is saturated and swollen by heavy rains and floods, and there are landslips, and people fall in, fall forwards and down, captured, absorbed by towering sticky walls of mud, then the gap presses back, closes again, a kind of eating, the earth draws us into itself and makes us part of it.

What was going on was this earth language, with Josephine now a part of its grammar, earth sentences, the earth was the speech she could hear, that spoke her and spoke to her, that attracted her into its structure and dissolved her into a part of speech, a part of earth. How terrifying at first, the fall, into the chasm that opened its brown lips and drew her in, and then what a flood of bliss, the rains pouring in torrents through the valleys into the parched fields. She belonged here. The earth was a great body and she belonged with it and was part of it. She and the earth were the same body. The one body was both of them.

Now she could see that the earth was alive, teeming with life, holding everything in a continuous dance, it was a vast memory swarming with past, present and future life, this was what God was, this profound understanding, in this untranslatable speech, that we were all made the same, part of each other, rocks and stones and trees and people all whirling about together living and dying and being transformed into each other and so reborn, and so, dying, held so lightly in that connectedness.

Nothing had been lost. Beatrice was there, and Ferdinand, and all her early joy, and everything and everyone she had ever loved, all held lightly, as on the open palm of an enormous hand, and she was not wicked, but utterly loved, there was goodness inside her made of the same stuff as the goodness outside her, she was part of it, rich and full and good as an egg.

There was a pebble on her table, that she used for weighing down her pile of papers. She took it up, and closed her fingers round it. The pebble was alive. A body full of joy. That was what she had been made for: to express this joy. Now she had to make something with what she'd been given. Testify. Bear witness to this joy.

She put the scrolls away again. Magdalena kept them in a cupboard in the kitchen, where the Inspectors would not notice them if they came poking around. They appeared to be part of the *batterie de cuisine*, rolling pins wrapped in yellow tea-cloths.

She read and studied. She struggled to record her visions. She did not know why. She was impelled to do it, and she obeyed the voice inside which said: write all this down. She continued to garden, to dance and play cards, to make love. She invented amusements with Isabel: card tricks, charades, costumes. They cooked together, fancy dishes to divert the evening guests. Spun caramel baskets of cold meats modelled in marzipan, meringue toadstools, sugar mouths and breasts and tongues, chocolate skulls and crossbones. She talked with Magdalena and Lucian, with Isabel. In the evenings she made up her face, put on her yellow satin dress, and went to work.

She tested out her plans for the future on her two friends.

She left Isabel out of these discussions, considering her too young, and not wanting to over-influence her by her own choice of life. She failed to reflect whether this would hurt her niece or not. She packed her off to bed with a hearty kiss and shut the door on her: night-night, darling.

Josephine, Magdalena and Lucian lolled side by side on the big grey sofa, feet up, shoes off, finishing the wine. All the guests had gone home.

Josephine described how she wanted to found houses for single women to live in, if they wanted to, but nothing like the overcrowded and ramshackle convent which she and Isabel had endured and which they were so happy to have left.

Each house would be a double house, looking two ways, with one entrance on one side and one on the other. The house would have two addresses, one on each street that it fronted. Nobody except the inhabitants, on entering the double house from either side, would know that the other half of the house existed. In one of those medical books of her mother's, that she had snatched a glance at so long ago, Josephine had seen a drawing of some Siamese twins. Now this served as her model for a house, and for how she wanted to live. Two houses together, back to back; two bodies joined by a single skin. But there would be ways through, from one to the other, for those who lived there and who had the keys to the communicating doors. The existence of the other side would be kept secret. Each woman who lived here would be able to live two lives: a double life; it was that simple.

One side would be a convent without Catholicism and Catholic beliefs. It would still be called a convent, to signify that when you entered here you gave yourself completely to the life within. You committed yourself. You abandoned yourself. Total giving. Total freedom as a result. This side of the house would be built to conform to the style of living perfected by the desert hermits, each of whom had a small hut set in a small garden, near to that of the others but at a sufficient distance to maintain privacy. In this house each woman could have her own cell, or hut, and she could join the others for meals if she wanted to, or she could choose to eat and meditate alone. She could have as much solitude as she needed, for whatever purpose. Each woman would have her own little garden to sit, stroll and work in, and she could join the others in the communal garden when and if she so wanted. The kitchen would be the chapel. The altar would be the table on which they prepared food. Mass would be a question simply of cooking a good dinner. They would not need priests because they would all learn to cook.

They would have the solitude they so desired. Some women thirst for solitude as for water in a drought. This has not always been recognised. A solitude of your own choosing, begun and ended at your own whim, can be a fine thing, if you have plenty of books and wine within reach, food, a garden, wood for the fire.

Josephine had realised that she wanted to be not a full-time nun but a part-time one. And so, when the inhabitants of her convent felt, as they regularly would, the need to live a different kind of life, they would walk into the heart of the double house, unlock the communicating door, and emerge into the other side. Here, they would be able to live the kind of life that hermit-nuns do not. The convivial, social, chatty, sexual, dancing and feasting life. This side of the house would be a mixture of club, restaurant, salon, dance hall, café-theatre, boudoir, opium den, and so on.

This would be the side of the house people ran in and out of casually, freely. You might sleep here, as often as you chose. You might move in. You might move out. But always, waiting for you, when you needed it, would be the other side of the house. The place of visionary bliss. The sensual convent, where God manifested in sensual joy.

Some women would spend more time on one side of the house, and some on the other, depending on mood, personality, inclination, change of circumstances, and so on. The changeover might be daily, weekly, monthly.

Magdalena and Lucian pointed out some of the flaws in this plan.

— What about married women? Magdalena asked: women with children? Are they included? Who would look after the children if the mothers kept going off?

Josephine was flustered.

— I don't know, she admitted: I haven't got it all planned out yet. I've begun with the single women because there are so many of us put away into terrible convents. Married women might want something different. I don't know.

— What about men? Lucian asked: if they are to come as guests to the salon side of the house, shouldn't they too have their own hermitages?

Josephine hesitated. Then she burst out.

— It's up to men to discover what they want and sort it

out. I can't do it. *You* organise the houses for men, Lucian.
You're a man!

Josephine wanted to found one of these houses in every
city in the country, to give all her countrywomen a greater
choice in how they lived. Magdalena persuaded her to begin
with her own city. She promised to help her find a house and
to pay the rent for the first year, to get the inhabitants started
off on a firm footing. They would earn their own livings by
the labour of their own hands, and thus be free from the
meddling and demands of patrons.

– I promise not to interfere, Magdalena said.

Josephine laughed.

– I don't believe a word of it.

Lucian insisted that there would have to be a conventional chapel and indeed chaplain, to save the nuns from
being investigated by the Inspectors. They would have to
seem convincing, to be apparently a conventional enclosed
house when viewed from the outside, in order to have their
freedom on the inside to do as they wished.

– If you look like an independent group of holy women
who've simply decided to live together, he argued: you're far
more likely to come under suspicion. The Inspectors don't
like such arrangements, as you know very well. They tend to
break them up and send the women into ordinary convents.
Whereas if you have a Rule, and keep the Blessed Sacrament
in the chapel, you will look perfectly normal, just like any
other nuns, and you will be safe.

What the world would see, if it bothered to look, would
be the establishment, one by one, of strict convents of the

Reform, gradually appearing throughout the land. Worldly people would shrug, and sneer, and not give a damn what a bunch of enclosed nuns got up to. They would be full of excitement, instead, about the new salons which were springing up in all the major cities, run by courtesans of a wit and elegance never before seen. Men and women alike would flock in, to talk, dance, drink, gamble, make love and generally amuse themselves, and the life of the country would be renewed and enriched, nourished by an additional, secret source of prayer and contemplation.

– In time, Josephine prophesied: the existence of the other side of the house will be able to be revealed. The double house will not need to be kept a secret for ever.

– But for the moment, Lucian counselled her: at the beginning, everything must be done in tremendous secrecy, to avoid giving rise to gossip and attracting the attention of the Inspectors.

Josephine looked from one to the other of her two friends, seated one on each side of her on the grey brocade sofa. All three of them were heretics now in the eyes of the Church, guilty of blasphemy and fornication also, liable to extreme torture before the final punishment of a slow and agonising death. She had rescued herself from such torment before. A second time, she might be less fortunate. She shuddered, because she knew no one could be brave in the Inspectors' prisons. It was the first thing they extracted from you, before their pincers got to work on fingernails, clitoris, teeth.

The Life of Saint Dympna

Dympna was born, on her father's side, from a line of Celtic chieftains. Her mother came from a different tribe, far away on the other side of the mountains. Dympna had the same hazel eyes as her mother, the same fresh skin, the same long golden hair. Most of the women of her father's country had blue eyes and black hair, so she and the queen were rarities.

Dympna looked very like her mother, and promised to grow up as beautiful. She wore her hair in two long plaits down to her knees, just like the queen did, and, as soon as she was tall enough, began borrowing all her clothes. She tried on her mother's blue woollen cloak and tunic, her leather belt, her silver brooch and bracelets and pins. In front of the polished steel mirror she jerked her hips this way and that, and smiled. The queen was so young looking that the two of them could have been taken for sisters. A stranger might, indeed, have thought Dympna the queen. She walked so proudly, and carried her head so high. She took after her father, and his people, who were used to being looked up to. His clan had ruled its neighbours for generations, by dint of brute force and with ruthless authority, so its members, Dympna among them, grew up believing that they were naturally far more important and of greater value than other people. Dympna's father told her constantly how she was born for great things and how she was infinitely superior to the rest of her sex. So she paced the halls of the castle with a small smile of self-satisfaction, conscious of all the people who passed in and out and admired her.

The clan's wattle and daub houses clustered around the great castle, guarded by a picket fence. On one side the castle looked out to the sea and on the other to the mountains. Here the chieftains had always lived, and from this stronghold they sallied out on raids against their neighbours. In summer they went out plundering and marauding, and in winter they shut themselves up against the salt winds, the gales and storms, and sorted through their spoils.

Dympna's father pulled her up onto the castle battlements and showed her the world, far below, at her feet: hers for the taking. He taught her to ride astride like a man, he taught her to hunt with a hawk, to set traps for rabbits, to kill deer with a well-aimed arrow, to pluck and skin the creatures she caught and killed. He encouraged her cleverness. He trained her up himself. He asked her riddles, or set her puzzles to solve, as though he were setting up jumps in a steeplechase. Then he watched as Dympna galloped round the track, flying over hurdle after hurdle. He set them higher and higher, and each time she whisked round the course and never fell.

Her gentle mother looked on in silence while all the clansmen admired her daughter's beauty and brilliant, imperious chatter. But her old nurse Gereburna muttered that there were more worthwhile things for a girl to learn. Dympna laughed at her. Her father's praise was her food and drink. Nothing else mattered.

While Dympna was still just a girl, her mother fell ill. None of the clan's healers could save her. Her desperate husband knelt at her bed and sobbed.

Dympna discovered she was fastened to the queen by a rope of death. Death stalked her, flung a noose over her head and neck, put her on a leash as though she were a dog. She tugged free. She spurred her stallion along the beach, racing the incoming tide over the flat sands of the estuary, or she fisted her hawk and went hunting, or took her dogs and ran through the forest with them until she was exhausted, or she climbed to the very top of the mountain behind the castle, flinging herself down on the springy turf and gazing longingly at the larks spiralling up over her head into the fathomless sky. Back at home in the castle, where death was closer, she engaged her father in hectic talks and conversations, or she caught the cats belonging to Gereburna and threw them across the room.

The old nurse did not spend much time with her darling girl any more, for she was busy attending to the dying queen. Dympna's only companion was her father. The castle had become a lonely place, as the young queen's life flickered out, as death usurped her place, as the kingdom became death's kingdom.

Just before she died, the queen rallied all her strength to speak to her husband one last time. She implored him to accede to her dying wish.

– I know you'll want to marry again, she said: but promise me you'll only marry a woman who is as beautiful as I am, and who has the same golden hair.

The king smiled at her through his tears.

– You know very well I love puzzles and riddles, he said: but the one you have set me is far too easy to crack. Since all the women here have black hair and blue eyes and can't come near you for beauty, I can easily promise you never to marry again! How could I ever find a wife as lovely and as gentle as you? It's impossible. Rest easy. You know that, and so do I.

The queen died. They burned her on a great pyre on the seashore, put her ashes in a gold box, and buried the box under a cairn of stones high on the mountainside, with gulls circling overhead and just the wind for company. She had been greatly beloved, and so she was greatly mourned. Everyone in the clan, and from all the country around, came to her funeral, and climbed the mountain to lay bunches of flowers on her grave.

Dympna was a chieftain's daughter, raised to be brave and not to show signs of weakness. She put on a stony face like a mask, so that no one could imagine she had ever felt a moment's grief.

Death had been booted out of the castle now. Death was clasped by gold locks in a small gold box, imprisoned under the earth high up on the mountainside. The cord was broken, and Dympna was free.

She was fifteen. In her spring time. Like the young trees juicy with sap rising along branch and stem, she put forth her green buds, her leaves and flowers. She flourished, grew. There was no stopping her. She bloomed into great beauty.

She plaited her hair, put on her mother's blue woollen tunic and cloak, fastened up her sleeves with her mother's silver pins and brooches, and assumed her mother's place. She ran the household. Suddenly she exhibited expertise in all those feminine arts Gereburna had despaired of teaching her. She looked after her grief-stricken father with gentleness, with patience and tact. At night she sat with him by the fire, very close, and listened to him, hour after hour. In his sorrow, he showed her his weakness, which he had always kept hidden. When he was with her, he did not have to be a chieftain, he could leave war outside, he could prop his leather shield against the door, unbuckle his leather breast-plate and throw it down, leave all his weapons in a heap on the trodden earth floor. With this young girl who nestled close to him, and gazed up at him with shining eyes, and revered him as though he were a god, he felt safe.

In time, his grief turned to irritability. The courtiers saw it was the moment for speaking to him. Their spokesman, one of his most trusted advisers, came to him and said: you really ought to marry again, too prolonged a period of celibacy will do you no good, and how can a chieftain rule without a queen at his side? For the good of your people, you must take a wife.

The king remembered his promise to his dying queen.

– Certainly I'll marry, he agreed: if you think I must, but only the most beautiful of blondes.

In that country of dark-haired women, there were plenty of beauties to be had, but none with the stipulated fair hair. The courtiers searched far and wide, but had to turn down all the candidates who offered themselves or were offered by their families.

While he waited, the king drew even nearer to his daughter. He thought he had never appreciated her sufficiently before now. He began to understand just how dear to him she was. Her presence comforted him, as no one else's could. He talked to her exactly as though she were an adult of his own age, because she was so intelligent, and because he did not believe in treating her as a child, and because he had to have someone to tell how he felt. In that lonely, remote castle, full of fierce fighting men, she was the only companion he had that he could be intimate with, who did not expect him to get drunk and rowdy when he wasn't in the mood. She was the only woman there, and he had brought her up to be womanly in just the way he liked. She knew when he needed her to be quiet and still, and when he wanted her to be lively and amusing. And with her fresh beauty and her golden hair, she was the very image of his dead wife.

Gereburna felt uneasy when she noticed how much time the young princess spent closeted away with her father. She felt she had neglected Dympna, at a time when the girl was going through anguish. She had abandoned her, and thought more of the dying mother than of the bereft daughter. She began to see that her father was the only person in the world whom Dympna felt truly loved her. But it was a love which was so possessive that it shut the door on everybody else. She took Dympna aside and tried to warn her of possible danger. She was so horrified at the thoughts which had begun to cross her brain that she didn't dare to put them into words. She mumbled vague strictures about how Dympna needed to mix more with young people of her own age, how she'd soon start taking an interest in boys and how that was only natural.

Dympna tossed her head at Gereburna.

– I don't like boys, or young men either come to that, she said: they're stupid and boring.

She pulled her nurse's grey locks.

– I like older men, she said: like you do, my darling anxious Gereburna. So do stop fussing.

Some days later the old woman tried again.

– Your father may want to marry again, she suggested: it's not to be expected that he'll want to go on for ever as he is now, so lonely and solitary.

Dympna's laugh was long, loud and contemptuous.

– But he's got *me*, she said.

She refused to take any more lessons from Gereburna, and had her sent away when she presented herself at the palace doors. The old nurse cursed herself for her tactlessness. Now that the young princess was so angry with her she

203

would no longer trust her. She would no longer confide in her. Little as she had ever shown signs of wanting to do so. Gereburna had thought that one day she could be a true friend to Dympna. But now the girl wanted nothing more to do with her.

– Interfering old busybody, that Gereburna, Dympna said to her father: dirty-minded old beast.

She gulped wine from her golden goblet.

– You won't ever marry again, will you? she asked her father.

He sighed.

– Who could I marry?

– Me, of course, Dympna joked.

Her father laughed, playing with his wine. He picked up the joke and tossed it back, like a ball. The most light and playful of balls bouncing amidst the litter of supper things on the table, the wine cups, the flagons of wine, the plates of meat.

– And what shall I give you, dear heart, to persuade you to marry me?

– For my trousseau I shall need three dresses, Dympna said: one golden as the sun, one silvery as the moon, and one as sparkling as the stars. And I shall need a fur coat!

She was laughing. Her face was radiant, soft. Both of them had drunk a lot of wine. It was as though the queen sat there, nodding her head at him, urging him to go on, assuring him that it was all right. If you have my approval, she seemed to be saying in her low, sweet voice, what does it matter what anyone else thinks? This way, my darling, we can never be parted. Didn't I carry her inside me, and won't you be loving me even more by loving her? We were one flesh once, she and I, I and you. How can it possibly be wrong? Love your daughter and so love me. Don't leave me, my darling. Be faithful to me. Never betray me with another woman. Marry your daughter, and you stay married to me.

The king saw his dead bride rise and approach him. She held out her hand. He heard her speak: I'll never love any other man as I love you. You're the only man I'll ever love. I will stay with you for ever. I will always love you, and I will never leave you, I will never go away.

Dympna was smiling at him. She was holding his hand. Her face was flushed, her eyes were very bright. She looked as young and beautiful as his wife had been on her wedding day.

– I'll fetch you the dresses you want, her father said: and the fur coat, and then you must keep your promise and marry me.

The following day, at noon, the sun shone high in the sky. In that heat it was hard to work, even to walk about outside. The servants slept in the kitchen yard, in the shade of the rose tree clambering above the cellar door. In the woods beyond the castle, Gereburna dozed on a pad of moss under an oak tree, her head pillowed on a heap of fresh bracken.

The king said to Dympna: take your clothes off.

She obeyed. She laughed at him, thinking it was some kind of game, and quickly shed all her clothes in a heap at his feet. There was no harm in going naked in front of her own father, she assured herself. And besides, she wanted him to look at her. She liked seeing his eyes on her. His admiration bound them closer together, made them more intimate.

The king seized her by the shoulders and spun her around. The sun enveloped her in warmth. It dressed her in cloth-of-gold.

– There's the dress you wanted, as golden as the sun, said her father: here and now I am giving it to you.

At night, after supper, he commanded her again to take off all her clothes, and again she obeyed. He took her by the hand and pulled her outside onto the battlements, high up under the starlit sky. Below them dozed the guards, and their dogs, and the hounds, and the servants. In the woods, Gereburna leaned against the oak tree's trunk and yawned.

It was the night of the full moon. Up she sailed, orange at first, then gold, and then silver-white. Moonlight poured down upon the earth, and upon Dympna's skin as her father seized her by the shoulders and spun her round. Dazzling moonbeams flowed all over her like white and silver satin.

– There's the dress you wanted, said her father: as silvery as the moon: here and now I am giving it to you.

The stars came out, one by one, steadily gaining in brightness. A net of silver, woven of silver cords, knotted with silver, thrown over Dympna's bare white shoulders, fastening her with loops and buttons of starlight.

– There's the dress you wanted, said her father: as sparkling as the stars: here and now I am giving it to you.

Filmy as chiffon, fine as cobwebs stretched over grass, the three dresses floated about Dympna in layers, golden and silvery and starry. She pirouetted for her father with gleaming eyes and a pouting mouth, she raised her beautiful arms above her head and pointed her toe, she posed for him against the midnight blue sky.

– But I'm cold, father, she said: where's that fur coat you promised me?

– Here, he answered.

He held it out for her, a coat made of richly striped and spotted and tortoiseshell pelts, the skins of all Gereburna's cats that he had had killed, flayed, and then sewn into this sumptuous furry coat with deep, wide sleeves you could wrap your hands in, a big collar you could turn up around your head and face, and long fur skirts swinging from the wide fur yoke.

– So now, my dear Dympna, said her father: you must keep your own promise, and marry me.

She ran ahead of him, down the twisting turret stairs, spiralling downwards, slippery stone that delivered her down, down, down, into darkness lit intermittently by torches, and far behind her she heard her father's footsteps, his breathing, his determined pursuit. But when she reached the bottom stair, raced out, and slammed shut the turret door, there he was in front of her, smiling and bowing and holding out his hand.

Gereburna slept badly because of the moonlight, a white glare which knifed under her eyelids and kept prising open her eyes. On and off she slept and dreamed by turns, tossing on her bracken bed which was not soft enough to cushion her old bones against the hard ground strewn with twigs and stones. The screech owls' cries flailed against her ears, and the scream of the mice they hunted and killed. Spiders descended on long threads from the branches of the oak tree above, their legs brushing against her cheek. The woods rustled and quivered as invisible creatures passed to and fro.

She dreamed of Dympna's wedding. There rode her darling on a grey horse, a crown of twisted gold set on her long yellow hair. She was dressed in flowing robes embroidered with motifs of the sun and moon and stars, a rich cloak of striped and spotted fur flowing back from her shoulders. Beside her, on his black horse, rode her husband-father, one of his hands laid lightly on his reins and his other hand gripping one of hers. The horses paced along and the bride and groom smiled at each other. They rode between lines of their people, who held up boughs of apple blossom and waved them as they passed, so that the petals of the flowers flew off and surrounded them like white hail. And there in the crowd was the dead queen in her white shroud, half her face rotted away and worms wriggling in the sockets of her eyes, waiting for the bridal couple to reach her, so that she could point at them with her fingers of white bone and curse them as they passed. Dympna put her chin in the air and laughed with triumph.

Gereburna woke up. A chilly dawn, with the dew falling, and her bones aching after her night on the hard ground. She looked towards the castle, where a light still burned in one of the windows. As she strained her eyes to see which tower, which window, the light went out.

She heard the hunters a long way off, the long wailing of their horns, the baying of their dogs, the shouts of men and the neighing of horses. A crashing and trampling in the undergrowth as wild boar and deer fled for cover. Then the king and his retinue passed by in a swirl of green cloaks and black bridles, the hounds yelping and barking as they scented their quarry. A swift beautiful creature like a leopard, or a large cat, with a rich spotted and furred coat, fled across the track just in front of Gereburna, and vanished in the greenery. Two minutes later, the dogs streamed past. The king was at his favourite sport. He was no longer melancholy. He was himself again. It was the hunting season. Every day he hunted, from morning to night, and every evening he returned to the castle with his men, to feast and drink and listen to minstrels singing newly composed songs praising his bravery and prowess.

Gereburna never saw Dympna again, for she died of old age in the forest. She shrivelled up like an old root. She buried herself under moss and branches and leaves, then died, and her body rotted into the earth. Dympna was killed in a hunting accident one morning in the forest, and her body laid to rest with her mother's, on the high mountainside.

THE STORY OF
JOSEPHINE

Magdalena laid on a grand party to raise money for the first year's rent of the new convent. The guests were to come in costumes and wear masks. She promised supper, dancing and fireworks, and a few surprises.

Isabel said to Josephine: tonight I want to play the part of a guest, not a hostess. Tonight I'm not going to help you. I want to enjoy myself for once.

She spat these words out like cherry stones, a fistful of crossness dropped, let rattle onto the floor. She was hardly speaking to Josephine at all but to herself. She put her arms around herself and began to practise her dance steps. This way it was impossible. She picked up a tambourine and began again. She threw it down.

– You play for me, will you?

The tambourine was square, mounted on a stick. You

shook it with one hand and struck it with the other. The wooden frame was painted pink and was decorated with ribbon streamers in the same colour. Josephine twirled it above her head and set the little bells clashing. Isabel placed her hands one on each side of her waist and jumped, neatly and precisely, pointing the sharp toe of her shoe up then down. She raised her arms, curved her elbows, writhed her wrists. The tambourine insisted shrilly and her feet rapped the floor in time. She scowled. Josephine read the message that her niece's high heels tapped out: why do we have to move house *again*? Isabel stamped and frowned while Josephine watched.

– I promised your father I would keep you with me until you were sixteen, she said: you know that. That's only another six months. Then you and he will decide what you are going to do.

– You mean you and he will decide, Isabel said.

She spun round fast so that her skirts flew up. Then she ran out of the room.

Josephine wore a mask like everyone else, though she felt that her yellow satin gown, well known to all the regular guests by this time, made it clear who she was. Isabel and Magdalena both got dressed in secret, so that no one should know they had exchanged clothes. Magdalena wore Isabel's green velvet skirt and waistcoat, her feather and her emeralds, and Isabel wore Magdalena's new balldress of black silk, cut very low and laced very tight. To Josephine, when they descended the stairs, it was immediately clear which was which, but she joined in the game and pretended to be taken in. Both had black masks edged with black gauze ruffles and sewn with shiny black sequins, and both carried black fans. They preened together at the mirror, very pleased with themselves.

The guests arrived, filling the big room with their cheerful noise. The women's skin looked soft and golden as wax in the light of the candles that gleamed down on their shoulders and arms. Tips of flame trembled and glimmered, reflected back and forth by the mirrors whose brilliant surfaces were like water you could walk into, that would close round you and take you deep down into another world, peopled by mermaids wearing bracelets of coral and pearl, darting silver fish. Josephine trod lightly through the room as though she were swimming. She laughed and chatted to a host of strangers who waved their hands gracefully like fronds of seaweed. She performed her role mechanically, withdrawn into a dream of the house she wanted to find. Her words and gestures were learned by heart, a code of manners that got her through the evening with ease and detachment, while she stood behind herself, floating in a reverie, treading water, buoyant and half asleep, while all around her people leaped and rolled and dived like porpoises in the exuberance of their conversation.

She did come back to herself, eyes wide open, when Lucian came in. He arrived as part of a group of men who were all very tall, and all dressed in black. They all wore identical black masks and flourished red lace handkerchiefs. Lucian could not be hidden. She thought: *I know him*, and felt her insides jump and loosen, soft as sea anemones. She watched his eyes swivel across the room and rest on the figure of Isabel in her Magdalena-costume. The same look all the men had been giving her as they came in. They could not help looking. She caught them with her display of bosom and confined waist, her high cone of dark hair scooped up backwards then tumbling down onto her bare shoulders, the play of her mouth as she pouted and half-smiled. Their gaze hooked on to her and they appraised her, slowly, looking her over, up and down. Isabel pretended not to notice. She tried to be haughty, lifting her chin and walking imperiously about, but she could not conceal her excitement, her glee. Her cheeks glistened red, and she sipped quickly at her glass of wine. Josephine thought: I couldn't do that at her age, I was too frightened, I didn't know how. But Magdalena did. She examined her friend. Magdalena was swishing her green feather in one hand, as though it were a riding whip, against the side of her dress. The other hand looped and circled in the air as she talked to the group of men in black, laughing. She exclaimed and pointed. She told each of them precisely why she recognised him. They, in turn, addressed her as Isabel.

To accommodate the large number of guests, Magdalena had opened up the cellars. These formed a series of interconnected rooms opening off a tiny central hall, built of stone that had been roughly plastered, and now, for the party, painted a glowing red. Each cellar was windowless, with a vaulted ceiling, and the fourth wall, facing the hall, made of stone arches, so that you could see across, into the room opposite. Fires in tripods muffled the air with warmth.

Lanterns of pierced tin hung from pillars and sent star-shaped patches of light careering across floors and walls. Isabel, peeping about, took in the number of silk-covered wide divans heaped with pillows and rugs. The invitation offered was to sink down on these, kick off your shoes, lie back. As indeed many people were already doing, alone or in couples. She could not quite make out, in the shifting spangled darkness, the precise patterns of limbs. The more discreet had wriggled under the silk covers, or behind the columns that supported the vaulted ceiling.

Upstairs Isabel went again, unwilling to be contained too soon in darkness. She wanted, first, to be remarked by everyone, like a comet trailing its tail of fire and gold feathers across the night sky high above the admiring crowd. She would not be extinguished yet under the weight of a lover's body. That could happen later, when she allowed the one she desired to track her down and catch her. But now she paced, displaying herself to the guests crowding the hall and salon, slipping in and out of the stream of masks, head held high, stretching out her arms to hold up her skirts in ballooning bunches of black silk, turning her head from side to side to show off her neck, her cheekbones.

People began crowding on to the terrace, to watch the ballet taking place in the garden. Flaming torches on poles were planted in the ground, like burning bushes, to light the scene. The dancers swirled across the black strip of grass in front of the chestnut trees, dressed in black, holding strings of bobbing lanterns. The crescent moon sat on a swing while a constellation of stars did somersaults. Creatures dressed in skins of phosphorescence ran in and out of the bushes, inviting the guests to follow them into the web of moonlight and shadow and get lost. Brief visions, like moths beating up close to the window then vanishing again. Last came a cascade of fireworks, a rainbow torn up and released. Curtains of blazing gold and silver flowers, a shower of meteors, and the show was finished.

Isabel danced with one of the men in black, whom she recognised as Lucian, though, to tease her, he refused to acknowledge his true identity and insisted, also, on addressing her as Magdalena. She was convinced he knew she was Isabel. She enjoyed enormously the pretence that both of them were other people. She took part in a piece of theatre while a second Isabel watched and commented and kept control. She had drunk enough wine that the music entered her and took hold of her. Her feet knew exactly what to do. Haze of drink and warmth and pleasure, all her shyness carried by the second Isabel like a coat, the real Isabel was dancing on a golden staircase gently pulling her to become ever more light airy dissolved, in fact not Isabel at all, not Magdalena either. In a moment of clarity cool and hard and cutting as glass she thought *I am Josephine* and she held out her hands to her aunt's lover who spun her close to him, clasped her in his arms and expertly swept her about, forwards and back. Lucian made Isabel turn and turn, whirling her so rapidly she was giddy, he reeled and rolled her in and out, he held her so firmly and moved her so fast she felt weightless as though they were flying.

The music stopped. Lucian drew Isabel out of the room

very smoothly as though they were still dancing. Down the stairs they went, down into the cellars, into the dark corner, subsiding among cushions onto a low bed that was springy and soft. Oh yes, Lucian was telling Isabel, I am certainly who you think I am, let me show you how certain, he began kissing her, before she expected it, and, taken by surprise, she felt fire start up inside. So she abandoned herself, there in the darkness, mask torn off and thrown aside with his, unable to see his face in the shadows and knowing her own was hidden too. Lucian knows it is I, Isabel thought, he is not deceived for a moment that I am Magdalena, he knows the shape of my face and body from watching me grow up all these years, and yet it's true that he does not know me, not *this* me, she is a nameless woman, we are strangers to one another, he is treating me as he treats Josephine, he has never touched me before. Who is he if not Lucian?

That moment. Just before you touch each other. When you shake with fear and desire together, wanting to fall forwards and give yourself completely, when you want, also, to run away and hide yourself, you can't move, you let it happen, you draw nearer until there is only a thin line drawn in air that separates you, then you cross over and meet. Hands, eyes, mouths, skin. Those tense minutes before that happens, when you move into the light, you look at each other, let your desire show in your eyes. Flinging down your stake and gambling, risking yourself. Offering. Inviting him closer. Daring yourself and him. Isabel wanted to stay in control. She wanted to go out of control and not care what happened. She played that game, dancing forwards then back. Ready. Not ready. To become lovers. All the time knowing it was Lucian, and all the time pretending that he was a stranger.

Lucian undid her dress very carefully. Isabel lay back and waited. His hands unfastened her silk casings, he pushed the dress off her shoulders, his fingers, grazing her skin, cool and quick, undoing buttons, laces and hooks one after the other. They grappled in the darkness, stealthy and rustling and not crying out, lest someone hear. All around them were similar noises: breathing, murmurs, heartbeats, hushed exclamations bitten into hands as lovers crawled, leaped, squirmed into each other.

Isabel must have fallen asleep. When she awoke Lucian was gone. The darkness around her felt empty. She flung back on those parts of her clothes which had come off, smoothed her hair, stroked her hands over her hot cheeks, cooling them with a spit-wetted handkerchief.

She went back upstairs to find that she had missed midnight, the unmasking. Guests were crowding out through the big double front doors onto the square. Gusts of cool air, calls of thanks, exclamations, laughter. Lucian, mask dangling from one hand, kissed Josephine on both cheeks, Magdalena too, and departed with his band of friends. Isabel watched him go. She hung back so that he would not see her.

Magdalena and Josephine closed the door on the last of the guests. They sank down on the stairs, yawning, grimacing with tiredness. They drank a last glass of wine together and shared a plate of macaroons.

Isabel clenched her fists in the pockets of her dress. She

walked up to the two older women who, quickly revived by the sugary cakes, were now gossiping merrily about the progress of the evening. Josephine had unpeeled her black lace gloves and laid them over her knee, like two dead moths. She smoothed them as she talked, patting the silky creases with her forefinger. Her eyes shone with amusement as she described to Magdalena the behaviour of one of the guests who had done an impromptu striptease in the salon, to brisk applause, while Magdalena had been in the garden with one of her admirers. Josephine still looked young. Her curly black hair had a silver streak in front, but her face was unlined. The nest of wrinkles round her eyes was part of the character of her face. The laughter that brought them into being was that of a child, Isabel thought, watching. In many ways Josephine had not grown up at all. She herself felt much older, more experienced. Worldly wise. World weary.

Josephine looked up at her niece and stretched out a hand to her.

– My darling, so there you are. Did you have a good time?

Isabel told her aunt what she had done, and with whom. She noted the shock on the two older women's faces, the stilled muscles, opened mouths, widened eyes. Power surged through her like juice, filling her up so that she tingled, her skin tight, a container for triumph.

Then Josephine laughed.

– What a story. He was with me all evening. It was someone else. Or perhaps you've made the whole thing up?

Isabel burst into tears. She pushed between the two old hags, so smug, sitting there fluffing up their feathers and squawking at her, mocking and humiliating her, and ran upstairs in tears. I hate you I hate you I hate you. The words tripped up, trailed into the distance, banged a door.

Later, when she had undressed and put on her night clothes, Josephine crept into the room she now thought of as Isabel's. She sat on the edge of the bed and patted her niece's rigid shoulder.

She whispered: I love you. I always have and I always will. Whatever you do. You can't stop me loving you.

Isabel cried out in a sobbing voice: oh leave me alone, please go away. Just leave me alone.

The following morning, Magdalena took Josephine to survey the house she had found for her. It formed the end of a packed alley of shops and tenements. It stood wedged into the tight gap between yellow façades, their balconies strung with washing. The lines met overhead, a flap of damp towels and shirts. This had once been part of the old Faithless quarter, before the Faithless Ones had been driven out along with all the other unbelievers. The little house was built on the site of what had been their prayer-house. More recently it had been a soap-making workshop. Soap still made part of the structure, fitted into cracks on the floor, like putty. You could scratch it up with your fingernail. It scented the house with lilac, peach blossom, lavender.

– Surely it's too small, Josephine argued.

They paced it out. There was room only for a kitchen-dining-room on the ground floor. Upstairs were two lofts which could be partitioned to give thirteen box-sized cells. But there was a small yard at the back, where the second half of the house could be built once they had found the money. The cowshed at the far end of the yard could be converted into a chapel. The tumbledown woodshed could house a privy.

— I know it's incomplete, Magdalena said: but it's a start.

Josephine collected together a group of her old friends from the Incarnation who were as dissatisfied as she had been with their style of life. The prioress was pleased to be rid of them. She sped them on their way with gifts: a few straw mats for them to sleep on, some rusty cooking pots she no longer needed. Magdalena donated a table, two long benches, thirteen plates and spoons, a frying pan, a breadboard, a knife. Father Peter begged candlesticks and altar vessels for the chapel. He assumed that he was participating in a renewal of conventual piety, and no one told him otherwise. The group of new nuns, led by Sister Maria, cautiously welcomed Josephine's plans for the future. They saw clearly that these were unlikely to come to fruition for some time. They were happy, in the meantime, to live as a small community of friends, to work for a living, and to adopt Josephine's reformed Rule, which was much less punitive than the one they had been supposed to follow at the Incarnation. As long as they respected each other's privacy, and need for silence and solitude, she left them free to do as they liked.

Isabel made the thirteenth in the group. Sulky, retired into herself, she was marking time until she should turn sixteen. Then, she promised herself, she would do something, show them what was what, force them to see how stupid they were with their chatter of desert hermits when all they were was a bunch of spinsters frightened of real life. She put on the brown dress and black veil, like the others, twitching and tugging them to hang becomingly.

– You're quite right, Josephine told her: you're much too young to take vows. Don't do as I did, and rush into it. Wait and see how you feel when you're a little older.

Isabel tossed her head.

– You always have to be so understanding, don't you? she said: why do you always have to imagine you know how I feel?

They were standing at the kitchen table, sacks wrapped about their waists to serve as aprons, making supper out of the basket of provisions Magdalena had sent in as a gift. Josephine was stabbing, with her knife, the thick violet skins of the aubergines lined up in front of her. She made slashes in their spongy, cream-coloured flesh. Into these wounds she packed a balm of tomato, onion, parsley, garlic and red pepper. She put the little corpses into a pan, poured olive oil and white wine around them, and left them to stew on the fire she had lit on the hearth built of donated bricks. The fireplace was against the front wall of the house. A hole most conveniently situated just above it, which they had taken care not to have mended, let the smoke out into the street. Isabel put more sticks onto the flames. She stood, hands on hips, critically watching them leap up then settle.

– Let's leave that, Josephine said, indicating the pan of food with a wave of her hand: let's go outside for a breath of air.

Dusk swathed the tiny yard with glittering blue veils. The deep mauve-lavender of the sky overhead was pierced by a silver crescent moon, Venus darting from its heel like a diamond spur. Josephine paced excitedly to and fro along the edge of the vegetable plot, throwing her arms wide, making large gestures, pointing. The salon will be here, the dance floor here, the dining-room here. Into the scrap of yard she packed a palace. She was one step nearer to the completion of that waiting house, she was certain. She believed in it, though she could see it, as yet, only with the eyes of her soul. The kingdom of God is within you. She would complete its building in this small brick-walled wasteland which boasted nothing but a strip of vegetable bed and a straggly vine and a well. She sketched the invisible other side of the house with her hands, stooping, measuring, retracing her steps to get the dimensions just right, constantly calling to Isabel: you see? Isabel watched her aunt step to and fro, drawing plans in the air as though the entire dark blue sky were cartridge paper she could sketch on, and she gazed with her but saw only empty space.

Thirteen of them sat down to supper for the first time in the new house. Afterwards they pushed the table and benches against the wall and danced. Later, while the others slept, Josephine sat on the floor of her cell and wrote. She got on with it urgently because she knew she had little time left.

She had been ill for months with the disease that was to kill her, but had ignored all warning signs in her haste to find her house. Now that she admitted she had cancer it was too late. Doctors, who could do nothing for her, she sent away. Magdalena came with remedies and medicines that soothed but did not cure. At night Josephine lit her oil lamp and wrote on small squares of paper. She wrote poems, translations, an autobiography. These were her gifts to Isabel. She hid the pages of her life story to keep them safe. They were the clues in a treasure hunt.

– I didn't expect death so soon, she told Magdalena: and I am very sad my time is cut so short, but I don't fear dying. My self will have gone by then. There will be no one left to be afraid.

They were sitting in the kitchen, close to the fire. Magdalena took her friend's hand.

– It's all my fault, she wailed: I should never have found you this damp, poky place, I should never have let you come to live here, I thought it was such a wretched house you'd get tired of it and come back to live with me, we had such good times, I thought you'd stay, living here like this has killed you.

Josephine sighed.

She said: why couldn't you take me seriously?

– The Inspectors would never have allowed you to carry out your plans, Magdalena replied: they would have discovered what you were up to, you would have been stopped.

– I have achieved very little of what I set out to do, Josephine said, sighing again: the one thing I have managed to do is understand something about language. That's all. That's been my life's work!

She laughed so hard she began coughing and spluttering.

– It's a joke, she gasped: let me tell it you.

Magdalena patted and soothed her.

– Later, she said: tell me later.

She persuaded Josephine to go to bed, and went home.

Josephine thought: well then, I shall try to tell Isabel.

THE LIFE OF SAINT UNCUMBER

Uncumber was the daughter of the king of Portugal. He was a morose man, who felt weighed down by his wealth and responsibilities but lacked the courage to get rid of them and live a simpler life. He was too used to comfort: to inhabiting a palace that was cool even in the height of summer, watered by the gardeners morning and night, the walls splashed with the water thrown from the spouts of their watering cans. A ballet of gardeners swinging bright metal cans, all stepping forwards and backwards and sending arcs of glittering drops to break over the thick stone walls. Inside, the floors were of glass, tile and marble, and the courtyard gardens were bright with roses and palm trees, and you sat well out of the sun under a loggia. You could shrink into the farthest corner and pretend to be a lizard. Servants ran to mop the sweat from the king's brow, to bring him iced drinks and plates of cold fish with mayonnaise and dishes of melons and figs. At night he sipped the finest dryest white or rosé wines. The lines of servants reappeared with their cans and filled up his bath, and he lay in it and felt gloomy. At night he slept on a carved and gilded mahogany bed between crisp sheets, and wrote melancholy poems about lilies and nightingales.

He was sad because no one loved him. His royal parents had never shown him affection, abandoning him to the indifferent care of a succession of nurses and tutors. His father had beaten him regularly while his mother said her prayers in an adjacent room. He had never forgiven them for their cruelty. When he married, he had not known how to love his wife, who had borne him a daughter then run away back to her family.

No one loved him and so he was very lonely. He nicknamed his penis the King of Sicily in order to have someone to talk to. With the King of Sicily he discussed the weather, the progress of the grape harvest, the behaviour of the servants. He went over and over the events of his miserable childhood. He often wound up getting angry and excited. He would storm around the estate shouting to the King of Sicily to calm down or goodness knows what might happen. At these times his daughter Uncumber kept out of his way, crouched in her hiding place under the lemon trees while he raged by.

Uncumber had grown up beautiful, olive skinned and black eyed, with long, curly black hair. Even though she was now thirteen years old the king went on thinking of her as just a child. She did not talk much. She watched. She held back. Ready to run.

Women, fumed the king, had let him down. His cold mother had held him at a distance, shutting him up in his room when he cried, wringing her hands over his defiance and disobedience but abandoning him to his father's harsh punishments. His cold wife had criticised him in bed and despised his craving for love and delivered him the final humiliation by walking out and making him the laughing-stock of the entire kingdom.

A child was not a woman. A child was trusting and to be trusted, loving and lovable. A child was accepting, open, not yet corrupted by the adult world. A child's innocence, so understanding and so special, let you begin again and offered you a second go at true love, at peace and joy. A child would not be frightened by the King of Sicily, who was just a boy seeking a playmate. His wife had disliked the King of Sicily, alternately mocking and resenting him. But if he began while his daughter was still young, before she learned to be frightened or to disapprove, she would not reject the King of Sicily, who was only looking for love, after all.

Uncumber inhaled the sharp lemon breath of the gnarled trees whose pointed green leaves closed over her head and wove her a roof. The trees were small, like she was, with low, twisting branches. She could wriggle in between them unobserved, and sit in this lemony cave until her father had gone past.

That night the king crept into his daughter's room.

– It's me, the King of Sicily, he whispered: wanting to make friends, wanting to play with you. Look.

But Uncumber was not in her bed. She lay, tightly curled up, between the gnarled roots of the trees in the lemon grove.

The king grew cunning. At night he prowled the palace, soft-footed as a lynx, to discover where his daughter was sleeping at night. In the mornings, when she appeared at breakfast, he seized her and sniffed her. But since she had already passed by the gardeners and run under their watering cans to get a shower, she simply smelled clean and fresh, of herself and nothing else.

One morning the King of Sicily, angry and desperate, insisted to the King of Portugal that they go out together for a walk. Even if Uncumber was nowhere to be found, perhaps they might come upon some serving girl or washerwoman's daughter, or suchlike, who could be coaxed into a game.

So they caught Uncumber crawling out of the bed space under the lemon trees and making for the cooling spray of the gardeners' watering cans. The King of Portugal seized his daughter in his arms. He inhaled with passionate joy the sharp tang of lemons on her clothes and skin, a cool smell so fresh and clean it made him think of frilled grey oysters in their sea beds just waiting to be plucked, for the knife blade to insert itself and force them open, that little fold of flesh lapped in salt water, that tiny pearl.

– My little darling, he murmured: now I've found you I'll never let go of you. And nor will the King of Sicily. All his life he's been looking for a companion, and now he's found you, and he's going to put you to bed and take care of you, you'll see, take care of my darling girl.

He grasped Uncumber by the hand. He led her into her room and locked the door. He pulled down the blinds so that the room was dark. He threw Uncumber onto the bed.

The room smelled of earth and grass and lemons, of sea water and salt. It smelled of two people's sweat and terror.

Uncumber pulled her thick, curly hair over her face, as a shield. A shield of hair? What use could that possibly be? For the king was panting on the bed next to her, crying out her name, gasping, searching for her with his enormous hands.

Uncumber twisted herself round in the darkness like the roots of a lemon tree. She turned herself rapidly like a fish slipping through the currents between grasping fingers of weed.

The king's sad and greedy hands found the dark curly nest of pubic hair, the soft lips just underneath. He shoved his penis in.

But Uncumber had covered her face with her hair. She had turned herself upside down and had presented the King of Sicily with her beautiful mouth surrounded by her beautiful curly mane. Not her cunt at all. Her cunt had no teeth.

Her father's penis was in her mouth. She bit it off and spat it out. Then the leapt off the bed, ran to the door and unlocked it, raced into the gardens of the palace, and disappeared.

The gardeners went on swinging their cans of water and dousing the palace walls with long arcs of cooling spray. Lunchtime came. They put down their tools and water pots and trooped out of the palace grounds. The extra gardener who had so suddenly joined their ranks shook each one by the hand and then ran away to the city.

No one knew her name, so, when she died of exhaustion after fifty years working as a cleaner, she was buried in the common burial ground reserved for the poor.

THE STORY OF
JOSEPHINE

Josephine might have died, but she did not finish with living. Her ways of talking, for example, her customs and gestures, all these took root inside Isabel. Her niece acquired her doings and sayings as though they had been willed to her. Gifts she could not reject or return, that were bred into her from all those years of living with Josephine and learning from her without realising that that is what she was doing. Copying her was like breathing. Isabel drew Josephine into her.

She found that she now dried her hands in exactly the same way that Josephine did, washing them very thoroughly first, so as not to dirty the clean towel with traces of earth or grease, then cupping them so as not to drop water on the floor, then going swiftly to the strip of linen hung on the hook behind the door. Similarly, Isabel discovered that she washed up as Josephine did, in two bowls of hot water, one soapy and one for rinsing, so that she didn't waste the precious liquid. When the water had cooled, she took it outside and threw it on the vegetable plot. Each time she performed a household task, making her bed or sweeping the floor, Josephine hovered at her shoulder and watched critically. She had known how to scold if she had to. Most of the time she had corrected Isabel with love, but on occasion Isabel had needed to resist, to put up her fists and fight, and had provoked Josephine to wrestle. With a wall of temper between them she felt safer, that she would not drown in the lush scent of the flowers. Afterwards they kissed and said sorry, and love felt bearable again because it was young and new. Love that was old and went on being there was a prison from which Isabel had to escape. It wasn't something she herself had made. She didn't trust it.

Another part of Josephine that Isabel inherited was her thrift. The thirteen nuns of the Reform at St Joseph's had to eke out very scanty resources. They had decided to earn their living from spinning cloth and selling it, so that they did not have to exploit the poor by asking them for alms. Since they did not have to depend on rich people's crazy whims, either, they were free. Josephine hadn't seen scraping and saving as mere penny-pinching. She enjoyed it as an art. One of her skills as a cook, a craft she had learned at Magdalena's house, was using leftovers. Some well-wisher might have given the nuns a small basket of sardines, say. Josephine would grill them for dinner, crisp and golden black with a sheen of oil, then, next day, she would flake any bits left on the serving-dish to make fish-cakes, mixed with a handful of sultanas, some ground almonds, a dash of red pepper. If there was an egg, she mixed it with mashed potato and made gnocchi. Similarly, a bowl of cold rice would turn into croquettes, flavoured with onion and herbs. She conjured sausages out of nothing: breadcrumbs, grated heels of cheese, minced sage. Soup the same way: water, garlic, bread, a tomato or an onion if there was one.

To her it was a game. Receiving inspiration from a motley assortment of ingredients that you'd been given, that in richer kitchens would have been thrown away or put down for the dogs. The element of chance was the challenge. Her eyes would light up at the sight of a couple of crusts, a cup of chick peas, some leek tops. As long as she had some olive oil, of which she cadged a steady supply from Magdalena, she could cook. Often the nuns ate bread, salt and olive oil for supper, and felt they lacked for nothing. And after supper, they would dance, especially on evenings when the supply of firewood had run low and they needed to keep warm.

Given Josephine's love of making do, her capacity to create with whatever lay immediately to hand, it did not surprise Isabel to discover, when she began trying to sort out her aunt's writings after her death, that this thrifty woman had used any odd pieces of paper she found lying around: the backs of recipes, prayer cards, bills, other people's letters, and so on. Subsequently she had reused them as the need arose. Isabel became most inventive at working out where Josephine might have abandoned a first draft or a quick note. She found manuscripts torn in half and screwed up to make stoppers for bottles of medicine or ink wells. Others masqueraded as petticoat linings and pads for elbow rests. Some were twisted into spills for lighting the oil lamps or the kitchen fire, or were folded and cut to make templates for patchwork, or were stuck together to mend broken windowpanes whose glass the convent could not afford to have replaced. Helping another sister stitch coifs, Isabel discovered that the paper pattern they were using had Josephine's writing on the back. In the privy she was distressed to find that the bent nail on the wall carried a stack of neatly torn-up squares of paper that Josephine had used for blotting poems. Isabel held the pages to a mirror to read them, then copied them down. The paper lace doilies that appeared on the refectory table on a feast-day appeared to have been snipped from a translation by Josephine of the *Song of Songs*. Opening a jar of quince jam Isabel realised that the paper lid had been cut from a sheet of Josephine's final draft of her story of the life of a saint. So it went on.

Josephine had become her own enemy. Preaching poverty and the reuse of everything serviceable, the endless and ingenious transformation of materials, she had ensured the destruction of her archive. Nonetheless, working against such odds, Isabel felt quite proud of herself. She collected a great heap of writings which she hid, temporarily, in a purloined potato sack placed under the mattress in her cell. The rustling sound of the paper was just like that of the straw with which the nuns' palliasses were stuffed. Nobody was likely to enter her cell, Isabel was certain, for one of the rules of the Reform was strict privacy to be alone, think your own thoughts, and get on with your work without interruption. So the bits of manuscript were safe.

Isabel slept on a palimpsest. In the night Josephine's words sprang up from their tidy layers under the bed and clicked about in the cell as though they wore tap shoes and carried castanets. In the night Josephine's words floated up to the ceiling soft as snow. They settled on Isabel, flakes of paper she brushed away from her face. Her eyelids were two torn discs of paper. The words got into bed with her, wove into her dreams, then woke her up and would not let her go back to sleep.

Having deciphered, more or less, in a rush, the writings she had found discarded all over the house like vegetable peelings in a bin or balls of fluff under a cupboard, Isabel was sure that more remained, hidden somewhere by Josephine, whether on purpose or by chance, and that it was up to her to work out where they might have been left.

Josephine had hinted often enough that she had written a second autobiography. Isabel grew dispirited looking for it. Her hunt for these papers concealed from her the grief she was feeling, but from time to time it crept up on her and threatened her with something close to despair.

She wished she could see Magdalena and talk to her, but she did not dare send her a message and request a visit. She was afraid of Magdalena's sharp tongue and felt unable to ask her for help. Magdalena, she was convinced, disapproved of her. Isabel could not bear, in her present state, to be criticised by anyone. Words of censure, looks of reproof, were like pins scratching and tearing her flesh. The memory of them stayed like mosquito bites, itching and irritating you to the point of frenzy where you rubbed at the red weals to break the skin and draw blood and so find relief. She did not want Magdalena poking and prodding. She fell back on Lucian. She counted on him as a friend, as did all the nuns. They liked him because he was kind. To women in general. He valued them and encouraged them in their struggles. This was not, Sister Maria was fond of saying, what you expected in a priest.

Nonetheless, Sister Maria made it difficult for Isabel to confide with ease in Lucian. She enforced the traditional code of etiquette governing nun and priest that had obtained at the Incarnation. They could talk to each other in the confessional. Nowhere else. The curtained-off corner of the cowshed-chapel which they were forced to use, with a holey blanket pinned up between them as grille, was not conducive to talking. Isabel could not confess her sins to Lucian. She kept silent about these, out of shame. She told him instead about trying to collect all Josephine's papers, how much this mattered to her.

Lucian sounded as uncomfortable as Isabel felt in this makeshift tabernacle rigged up by Sister Maria. He confessed his faults to Isabel as though she were the priest.

– I burned all Josephine's letters, he said: fifty or more of them, that she wrote to me from Magdalena's, while you were both living there. I felt I was too attached to my memories of her. Now I realise they were all I had. All gone. I'm sorry, Isabel. I should have kept them and given them to you.

His voice made her think he might be crying. That was not a sound she wanted to hear, so she said *amen* loudly, got up and tugged the curtain aside, and went out.

The little yard was filled with warmth, the golden sweetness of an October day, when the air both caresses and stings, heat overlaid with cold. Isabel could not be unhappy in weather like this. She unclenched her fists and let her hands drop to her sides. She leaned against the rosy brick of the garden wall, watching two wasps fly in and out of one of its crevices. From the street outside came the sound of voices, the scent of apples and manure. Her fingers strayed across the rosary beads slung from her belt, and she decided, as a last resort, to try and pray. She went indoors, and up to her cell, like all the others a small plywood box, but nonetheless, a private place, where she could be alone and undisturbed.

Saying the rosary had always bored her. Her mind drifted angrily off. She disliked all vocal, repetitive prayers of that nature, and preferred praying, if she prayed at all, without words. If she wanted to meditate on the life of Christ, she preferred to pick the scenes for contemplation according to her own desire, not in the order someone else ordained. The rosary was ever the same. Round and round it went, never altering or varying. Saying it became mechanical. You droned, drifted off. Not into religious rapture but into daydreams. Other stories which you told yourself.

Nonetheless, just as an experiment, Isabel sat down on the floor, hauled Josephine's rosary between her hands, and dutifully slid her fingers onto the first bead. This signified the First Joyful Mystery, which was the Annunciation. The weight of boredom which immediately descended on Isabel made her stop muttering the Our Father. It seemed so pointless. Then she remembered Josephine enjoining her to use her rosary after her death. Not even for her aunt could she pray well. She felt cross all over again, and ashamed.

In her irritation Isabel was picking at the beads with her fingernail as she slipped them through her fingers. They were gilded papier mâché beads, lightweight, little flattened globes slung on a gold string. Now Isabel's fingernail flicked up an edge of paper on one bead. She scratched at it, pulled it gently. The bead unpeeled. It was not solid papier mâché at all as she had thought. It was made of a small square of manuscript squeezed together and rolled up around the thin cord on which it was strung. The glue and the lick of gilding holding it together had worked loose under the fretting of Isabel's fingers.

She flattened out the tiny page and peered at the shrunken handwriting. She knew that she was looking at the first sheet of Josephine's secret *Life*, even before she made out the opening words. *I wrote my first book under obedience.*

The beads were spindle shaped, plump as buds. Greedily Isabel eased them off the string one by one, as though they were ripe blackberries she was picking to eat. She hurried too much. She pulled off too many beads at once. The palm of her hand was full, and overflowed. Rolls of paper spilled across the floor, and Isabel realised that she no longer had any idea of what order they had been arranged in. She picked some up, and opened them out. Bubbles of narrative, that burst in all directions. A chaotic pattern which made no sense. The bell began to ring downstairs. She scooped up the beads. Her cupped hands were full of words which ran about like balls of mercury. She hid them with all the others, under her mattress.

On the following day, in chapel, Isabel noticed a powerful, sweet smell emanating from the stone cupboard behind the altar where Josephine's body lodged.

The digging up of Josephine's body followed, and the discovery that it was incorrupt. Soon afterwards, Isabel witnessed the destruction of the body, when it was cut up for relics on the orders of Sister Maria. Isabel was there, looking on, and did nothing to stop what happened.

The following day she fell ill with a fever that seized her like an enemy, shook her about, stabbed her abdomen with violent pains, racked her joints. She sweated and vomited. She flopped, weak and limp, on her damp pillow, feeling so sick that throwing up was a relief. She was dimly aware, at one point, of being carried into Sister Maria's cell. The face of the prioress glimmered close to her own. Someone sponged her brow and dragged a clean nightdress over her head. Even in her delirium of bodily wretchedness Isabel was aware that Sister Maria was treating her with scrupulous care, sitting up with her day and night and listening in compassionate silence to her rantings and babblings. She assured Isabel constantly that these were the purest nonsense, and not the work of the Devil, and that Isabel was not to be afraid. She administered this comfort as steadily as she administered purgatives. Isabel was so enfeebled by this treatment that it took her over a week to feel strong enough to get out of bed. When, finally, she crept back into her own cell to check on the safety of Josephine's papers hidden there, she found, to her great distress, that the cell had been emptied and scoured out, the bed and bedding removed, and the sack of writings gone.

The Life of Saint Marin

The holiness of Marin was hidden. No one saw it. Not in his lifetime, certainly. Only after his lonely death, when his brother monks came to lay him out in his cell on a black bier surrounded by candles, as was the custom in that monastery where he had lived, did his holiness become visible. As though it broke forth and shone, like a gold flare. It was revealed, like a lost jewel buried in the earth then dug up.

His fellow monks gaped at his naked dead body, which they were about to wash and anoint. They rolled their eyes from side to side, shook their index fingers in the air, nodded their chins up and down. They spread their palms wide, puffed up their cheeks in balloons of air then blew these out again in small explosions. They crossed themselves and collapsed onto their knees in a circle around the corpse. Marin's cell was thick with the scent of honeysuckle and roses and some other flower they couldn't quite name. Snow lined the window-sill like cut plush. Snow fell, piling up in the corners of the cloister in light drifts, putting a white skull-cap on the dome of the monks' church, a great hush on the grove of pine trees outside the monastery gates. Snow dragged down the branches, caped them in white.

The Abbey of the Treasure of God gripped the mountaintop on which it was built in the way an eagle clenches its talons around a branch. A nest of eagles; a nest of monks. Balanced so high up you felt, as you were meant to feel, that heaven could not be far away. Fastened into their lofty citadel, almost flying, one with the clouds, the monks were not only far removed from the world but well superior to it. Just as the mountain strove upwards with all its force, so the monks aimed to raise themselves even further into God's atmosphere. A kind of weightlifting. Hampered by the body rather than helped by it. They kept in training. They sang the Divine Office at the appropriate times of day, they practised meditation and contemplative prayer, they begged for forgiveness for sinners, they mortified their flesh which stopped them rising up to meet God.

All the windows of the monastery faced inwards, towards the mountain. Anyone trying to look out and admire the view was admonished by slabs of sheer rock hurtling upwards. God was not the free air, the wheeling buzzards, the tops of spruce trees far below. He could not be grasped in the hands. His was a stern beauty: he was flawless stone, a king made of granite. He had made Himself man, once, long ago, but now He was risen into majesty: He was the glacier hidden under deep snow which no one had ever crossed, the sheer face of pitiless cliff up which no human being could ever climb. To try to cling to him was to be flung back, to plummet into the bottomless drop of despair, to be lost for ever. So the monks placated Him with prayer, and set a guard on their senses. They tried not to let themselves want anything, for that was dangerous and led to death. They tried to root out all their desires.

They denied themselves pleasure, which was a distraction. They did not speak to each other, for example, but used gestures if necessary. Communication was a sign of failure: God was supposed to be more than enough. So they tapped their breasts to say *sorry* before asking for a piece of bread, or a spoon, if the refectory servers had forgotten to lay the tables properly, or were especially slow in coming round with the cutlery and the break-baskets. The bread was always at least two days old, and had to be dunked in the soup to soften it. The spoons were of cheap tin, often green with verdigris. No salt, garlic or herbs were used in the cooking, no sugar or spices. The wine and beer were well watered. A flask of olive oil, in the abbey kitchen, lasted a very long time.

The monks grew their own vegetables in their big kitchen garden behind the church, but their olive oil and bread they procured from the people working the farmlands lower down the mountain. All the foodstuffs the monks could not produce themselves came up the steep path to the monastery on the backs of donkeys. The monks' prayers were offered in return.

The village of the Treasure of God clung to the side of the mountain like a flea to a dog. Squat, red-roofed houses clustered around a tiny square that boasted a bar, a fountain, a well and a church. Chickens scratched in the dust for vegetable peelings and scraps. Goats, wagging their pointed white beards, tugged at the ropes tethering them to stakes at the roadside. The sheep were pastured higher up, beyond the cherry orchards and the small terraced vineyards. Under the trees and in between the vines grew cabbages, lettuces and beans. The villagers worked so hard extracting a living from the harsh land that they had little spare time for praying. That was the monks' job: to do it for them. They went to Mass on Sundays and that was enough.

Once a year, however, on the feast of Our Lady of the Blackthorn, in the middle of May, all the fields and houses emptied. The villagers put on their best clothes and climbed the mountain to pay their respects to the statue of the Madonna that gave the Abbey of the Treasure of God its name. This statue had been discovered, centuries before, by a shepherd girl, underneath a blackthorn bush at the edge of a field. No one knew exactly how old the Madonna was, but she was believed by all the monks to have been sent as a sign by God to the founder of the monastery, the first abbot. He had taken her from the shepherd girl, and put her on the altar in the abbey church, and asked her to bless his house of monks and let it prosper.

The monks' Rule taught them to despise the beauty of this world, which was, like the beauty of women, a lure and a snare, designed by the devil as a trap to catch sinners, like a honeypot, stinking with sweetness, set to drown wasps. The only woman the monks dared to notice was their Virgin. She was not soft, as women are commonly supposed to be, but strong to the point of hardness. If she was beautiful, hers was the kind of beauty that men, too, can possess. She was small as a year-old child, carved of olive wood smoothed and polished by the passing of time, rubbed free of inessentials. Her black face was patched with squares of gold leaf. One black hand curved around the child, who leaned out from her hip, and the other stretched forward, palm tilted to tip grace onto her visitors. Her black toenails were gilded. Her power was to work miracles of intervention and healing. She enabled girls to find husbands, she helped infertile women get pregnant, she consoled widows. Her mystery was that her face, with its half-hooded eyes and flattened cheeks, looked impassive, almost severe, yet when you got close enough to kiss her foot and implore her intercession, you tracked the trace of a smile just departed from her wide mouth. The power and the mystery fused together in the longing, fierce as a thorn, with which she pierced your heart before she gave herself to you. She opened you, like a lance, then poured herself in as balm.

The pilgrimage to the Madonna began very early in the morning, before dawn. The villagers started their long climb in chilly darkness, the women carrying their babies strapped to their backs and the men carting baskets of bread and wine as presents to the Virgin. The old people plodded up on donkeys, clasping the small children straddling the saddle in front of them. The young men waved branches of blossoming blackthorn and the women clutched nosegays of lilies of the valley. All these gifts were piled on the ground in front of the abbey gates once the pilgrimage reached the mountaintop.

The villagers sat down in little groups and rested. They waited in silence, while the darkness of the moonless night shifted imperceptibly, second by second, towards the grey mistiness that signalled the coming of dawn. Then, as the first pink streak marked the sky to the east, the abbey gates swung open and the people stood up and poured forwards. There was the Madonna, held in the arms of the youngest monk. Behind her stood the community, the monks carrying lit tapers and the Abbot swinging his censer. They sang a Latin hymn whose tune everyone knew, as familiar as their own breathing, but whose words no one could understand.

All year the Virgin of the Blackthorn was hidden in the darkness of the monks' church. On this one day in the middle of May she emerged and showed herself to those who loved her despite her invisibility, her silence, her remoteness. On this one day she showed herself as a shining black presence, she created new words on people's lips and moved them to shouts and tears, she was carried close enough to her devotees that, one by one, they could kneel and kiss her gilded feet. They trusted her to have their good at heart. They supposed it would be too much trouble for her to reveal herself more than once a year. So the strength of their prayers on this day was very great. Similarly, their feasting, drinking and dancing in the village that night was uninhibited and unrestrained.

The Madonna's miraculous powers attracted pilgrims from all the districts round about. Every year, the crowds increased. As did the prosperity of the villagers, for, as the Abbey had no guest-house, the visitors were put up in the lofts, barns and outhouses of the homes down below. Meals and wine were provided for them by the family running the bar. Some of the pilgrims, moved to a love of God that pushed them to change their way of life completely, stayed on and entered the monastery. A steady supply of monks was ensured. The Abbey flourished.

One of these new arrivals was Frederick, a man of about forty who had been a soldier and killed a great many pagans on the Crusades. After assisting at so much bloodshed, he wanted to end his days in peace. He brought with him his son Marin, a handsome youth of fifteen, and begged the Abbot to receive them both as monks. His wife was dead and he had no other child except this son whom he loved passionately and from whom he could not bear to be parted. On their knees, Frederick and Marin implored the monks, assembled in the abbey courtyard, to receive them into the community. The monks and the Abbot withdrew to the Chapter-House, to consult with one another. It was an unusual request, they agreed, but they could find no objection. And so first Frederick, and then Marin, were given the rough grey woollen habits of the Order, and the names, no longer of father and son, but of brothers.

They proved themselves unexceptional monks, characterised mainly, perhaps, by their devotion to each other, but taking care to be courteous and cheerful towards all. They sang the Divine Office in choir and laboured in the kitchen garden and appeared content. Marin, surprisingly for one so young, adapted easily to the rigours of the life. Digging and hoeing gave him the muscles he had hitherto lacked. The exact obedience required of him at all times made him wrinkle up his nose and smile. At suppertime he would fall upon his scanty meal and devour it with enjoyment. The ugly tonsure and awkward, bulky habit could not conceal his large dark eyes, fine olive skin, slender build and graceful movements. His youth made him appealing, as did his openness, born of ignorance. He had not yet learned to put up a guard of reserve around himself. He looked at people gently, earnestly, sweetly. He had not yet mastered the monks' practice of custody of the eyes, of keeping them lowered at all times. He liked to watch the larks spiralling overhead, to notice the colours of the mallows and the violets blooming in crevices of the wall, to follow the changes in the shapes of clouds. Frederick, the old soldier, would signal vigorously to his son: eyes down!

The older monks began to shake their heads over the new novice. They pursed their lips and frowned, they rubbed their noses and stroked their chins. They shrugged their shoulders and snorted.

In early May the year after Marin had entered the monastery, when the Feast of Our Lady of the Blackthorn drew near, the Abbot instructed him that it was he who would hold the Madonna in his arms, in the annual ceremony, and show her to the people. He was the youngest monk and so, following the ancient custom, he would be the

one to walk among the crowd of people and offer them, one
by one, the Virgin's feet to kiss.

Very early on the day of the Virgin's feast, the monks sang
the Divine Office in their church and attended Mass, as
usual. Then the Abbot lifted the little statue of the Madonna
out of her dark, shadowy niche high up above one of the side
altars, and put her into Marin's arms.

As his hands came into contact with the smooth, stubby
piece of olive wood, Marin felt an explosion under his skin,
like dawn breaking behind his ribs, like rays of sunlight rippling up his spine to topple over, little waves of pleasure, in
his heart and throat. His fingers clung to whatever it was he
held and that held him. He said to himself that he would
never be able to let go of her now. She had him. The cool
olive wood of which she was made burned and stung. His
tears spilled down his face.

The monks assembled in the courtyard. The pale moon
above was almost transparent. The stars had vanished. They
could hear the waiting crowd outside, its patient breath.
Then the Abbot nodded, and Ferdinand swung back the
monastery gates, and Marin walked out, at the head of the
procession of monks, holding the Madonna in his arms.

He had been coached in the ritual. He knew what to do.
He moved among the pilgrims as though they were all part
of a village dance, each one turning round to perform the
necessary steps.

One group of girls was boisterous and irreverent, as some
girls will be, before they settle down. Egged on by her
giggling friends, one bold young woman stared Marin in

the face as he approached her and caught his eye. She called out: oh, what a pretty monk!

People peered and stared. He was the focus of the crowd. He retreated, blushing, towards the Abbot. Having surrendered the Madonna to the older man, he pulled his cowl forwards over his face and bent his head, plunged his hands deep into his sleeves and crossed his arms under his scapula. Then he backed away until he was standing behind Frederick, safely hidden from view.

The bunch of bad girls in the crowd was irrepressible. They continued to laugh, to whisper and point. Marin caught the drift of their taunts and compliments as though these were thistledown that floated past and brushed against him. His cheeks burned. Too late, he did what he had been taught by his novice-master and shut his ears.

Later that day, when the rabble of pilgrims had disappeared down the mountain for their evening feast and dance, Marin and Frederick went out to bring in the baskets of offerings that had been left just outside the monastery gates. Marin turned to watch the sun setting behind the far grove of pine trees and the disused swineherd's hut that stood next to it. The dying sun reddened the thatched roof, and the face of the laughing girl who lounged in the doorway and waved at him.

– It's that girl from the bar in the village, Frederick told his son: the same one who was kicking up a fuss this morning. Don't take any notice and she'll go away soon enough, you'll see.

Frederick rarely broke his vow of silence. Marin felt

ashamed. He picked up the largest and heaviest of the baskets and turned.

The bar-girl swung her hips and called out. Marin concentrated on his basket, staggering with it inside the monastery gates.

In the following months, as usually happened after the showing of the Madonna, several of the village women found that they were pregnant. To have received the Madonna's favour was a great blessing. Everyone gave thanks. The proud husbands stood rounds of drinks in the bar.

The bar-girl was pregnant too. Her shame and disgrace were compounded by her refusal to name the father of the coming child. Her mother beat her with a stick, her father with a leather strap, but to no avail. They flung her out of the house to sleep in the cowshed. They bolted her in, so that she couldn't run away. She lay on a heap of filthy straw and cried.

Autumn was drawing near. A cold season in that high mountainous district. The bar-girl shivered, for she had no blanket, no woollen stockings or jacket. She had a thin petticoat to wear and nothing else. The heat of the animals kept her warm, and their mild presence, their massed bulk stamping and shifting in the manure-scented darkness, kept her from going mad. She clasped her belly, and felt the baby kick, and cried. She slept in the mud and the cow-pats. The animals were kept clean but not she. She lay in her own shit, worse than a beast.

Meanwhile Frederick fell ill with a recurrence of the fever he had picked up years ago on campaign in the Holy Land

and never shaken off. He was carried to the infirmary, where Marin nursed him. The deftness and tenderness of the son towards his father were a marvel to see. Marin bathed Frederick, held cups of medicine to his lips, cleaned up his vomit, helped him use the chamberpot, held his sweaty hand and stroked it. Frederick muttered, in his delirium, about the overpoweringly sweet smell of blackthorn blossom, the coolness and freshness of the white flowers, the dark tangle of surrounding thorns. Marin listened.

Frederick drifted deeper into illness. His mind walked off and did not come back. The fever let him perfect his training as a monk and detach himself completely from worldly desires. He seemed to feel little pain. He no longer recognised his son. He did not hear the great bell rung to summon all the monks to an emergency meeting in the Chapter-House.

The bar-girl was in her eighth month of pregnancy. Half-starved and nearly crazy she lay in her own excrement in the sodden straw of the cowshed and screamed. Her parents loomed over her. Her hopes centred on the ending of pain. She could no longer imagine clean clothes, something good to eat, a kind hand smearing ointment on her cuts and bruises. She felt that one more beating would kill her and push her down to hell. She looked at the horsewhip in her father's hand and she choked out some words.

– Brother Marin did it to me. It was Brother Marin.

Frederick twisted to and fro. He was in the Holy Land with the army. He was lost in the desert, which rose up around him and groaned, which would suffocate him with loneliness. A dark-skinned woman came towards him with her arms outstretched, laughing. She pulled up her skirts above her waist and danced around. His mouth was full of sand. He croaked the name of his son.

Marin lay face down on the floor of the Chapter-House, his arms stretched out, in the shape of a cross, at the foot of the dais on which stood the Abbot's throne. The monks sat in grey rows on long benches and stared straight ahead. One or two of them sighed as sentence was pronounced. One or two shuffled their sandalled feet. One or two smiled. Most of them nodded and frowned.

Marin was banished from the monastery. His punishment was to be deprived of his life among the monks, whom he had betrayed by breaking his vows. He was to go and live in the swineherd's hut on the edge of the pine grove where his brothers would not be corrupted by the sight of him. In this solitary confinement he was to do penance for his sin. He was to go barefoot, but to keep his habit, as a reminder of his former virtuous state. As a mark of his disgrace, and to teach him humility, he would sleep and eat like the pigs did, in mud and dirt.

Marin crept out of the abbey. He lay sobbing in the swineherd's hut. He knew that Frederick was dying.

Frederick died that night. Marin heard the bells toll for him, and, later, he heard the funeral Mass being sung in the monks' church. The wind carried the Latin chant over the monastery wall and into the hut.

Grief trampled him down. He lay, battered and sick, missing Frederick. He felt as though his arms had been torn off.

Later on, he felt his guts twist, his stomach shrivel and ache. Hunger drove him out to find food, and saved him.

From time to time a handful of stale crusts was flung over the monastery wall for him, as you'd throw kitchen waste into a pig's sty. Or he might be hurled some potato peelings, or cabbage stalks, or apple cores. He ate as well, he decided, as the chickens down in the village did, and, like them, he learned to forage. Wild strawberries and chestnuts and mushrooms were his luxuries. He chewed sprigs of rosemary and thyme, that he found growing in abundance around the mountainside, together with mint and fennel. He drank water from the streams, pure and cold. At night he lay on a bed of bracken in his hut and stared through the holes in the roof at the stars. At dawn he was awoken by a chorus of chaffinches and blue-tits. Since he shared his food with them, they flew about the hut all day long, and would eat from his hand, and so he had a sense of being kept company.

The bar-girl gave birth, in the cowshed, to a daughter. The baby fed on her mother's milk for three months, got a good grip on life. Then the grandparents tore her from her mother's arms and took her away. They considered abandoning her on the mountainside, to be eaten by bears. They certainly did not want to keep her, as a constant reminder of their daughter's shame. They decided that she was the monks' responsibility. Since it was now the time of year when everyone went up the mountain to pay their respects to Our Lady of the Blackthorn, they took the baby with them and handed her in to the Abbot.

The bar-girl tore her hair and howled. She ran up and

down the piazza half-naked, bright-eyed, looking for her baby. Her breasts leaked milk. The villagers feared she would try to damage other women's children. They feared she was possessed by evil spirits. So they drove her out of the village, warning her never to come back.

She became a byword in the village for immorality, a bogey figure with which to frighten naughty girls.

– You don't want to end up like *her*, mothers would warn.

– Don't you start behaving like *her*, fathers would threaten.

– You're as bad as *her*, brothers would taunt their sister.

The worst thing that one girl could say to another was: you're just like *her*.

The Abbot placed the baby in her basket just outside the monastery gates, for Marin to find and care for. Part of his punishment. She was certainly his responsibility, in any case. Marin looked rather too well and healthy for someone who was supposedly living a penitent's life. He was heard to sing sometimes. He had been observed picking wild flowers and capering about on the grass. The Abbot decided that the errant monk needed an extra burden, to weigh him down.

Marin called his tiny charge Marietta. He rocked her until she stopped crying, then washed her in the stream. He washed her in the white tumble of water and she kicked and laughed. He wrapped her in the torn-off sleeves of his habit, and tore up his scapular for nappies. He fed her on the milk he coaxed from the udders of the wild mountain goats, who stood patient and still for him, their kids looking on, and then later, as she grew, he gave her bread and milk, a paste of mashed chestnuts, bits of honeycomb filched from the wild bees among the rocks, wild raspberries picked in the forest. The baby flourished. So did Marin. When he went for long walks around the mountainside, he took Marietta with him, tied on his back. She jiggled up and down, cooed and dribbled into his neck. Together they watched the deer, and the eagles, and the bears. They climbed trees, they stood under the waterfall, they rested on the softness of pine needles and dead leaves and bright green moss. When winter came, Marin wove two coats and two blankets of bracken threaded with goats' hair and the tufts of sheep's wool he found hanging on bushes, and so he managed to keep both himself and the baby warm. She began to crawl, to stand, to take tottering steps. He walked behind her, leaning over her, holding her hands. She was his joy and his delight. He talked to her, to tell her this, and discovered, after his year of silence in the monastery, how much he loved words. They tasted like wine vinegar, like pepper and salt, like marzipan.

– Your father's name is Frederick, he told Marietta: my little half-sister, that's who you are.

The blackthorn bushes broke into white blossom. The time had come round again for the annual pilgrimage to the Madonna of Blackthorn. May arrived, the month of her feast.

Marin could not keep away. He wanted to see what the little black Virgin had in store for him this year. He cut himself a switch of flowering blackthorn, and he picked a bunch of lilies of the valley. He tied Marietta by a string to the door of the hut, but she set up such a howl that he felt obliged to untie her and to take her with him.

Night was dissolving. Moonlight showed the path. Carrying Marietta on his shoulders, and with his arms full of flowers, Marin walked towards the monastery. A thin figure in a kneelength, sleeveless grey garment almost unrecognisable as a habit, he was barefoot. His skin was sunburned and his black hair unruly, and his dark eyes seemed bigger than ever in his bony face. The baby girl riding high on his shoulders, clasping her tiny hands around his forehead, babbled and chuckled with pleasure. Together they came bursting out of the darkness, into the pre-dawn grey light, the crowd of villagers.

Of course everyone stared at them. Of course Marin lost the child. Once he had set her down, she would not stand still beside him. Once the Madonna appeared, Marietta toddled forward, chirruping and laughing.

The bar-girl's parents remembered that this was their grandchild. One glance at the healthy, lusty, crowing child reminded them how much they missed her and wanted her back, how delighted they would be to have a young girl about the place again. They were getting on in years. With their daughter gone, they had no one to look after them in their old age. So they swept Marietta up, tutting and scowling at her unkempt, savage-looking foster-father, and departed with her down the mountain.

The Abbot decided that Marin had atoned for his sin. He took the young man back inside the monastery and put him in charge of cleaning out the privies. These emptied themselves into a large foul-smelling pit, which filled up all too quickly. Marin's job was to shovel up all the shit into buckets which he emptied into the deep trough he dug at the far end of the kitchen garden.

He felt that his heart had been pierced too many times. His life was leaking away through the holes. The Virgin had stabbed him with her eyes, which were as black as the bush she'd been found under, as sharp as its little black spines. At night, when he couldn't sleep, he would come down to the church to pray. He knelt in front of her and stared up at her. She was remote and unknowable. She could tell him nothing. She was unreachable. She was indifferent to him. She had forgotten his name.

Marin died in December of that year. No one knew what he died of. No one wanted to nurse him, for they were sure he smelled too abominably of the shit he dug out from the latrines. Surely the shit clung to him, was clotted under his fingernails, between his toes. So the monks kept away from his cell, once they realised he was ill, and let him die alone.

They came to his cell the following day, to strip and wash the body, preparatory to laying it out, clothed in the habit once more. They came slowly and unwillingly, expecting a putrid stench.

Marin's cell smelled of roses and honeysuckle, of lilies of the valley and blackthorn blossom. In the middle of December, when no flowers bloomed and snow lay on the window-sill like cut white velvet, when the monks' frosty breath hung in the air in stiff white clouds, Marin's dead body gave out, freshly and persistently, the perfumes of summer.

There lay in front of them, the monks discovered when

258

they peeled off the filthy ragged clothes, not the body of
Marin but that of Marina. Wasted and emaciated as she was,
her breasts proved her a woman, the shape of her waist and
hips, her small round belly, the triangular patch of curly
black hair which grew at its base, in great profusion, the
folded lips which touched each other softly.

The longer the monks gazed at Marina, the more the
room filled up with sweetness.

They wrapped the body of the servant of God in a black
cloth and laid it on a black bier and surrounded it by
candles. They sang their farewell, standing packed tightly
into the cramped space of the cell. Then they took the bier
down to the church and laid Marina out for her funeral
Mass.

The village people were allowed, as an extraordinary priv-
ilege, to attend the ceremony and witness the fragrant body
of she whom they were already calling a saint.

One of the mourners was the bar-girl, who had crept in
behind everyone else. No one knew she had returned to the
village. No one took any notice of her. She knelt at the back
of the church, asking Marina to forgive her for the lie she
had told, and asking her to perform a miracle and grant her
some hope in life.

The bar-girl's parents died shortly afterwards. The bar-girl
moved back in to the house, to care for her daughter
Marietta and to run the bar. This flourished more than ever,
for the number of pilgrims greatly increased. People travelled
great distances not only to see the Madonna but also to
touch and see Marina's body, which was shown to them at

the same time, and were glad of clean beds and hot meals after their arduous journeys.

Eventually, with a change of abbot, reforms were instituted and superstitious rituals got rid of. The black Madonna was sold to a passing merchant, and Marina's body taken out of the abbey church and buried anonymously, no one remembers where.

THE STORY OF
JOSEPHINE

Josephine kept leaving Isabel. She kept uprooting and unsettling her. She consented to having her fetched from the Far Country without consulting her. She abandoned her at the Incarnation while she jaunted off to enjoy herself with Magdalena. She wrenched her away from the convent, just as Isabel had found her feet, and moved her to Magdalena's, then forced her to live at the new foundation of St Joseph's. Then she died.

Here and from henceforth I must say 'I'. I, Isabel, write this account of my aunt's life. I shall no longer write in disguise, pretend to be a calm witness when I am not and never was. How can I recount the story of Josephine and not admit I am making it all up? I was not there, after all, for so much of her life. I am relying on hearsay, the stories she herself told me, the bits I put together for myself. It was easier, at first, to write this as though I were someone else. But I cannot do that any more.

She died. I was alone in the world. My father decided to stay in the Far Country for the time being, overseeing his estates and slaves, because he was very busy there, with my brothers, amassing more wealth. He wrote to me that I should stay at St Joseph's for the time being, while he thought about what should be done with me. When I write how frightened I was, how bereft and lonely, my breath is tight in my breast as though a vice were clamping me, I'm clenching my pen hard enough to snap it in two.

I was sixteen. All on my own, with no one to help me. Magdalena was so angry and distressed about what happened to Josephine's body, after she had taken such care to have it well buried, and protected in every way, that she would not come near the convent. I knew that she and Sister Maria quarrelled over money. We all knew. Magdalena said our first year was up, and that therefore she was ceasing to pay our rent. Sister Maria accused her of withdrawing financial help too abruptly, by way of punishing us for what happened, after death, to Josephine. Magdalena retorted that we had acted on the basis of a ridiculous mistake. What we had called the odour of sanctity was merely the sweet smell lingering from the days when the convent had been a workshop for making soap. And the body was not incorrupt at all, she asserted, but simply well preserved from having been buried in dry sand. Sister Maria said that dryness was not a word she would have used, for, on the contrary, the convent was remarkably damp and we poor nuns should never have been forced, by our selfish and uncaring patroness, to live there. The letters winged back and forth like poison darts. Sister Maria read them out to us at mealtimes.

I wished I could see Magdalena and talk to her, but I still did not dare to send her a message asking her to visit me. I was sure she despised me, after the way I had behaved to Josephine in front of her, that night. Lucian and Peter could not give me advice, for they were both absent. A priest whom I did not know came in every day to say Mass for us. Peter, Sister Maria had informed us, had gone on a retreat, to pray for Josephine's rapid canonisation. Lucian had departed for Rome, on a special mission to the Holy Father. He was taking him, as a gift, Josephine's right hand. I had said good-bye to neither of them, for I was too ill.

There was no one to speak to. I wanted to say to Josephine: I am sorry. But it is too late now. She is dead and gone. I will write it down here. I am sorry.

I always knew there was a lot more she could have told me, but chose not to. She was waiting until I was older, when I would understand more. But she died before I got to know her. How could she go away and leave me like that? She abandoned me. I had nothing left once she was gone. An enormous nothingness chilling my open hands and banging inside me like a winter sky. I rolled around in that vast bleakness, belonging nowhere. Home was wherever she was and now her bones were separated and I had no home.

I did not have the time to find out what she thought and felt about so many things. What her life had really been like. That first autobiography was written for the Inspectors, in priest language, and it did not satisfy me. It was pap. She had hinted to me of the danger she had been in, at that period of her life when Christ appeared to her and talked to her. She had stressed the importance of getting her story right. One mistake, and they'd have been ironing her flesh in that spiked frock-press they kept for arrogant nuns.

I searched all over the convent for those other writings of hers, which I lost when they were taken away from me while I was so ill. Sister Maria denied all knowledge of them when I asked her. She said dangerous texts like that, if they had ever existed, which she doubted, should not stay in the house and put everybody at risk, so we were well rid of them, whatever they were.

I sat with Sister Maria in the kitchen, where I had so often sat with Josephine. Sister Maria sat in Josephine's place, and I felt sorry for her, for I was sure she understood she could not replace our Foundress in our hearts. That must have made her bitter. She was not the one we wanted.

Sister Maria moved her arm impatiently and tossed her hand in her lap. I read her as saying: *I* am prioress, this is *my* house, it is *I* who make the decisions here not you girl.

It was a cold morning, but we had no fire because we had no firewood. I put my clammy hands in my sleeves to try and warm them, and held my bare sandalled feet stuck out in front of me, off the icy floor. It was my first day up out of bed. When I walked I wobbled.

— If you are not going to join us, Isabel, Sister Maria said: then perhaps it is time for you to move on. You have had enough time given you, I think, to make up your mind.

There are plenty of other postulants on my waiting list, only too anxious to take your place. Especially now that Josephine's holiness is becoming more widely known. I think that eventually we shall have to move, this building is far too small, I see no reason why our little community should not expand into something really sizeable with an important part to play in the spiritual life of this great city!

I was thinking how the reason we had no firewood was because I had been too ill to go and fetch it. Magdalena had stopped paying our rent, but she still gave us wood, which I was supposed to go and collect, being the only one who could leave the house. Now a chill lay on my skin and my teeth were chattering.

I blurted out: but Josephine was so definite. Only a small community could possibly work. It's in the Rule.

Sister Maria said: Josephine's Rule has unfortunately been lost. But in any case, the Rule has not yet been ratified by Rome, nor by the Father Provincial of the nuns of the Incarnation, nor by the Archbishop. We must be practical. A large convent, well endowed by influential and reliable patrons, is far more likely to survive than a small one dependent only on its inmates' labour. Josephine herself would have come to see that, in time. You mustn't fret, little one. You'll make yourself ill again.

She nodded at me, and raised her hand to sketch a blessing. Her words were so sweet but I felt her dislike, like a rash on my skin.

– Off you go, my dear. Run away now and get on with some work.

I went out slowly, and trailed across town to Magdalena's house, to fetch some firewood. She had left a great bundle of brush and twigs on the steps. I did not dare try to go in. I hoisted the wood onto my back and plodded back to St Joseph's. It was late morning, the sun beginning to burn through the golden mist and wash the streets with warmth. I steered through the noisy squares and alleys with careful steps, feeling my strength return under the caress of the sunlight. I was pleased that I had left my heavy cloak behind. Instead I wore a coat of summer heat. The autumn day was golden, as sweet as ripe pears. I looked about me with great delight. I belonged here, with all these people, in this city. I was glad our house was right in the heart of town. Life sang and banged and clattered all round us and we were a part of it, with everyone else. I walked up to our door thinking that perhaps I should stay in the convent and take vows and try to put Josephine's vision into practice, however difficult that might be and however long it took.

Two men in red livery trampled past, yelling to me to shift out of the way before I was knocked down. A messenger on horseback, both man and horse decked out in red, came up, whistling. He threw down a letter at my feet, while the horse kicked out and sent my bundle flying, then rode off. The letter was studded with thick red seals. I took it inside with the firewood and put it in the kitchen for Sister Maria to find. Then I got on with my work, which was hoeing the weeds from the rows of vegetables. I pretended each weed was Sister Maria, and swung my sharp-edged tool with gusto, slicing her off at the neck, chopping her up at the roots, and finally throwing her onto the rubbish heap and burning her.

After three hours of this I was tired and hungry. I thought I would steal indoors, even though it was still far off dinnertime, to rummage in the larder and find something to eat. I cleaned the blade of my hoe free of mud, wiped my feet on a tussock of grass, and cleared the sweat off my face with my apron. I walked across the yard and pushed open the kitchen door.

Astonishingly for that time of day, the place was in use. Hot in my face came a breath of cooking, something meaty and sweet. Even more odd, Sister Maria was the cook. Normally at this hour she was in her cell, doing her accounts or drawing up rotas of whose turn it was to clean out the privy and empty its contents into the deep pit at the back of the yard.

She had her sleeves and veil pinned back, and was swathed in one of Josephine's old aprons made from bits of worn sheet stitched together. I recognised it from a tiny bloodstain in one corner, faint after repeated washings. Linen, so thick you could see the coarse weave of the threads. Josephine had darned a hole in the front. I knew her bold, lumpy darning, flattened by the iron to a proud white grid. Now Sister Maria had drawn Josephine's sewing around herself and had spattered it with grease.

She was standing over a large iron pot that was hung over a good red fire on the brick hearth. The pot's pouting lip was low enough that I could see in, a mixture that looked like pork stew. Sister Maria was stirring this with a wooden spoon as long as one of the poles we used for pounding the washing. She spoke to me in her false, honey voice.

– Isabel dear. What are you doing here? You should be upstairs in your cell.

She moved the pole gently to and fro. I could hear the heavy, thick swish of the fat and juices in the cauldron, the clunk of bones. The meat was disintegrating, very slowly. It simmered in its great pot, a seethe and a bubble on its golden-brown surface, the colour of resin, an amber ooze heaving back and forth as the bits of pig began to liquefy.

Sister Maria clearly loved her cooking pot. She moved to stand protectively in front of it, so that I could no longer see into it. She wanted to keep the food all to herself. But she couldn't smack her lips over her pork feast with me scrutinising and crowding her. She jerked her chin at me so that I stepped back, away from her. I sat down near the table, on one end of the bench, so that she would realise I belonged in here just as much as she did.

She told me, as she stirred and prodded her swimming chunks of meat, that the Inspectors had sent her a letter announcing their imminent visit, in two days' time. They had decided it was time to see for themselves what went on in our little house. They had heard about the incorrupt body of our holy Foundress, and were coming to investigate.

– So I am very busy preparing for their arrival, Isabel, Sister Maria said: and one way you can help me is by not being a nuisance.

She was keeping the mixture in motion, poking and lifting it, so that it didn't catch, and burn.

– Of course, Sister Maria said: the Inspectors remember Josephine very well from all those years ago, at the Incarnation, when they graciously encouraged her to write her *Life*. And now they will discover that our dear Josephine was not just a true daughter of the Church but a great saint!

Her face glistened with moisture, like a film of pork grease. It was very warm in the kitchen. I could smell her sweat, and the sweet odour of the simmering pork, one harsh and acrid and the other more savoury.

– A saint? I said: Josephine? How do you know?

Sister Maria's voice went up squeakily, like a missed note on a violin.

– I lived with her at the Incarnation, she said: all those years. We all saw how pious she was, and we all knew about her visions of Our Lord. She could not hide her rapture, her heaven-sent joy. Of course she was a saint. Her *Life* makes that clear. And now her incorrupt body! All those relics!

I felt stupid with heat and hunger. The aroma from the big cooking pot swirled out, a rich steam, almost overpowering. Potted pork. I'd watched Magdalena make it many times. After twelve hours' slow cooking, the pieces of pig dissolved, the fat melted, and the flesh became as yielding as butter, rendered so soft, eventually, that you could quickly shred it, using two forks, before you packed it into earthenware jars, sealing it with the white fat, poured on top, which hardened to a lid like a cake of wax.

There was a lump in my throat. I kept swallowing but it would not go down. My words rolled up into a ball of fat which would choke me unless I spat it out. Sister Maria's high voice chafed my ears. She went on and on, chattering, red-cheeked, digging her pole into her smoking vat of jointed parts. Her story was that prayer to Josephine had produced a miracle. Josephine's body, some of it, perhaps most of it, had been returned.

I thought that my illness had crept back up on me. My back weakened and slumped. I put my elbows on the table and leaned my forehead on my hands, as a wave of sickness passed through me and left me trembling. Sister Maria's shrill words poked at the back of my mouth like fingers forced in to make me vomit. I must have eaten something bad. Or else I'd been poisoned. Scraps of what she was saying reached me, but I could not understand them. Afterwards, when I had got myself out of the house, I tried to piece back together what I had heard. There were too many gaps for it to make sense. I had to fill them in.

miracle   dream   body is hidden   the river   you will find bones   cache of bones   body damaged flesh removed most bones intact wickedness relic-hunting thieves God's power mercy because miracle   miracles this sign Josephine's intercession heaven   many bones how pleased the Cardinal will be of course our holy father the Pope

Sister Maria's gabble jumped at me like boiling oil sputtering from the frying pan. I backed off to avoid it. I ran over to the ladder up to the sleeping-loft, got myself up it as fast as I could, and went into my cell. I threw together a bundle of my clothes and jewellery, slid back downstairs, past Sister Maria and her pole and her pot and her evil cookery, seized my cloak from its peg by the door, and left the house.

I leaned against the alley wall for a second. The smell of the kitchen rose up from my stomach along my throat into my mouth. I bent over the gutter and emptied my guts into it. Nobody took the slightest bit of notice of me. They hurried past with their baskets and burdens, brushing against my skirts without looking, as though I were a dog lifting its leg for a piss. I was grateful. I could not have spoken to anyone just then. The indifference of my fellow citizens felt like acceptance, even love. Out here in the street my distress was not remarkable, but simply part of what went on. This gave me a chance to recover. There was a standpipe at the corner. I splashed water over my face and hands, wiped them on my cloak, and set off into the centre of the city.

I needed somewhere quiet where I could sit and think what to do next. I hauled myself into the cathedral, for, having no money, I could not think of anywhere else to go. I sat down in a dark corner at the back, near a statue of Our Lady of Solitude. She was clothed in white satin and lace, with a blue jewel pinned on her breast. In front of her, someone had put a pair of high-heeled shoes, bright red, presumably as a thanksgiving for grace received. I did not take a great deal of notice of my surroundings as my sight was blurred with crying.

I wept for a long time. When I had finished, I searched the pocket of my cloak for a handkerchief, and instead found a letter, and a tiny parcel, that felt to me, in my confused state, like a small cigar.

The letter was from Lucian. He had put it into my cloak before going away, he wrote, so that I would know he had thought of me and said goodbye and wished me Godspeed. He was departing for Rome, and was not sure when he would return. He had removed the sack of Josephine's papers from my cell, he told me, and had given it to Magdalena to look after for me.

I unpeeled the wrapper of the little packet. On the outside of this Lucian had written: Father Peter gave me this as a farewell gift, to keep me safe on my journey. But I have no need to be kept safe, and so I am giving it to you.

Inside was the thick, dry stem of a reed, a hollow container for some dust and something withered. I shook it out onto my palm and peered at it. A strip of wood? It was the little finger of Josephine's right hand. Brownish. The nail pointed and yellow. It sprang into my awareness like an exclamation mark. No bigger than an anchovy preserved in salt. It stood for Josephine. I laid it on the prie-dieu in front of me.

Sister Maria had said: she is a saint.

She was my aunt. The frail pole to which I tied my boat, having no other mooring place. She got on with her life while I bobbed up and down. She could be passionate, withdrawn, tender. Those words are meshes in a sieve that she slips through. She loved me, and she also failed me. An inspiration would seize her and she would wander off, absent-minded and abstracted, to return hours later. She kept going away then coming back. She appeared tolerant and generous but she was selfish. She did what *she* wanted. She did her writing, and spent hours in bed with Lucian behind locked doors, making love and laughing, I heard them, or she sat about gossiping with Magdalena and trying on her clothes.

Now they were calling her a saint. Could a saint be Josephine?

A saint is: what I am not. A saint is: over there. Not here. A saint is invisible, I can't see her, she has run away out of sight, she hovers just ahead of me, the air trembles with her departure, she has gone off and left me, she is the woman I want and whom I can't reach and can't find. She is a woman who is dead. A saint is absence. Always somewhere else, not here.

Josephine's mother was a saint and so was mine and both are dead. I was six years old when my mother died. She lay in the house for three days, while messengers rode to the city to fetch a priest to sing her requiem and pray over her soul. I felt her restlessness at night, as she waited. She roamed about the house and broke a mirror and flew down the stairs towards me in her white nightgown, her arms stretched wide in the moonlight, calling daddy, daddy. She sleep-walked looking for my father and she should not have done, she should have lain quiet like a good girl and not got up to see what was going on. I wanted her well dead. I screamed get her out of here and I floated up and down the stairs in a white velvet shroud. She rotted. How could she not, in that heat. They surrounded the bier with banks of flowers, hoping that the rich scent would mask the stink of putrefaction, but they simply blended together. The thick, choking perfume of orchids and lilies, which drowned me, and the stench of dead flesh going off. Her face was green wax, sweating a little. At night she opened her eyes and stared at me and accused me of wanting her dead, she sat up on the bier and grinned her skull grin.

On the fourth day, they burned her. The church was not yet built, in our province in that country we were sworn to conquer, and so there was nowhere consecrated to bury her. No hallowed ground. The pagans wanted her to join them, they sat up in their earth beds and cried for her and asked her to come to them. But my father said his beloved's body must rest in safety just as her soul lay in the bosom of the Lord in heaven. He trampled the pagans down and stuffed earth into their mouths and they lay back and were hidden again under the ground. Her rich flesh crackled like roast pork, jerked and twisted, blackened and hardened to pork rind. Her skin fell off her like clothes and she was stripped to white bone and then, I was sure, the fever left her and she was at peace at last. Except at night when she came back to visit me and blame me and the moonlight moved across the floor and reached up cold hands towards my bed.

Josephine tried to rescue me from those bad dreams. She would wake me up and hold me in her arms and soothe me. Slowly her body became the reality, her soft plumpness under the scratchy nightgown, her fingers patting my hair and face, her warm bed smell, her voice crooning to me not to be afraid because she was here and all was well. The nightmares receded, shrank. Until the following night. They were there and so was Josephine. On and off she was there. Just as I had learned to trust her, that love was more or less reliable, she too started dying.

The Life of Saint Barbara

Barbara's mother died when the child was only twelve years old. Her husband had loved his wife so much that he wouldn't allow her, after the funeral, to be put in the town burying ground. He had a grave dug for her in the garden of the house where she had spent all her married life. The alabaster jar containing her ashes he put in a hole in the ground, right in the centre of the garden, and he marked the place with a pile of white boulders, and planted a pomegranate tree there in her memory. Around the place there grew up a hedge of wild roses, and in the green grass there bloomed tiny anemones, red and blue and purple.

Barbara's father kept away from the spot after that, in order to forget the pain of his loss, and he commanded his daughter to do likewise. No one tended the grave. The grass grew high and tangled all around it, and moss crept over the tumble

of stones. Bright ferns sprang up in their crevices. Ripe pome-
granates fell onto the ground and split open and spilled out
their seeds. As time went by, this little wilderness inside the
rose hedge at the heart of the garden became simply a refuge
for animals and insects and reptiles. Hummingbirds and parrots threaded the air overhead. Lizards and snakes basked in
the hot sun on the sprawl of rocks. Dormice and voles capered
through the grass. And spiders spun webs between the twigs of
the pomegranate saplings which had sprung up all around, in
which they caught blue and gold flies.

Barbara's father was a merchant who spent his life amassing wealth. Treasures passed in and out of his hands, but his
daughter he swore always to guard and cherish and never to
part with. He lavished presents on her. He bought her a cage
of canaries, a pet monkey, a sandalwood chest filled with
hair-ribbons and a pearl casket full of bangles and rings. He
bought her curly-toed slippers of blue velvet embroidered
with silver thread, tunics of pink silk tied with sashes of grey
brocade, and veils of all the colours of the rainbow of the
finest chiffon dotted with gold spangles. If ever Barbara
wanted something which the household could not supply, a
servant was despatched to fetch it from the city bazaar. She
had no need to go beyond the grounds of her father's house.
Everything she could possibly desire was enclosed within the
white marble walls which surrounded the property. And it
was rare that Barbara asked for anything, for her father was
so quick to anticipate her every wish, by means of the presents he showered into her lap, that she was not aware of
feeling any lack at all.

She was not required to dirty her delicate hands with housework. Her father kept servants for that. Sometimes she wandered into the kitchen and amused herself making sweets of almond paste and rose-water and chopped pistachio nuts, which she ate when she was bored. Sometimes she sat in front of her mirror and tried on her hundred different pairs of earrings, considering the merits of amber or amethyst, topaz or ruby. Sometimes she took two or three baths a day, just to while away the long hours between lunch and supper. Sometimes she rambled in the garden, whose beds and lawns were laid out in precise patterns like those on a carpet, but she was always on her own, for her father was extremely busy. Sometimes his work took him away from home for weeks at a time. When he returned from these trips he would shut himself up in his counting-house with his ledgers and account sheets and the brass scales on which he weighed out his gold. Even when he sat at supper with his daughter he might have an inventory beside his plate, so that he could check it as he ate.

All this work was for the sake of his daughter. Barbara could not complain of his lack of care, his lack of concern. Didn't he spend his life making money so that he could spend it on her? Wasn't she his precious darling for whom nothing was too much, nothing too good? She was his little princess whom he adored. So she strolled in the garden, and played with her money, and told no one she was bored. In any case she had no one to tell.

One day her father sat in his counting-house as usual, glancing from time to time, as was his custom, out of the

window, to see what Barbara was up to. For though he could
not afford to spend much time with her, he anxiously kept
an eye on her. He needed to feel sure that she was safe. He
didn't like it when she wandered away out of sight. Sooner or
later he'd send a servant after her, on some pretext, to fetch
her back. On this occasion, as he watched her running to
and fro on the grass, playing with her pet monkey, he realised
that she was no longer a child. She had grown up into a
beautiful young woman. She was now, after all, fifteen, the
same age as her mother when he met and married her.

Barbara's father looked at her long chestnut hair, only
half-concealed by her muslin veil of burning yellow, at her
pajamas of thin red gauze blown back against the curves of
her body. He watched her for the rest of that day, and saw
how the servants did too. All of them were aware of her: the
old man squatting to grill pigeons spiked on rosemary sprigs
over the charcoal fire set on the edge of the terrace, the
middle-aged man carrying up jars of water from the well,
and the young man weeding the gravel paths. Barbara
romped in front of them, and they peeped at her from under
their downcast eyelids. After supper, she lounged by lantern
light in her hammock slung between two peach trees, and
her father sat nearby in his garden chair, taking a pull on his
pipe, and was aware of the three servants hovering behind
them in the shadows, looking on.

Late the following afternoon, hunting for Barbara, he discovered that she was taking a bath, and that, presumably
because of the heat, she had left the doors on to the terrace
wide open. Only a flimsy blue linen curtain separated her

from anyone who might be passing. He knelt behind one of the doors and peered through the crack between the hinges.

There lounged his daughter in her tub of bronze, one brown leg hooked over the side, soaping her arms and humming to herself. Clouds of jasmine-scented steam blew about her, as though she were outdoors in the open air lying under the pergola planted with morning-glory and honeysuckle and roses. The smell was so powerfully sweet that it was impossible not to want to move towards it, to find its source. It was impossible not to want to go on looking.

Barbara's father backed away. He stubbed his toe, in his haste, on the marble step, and swore. Barbara jumped out of the bath, threw a towel around herself, and ran to the doorway. Lifting aside the curtain she peered out into the darkening garden but could see no one.

Her father sat in his counting-house with a heavy heart. Barbara was dearer to him than all his bales of silk carpets, his heaps of shining coins. She was his diamond and pearl, his spices and ivory, his fine porcelain, his cloisonné, his filigree, his rose crystal, his elaborately wrought glass. She was as necessary to him as water. She was his air. But now he was frightened for her. She was vulnerable. She was in need of protection. Her flame was the light he wished to guard, so that it might burn, delicate and steady, in his house for ever. Her virgin earth, he swore to himself, he would prevent others from trampling on.

He prayed to the gods for guidance, and it came. Just a few weeks before Barbara's sixteenth birthday his prayers were answered and it was clear to him what he must do.

A band of workmen arrived from the city, carrying picks and shovels. In the very centre of the garden, in the over-grown wilderness at its heart, they cleared a space, felling the thicket of pomegranate trees and cutting down the rose hedge and scattering the rubble of white stones. They built, according to the plans drawn up by Barbara's father, a sturdy tower, and inside it a fine new bath-house, walled and floored in aromatic cedarwood, with a large sunken bath inlaid with mosaic of lapis lazuli. Two heavily barred windows were set high up in the walls, near the ceiling, so that if male passers-by would not be able to peer in at Barbara as she lay in her bath, then certainly neither would she be able to peer out at them.

Barbara walked up and down in the garden while the work went on, at some little distance from the building site. Not too far away, however, that she couldn't direct towards the workmen a few curious glances from behind her veil. Her father saw this, and thought: I'm only just in time.

The new building was completed. Silver ewers stood by the bath in readiness, a pile of linen towels. The open pink palms of sea shells held soap and henna. All that the bath-house lacked was a bather.

The following morning Barbara's father wished her happy birthday, then conducted her to the tower. He opened the door to the bath-house and showed her in. He raised his hands to quell her dutiful exclamations of pleasure.

– All this is yours, my darling daughter, he said: think nothing of the cost and the trouble. I did it for you. You know I would do anything to please you. The only thing I ask is that you promise to stay inside here, and not go wandering about outside. Promise me that you'll stay in your beautiful new bath-house and never leave it.

Barbara had never needed to say no to her father, because he had always given her everything she wanted and had demanded only her presence in return. Now, however, for the first time in her life, she set up her will in opposition to his. And it was perhaps because he had loved her so much that she was able to discover the strength to resist him.

– No, she said: no I can't promise that.

Her father flew into a violent rage. He turned red in the face and panted heavily. He cursed Barbara and grabbed her by the arm, and shook her. He raised his hand to hit her. She tore herself from his grasp and fled into the furthest corner of the bath-house. He locked the door upon her.

– There you are and there you will stay, he yelled at her through the door: for ever! You'll never come out again, d'you hear me?

He leaned his forehead against the tower door and talked to it: you are mine, all mine, and now you can never leave me.

And so saying, he dropped the key to the bath-house down the open mouth of the nearby well, and went away.

Barbara sat on the bath-house floor and looked up at the two barred windows, high above her reach. She felt overwhelmed by hopelessness. She was alone. She had been abandoned here, a prisoner until the day she died. She thought of her dead mother, put her head in her hands, and began to cry.

The floor gave a sudden heave. Barbara looked up. The floor gave a loud crack, a report, and another, like the sound of guns going off. The planks of cedarwood began to buckle and split. Up through the gaps between them thrust slender green shoots, which lengthened, and thickened, and turned into green stems, which sprouted fast and tall and waved with green leaves. Soon branches appeared, and then tree trunks. Green fronds and tendrils swarmed up the bath-house walls. Green buds opened out into scarlet pomegranate blossoms. Red pomegranate fruits fattened then exploded, scattering their seeds across the floor, which was now carpeted with wild anemones, red and purple and blue.

Two of the pomegranate trees pushed so hard against one of the bath-house walls that it collapsed, leaving only a low parapet of masonry. The two trees bent in opposite directions, stretched and flattened out the reach of their branches, as though invisible hands espaliered them, and shaped themselves around the opening in the tower wall. They formed themselves into a window frame and instead of glass they held the air between them, steady and cool.

Barbara sat at her new window, on her new window-ledge made of pomegranate tree, half in and half out, dangling one leg over the sill. She saw her father approaching from far off. He was red-faced with fury and anxiety.

– What have you done, witch? he bellowed.

– A third window was necessary, father, answered the girl: we had one window for the father, and one for the daughter, and we needed one for the holy ghost of the mother so that she can fly in and out as she pleases.

Her father leaned in through the arch of pomegranate leaves and flowers, grasped his daughter by the hair, and dragged her out. He dragged her all the way to the city, to the magistrate's court.

Barbara was condemned to death for worshipping false gods. She was sentenced to be beheaded. Just as the sentence was being carried out, however, a bolt of lightning struck her father, set him alight, and killed him stone dead.

Barbara's body was carted to the city gates, to the ravine in the hills beyond it, and thrown in to that deep gash in the mountainside, and the vultures came, and picked the bones white and clean.

THE STORY OF
JOSEPHINE

Try to tell the truth. Some of it is clear and can be put down. Admit that I was not with Josephine when she died. I made that up. I wrote that because it let me look loving. Whereas in fact I was a coward. I believed Sister Maria that I was too young and emotional to attend a deathbed. I was grateful to her I think, I don't know, I can't remember. I see now it was not my upset she was concerned about, but her own. She had to deal with her own sorrow and she did not want to have to deal with mine. So she named me sorrow and sent me away. She banished me from the deathbed so that she could remain calm. For Sister Maria I was grief and rage and rebellion, everything she had struggled all her life as a nun to suppress in herself. I woke her up, I think, I reminded her of what she might have been. I threatened to crack open her peaceful ground, I was bramble and nettle, she had to stamp on me and get rid of me.

I took a book and sat in the little yard, pretending to read. I listened to the sounds of the city from over the wall. I let others tend my dying aunt. She died when I was not there. I should have stayed and been brave enough to hold her hand and speak to her. Nobody held her. If she needed comfort, nobody consoled her. They knelt, a huddle of tired nuns, at the foot of her bed, and chanted the prayers for the dying. They yawned and tried to stay awake. Josephine did not die in my arms, as I put. That was a lie, to make myself feel better, to convince myself that I had done all for her that I could, and that she was not terrified and lonely as death approached. She told me a week before she died that she was not at all afraid. It was not Christian faith that upheld her, for that had gone from her long ago, but something quite else. Now I can see that it was I who was terrified and I who was lonely.

The sight of her suffering was intolerable. It wrenched me apart, because there was nothing I could do to make her well again. Sister Maria was a skilled nurse. She did not simply have to witness Josephine's pain. She got involved with it, she struggled to make her patient better. All I could do was watch, and I could not bear it. There was nothing I could do or give. Others changed dressings, washed her, applied compresses and balms. I was considered too young to help.

I spoke little to Josephine, in her last weeks. I came in to see her, but there was always someone else there. We had few chances to talk to each other alone. But I did not know how to. Glaciers loomed up and locked me in their embrace. My skin stuck to their ice. I could not tell Josephine, for the ice choked me. There was a stone in my heart that sealed me up, like the door of a tomb. Sister Maria said I neglected Josephine and that I had a hard heart. I heard her whisper to Lucian: Isabel hasn't cried once, unnatural girl. She blamed me and I blamed her. Josephine was dying and we were squabbling over who felt what. Such a muddle of griefs. We were so angry that Josephine was ill, our sorrow roared like bulls and we had nowhere to put it. We unleashed it on each other, such rage inside us, and in the midst of this Josephine went on quietly dying.

All the stories of the saints that I had ever read declared that they died noble and inspiring deaths. The martyrs, even as they were torn to pieces by the fangs of wild beasts, uttered cries of love and exhorted each other to greater courage. While their eyeballs were poked out and their stomachs slashed open, they screamed out their faith in God. They acted as an example.

Just before Sister Maria sent me out of the room, observing that I was tired out and needed some rest, Josephine turned her head on the pillow, to face me. I had my hand on the latch. Her eyes searched for me. I squeezed past the kneeling nuns and knelt beside the bed so that my face was close to hers. She smelled of illness, sour and sick. Her face, inside her white invalid's cap, was shrunken. Her gleaming smile was trying to reappear. The corners of her mouth twitched. She had a message for me, so I waited, though my muscles wanted to clench and spring me up and run me away. She hardly opened her lips. The words fluttered through, as though they were tired out, and felt strange.

She whispered: it's a joke. Once you understand, it's funny.

– What is? I said, loud enough to be heard by all the others: what's a joke, dear aunt?

Sister Maria bent over me and put her hands under my armpits and pulled me to my feet. I heard Josephine mutter something, but I was not sure what. A faint, foreign sound. I think she said *metaphor*. I was bundled out into the yard, where I sat on the ground and clutched my book and listened to the singing drifting out of the casement window above. Caterwauling, Lucian called it. He did not think nuns ever sang well. His voice did not join theirs.

Josephine died the next day, early in the morning, attended by Lucian and the sisters. I sat outside, reading. Hers was a beautiful and peaceful death, Sister Maria reported. With her hands crossed upon her breast and her eyes raised to heaven, Josephine called upon the nuns to witness that she died a faithful and true daughter of the Church and that she begged God's mercy on her sins. A year later, Sister Maria wrote an account of the final moments, complete with all the edifying ejaculations Josephine had uttered. She would be able to show it to the Inspectors, if necessary, or to anyone else who asked for such a document to be produced. She corrected the words that I had misheard. What Josephine had said was: it's for the Pope. He'll understand. We need the money. This was sufficient permission, Sister

Maria considered, for her to pursue her plan of turning St Joseph's into a site of pilgrimage attracting the faithful from all over Christendom.

I slumped, worn out by crying, in the corner of the pew close to the statue of Our Lady of Solitude. I made my bundle into a pillow and rested my head on it. I was not ready to move from the cathedral because I had no idea where to go. I just waited. This was something I had learned from Josephine, who always sat on the floor of her cell when she wanted to concentrate on something. She called it attending. If you were tired, it didn't matter. You just emptied yourself out, like a bowl. You didn't want anything. Nothing was required of you except this peaceful alertness.

People call it day-dreaming. Or, just your imagination. But when you're there it's the most real place. Sceptics and unbelievers, should they read this, will think I am stupid, self-deluding, mad, and should be silenced, or they will simply shrug and scoff and put the book aside. Never mind. It doesn't matter. It's true, that's all, that when you roam through the long twisting tunnels inside the city, when you sail down the narrow streets of water, when you enter the honeycomb house, finally you discover the place where you are at home.

Inside me, I found out now, there was a cathedral built of gold. Soaring ribbed arches, a fan-vaulted roof like cockle-shells, two side chapels airy and delicate as twisted blown glass. A church that opened like an underwater flower, that spread its waving tendril-petals like a sea anemone. I was inside the gold cathedral and the gold cathedral was inside me. It was a golden flower that enclosed a pearl, as the oyster does. It was constructed with the precise engineering of love.

And here was the couple and the child, the three-in-one. Here was the woman in her golden dress, holding her girl on her hip, balanced against the crook of her arm, and the other arm wrapped about her man. They trod water, they floated in the air above me, they danced on buoyant pin-points of light, the three of them clasped so close that they were one. They were spun out of gold. They were radiant with the gold light streaming from them, they were a sun revolving then whirling in the darkness, they were the catherine wheel flaring and sparkling and shooting out stars, they were the single great eye of the sunflower. Love forced them to rise into the air and dance for joy. A figure of gold enclosed by crystal. The light that shines in the depths of the sea. The light inside the burning trees irradiated by the midnight sun.

The woman was my golden mother. I had damaged her beyond repair I thought, but it was not so, for she returned to me, she spoke to me with love and called my name, she wanted me so much to be born in the golden cathedral that was her house.

– Isabel. Isabel.

A familiar presence was stooping over me. Magdalena was stroking the side of my face. I returned to myself, to the corner of the pew.

She pulled me to my feet. I collected up my things. The relic of Josephine, which I had left on the prie-dieu in front of me, had vanished. Somebody must have stolen it while I slept. I put Lucian's letter back into my cloak pocket, scooped up my bundle of clothes, took out my emeralds and dropped them into the poor box, and went home with Magdalena.

I am finishing this writing in Magdalena's garden. I have carried my table and chair outside and set them on the gravel path beyond the row of chestnut trees, under the pergola, the wild green canopy of the vine. The rain has ceased, and the wind blows the white clouds away from the brilliant blue dome of the sky. On my face I feel the heat of the sun. The smells of the earth rise up. Raindrops lie in the red cups of tulips and glitter. Wetness and warmth. And the presence of Josephine.

I invent her. I reassemble her from jigsaw bits and pieces of writing; from scattered parts. I make her up. She rises anew in my words, in my story. Mended; put back together and restored; between my hands.

Magdalena said to me as we walked to her house: you can live with me for as long as you like, and you can work with me, if you like, as Josephine did when you both lived here before. She enjoyed it you know, she had a light touch.

I thought I should like to see some of those male guests again, particularly the young ones, and enjoy myself with them, flirting and playing and making love. I thought I should like to travel to the Far Country and visit my father and brothers. I wanted to walk in the city and discover all its pleasures and secret places. I wanted to find Lucian and hear his tales of Josephine. I wanted not to rush into anything too quickly. I wanted not to hold back but to go forwards into the unknown without fear. So I said yes.

I slept that night in my old room, that I used to share with Josephine. I slid into bed and pulled the covers around my face.

Quite distinctly, in the blackness, I heard her voice. She was in the middle of telling me something, as though we'd been talking for some time and she was continuing what she'd begun.

— This bread is my body. This wine is my blood. If you believe that you'll believe anything. My father is my lover. Do you realise, I spent thirty years of my life being afraid of a figure of speech? I never could remember its name.

She was laughing fit to burst.

The Life of St Mary of Egypt

For thirty years Zozimus was parish priest at the Church of the Holy Rood in the village of Blodwell near Nailsworth, near Stroud, Gloucestershire. He looked after the Catholics for many miles around, who came in by car for Sunday Mass, confession and the other sacraments.

His was an uneventful life, if you except his housekeeper, Mary, a maiden lady of uncertain age, running away in the middle of the night and last seen boarding a train at Swindon station, destination unknown.

All year round Zozimus worked hard, organising the flower and church-cleaning rotas, the Sunday School, the catechism classes, the First Communion classes, the Confirmation classes, the young mothers prayer group, the Knights of St Columba, the youth club, and the senior citizens luncheon club, and not forgetting to attend the Nativity play, the carol concert, the May pilgrimage to Lourdes, the Friday night whist drive, the Saturday afternoon bridge drive, the summer fête and the harvest supper.

Every July, for two weeks, Zozimus went to Blackpool with a group of other priests, for his holiday. They strolled on the beach and the pier, played bingo, drank a pint or two before high tea, and watched television or played cards in the boarding-house lounge in the evening. At night they took a sip of whisky, discussed the racing news and said a decade of the rosary together, then fell into bed exhausted by the bracing sea air.

Recently, however, Blackpool had been becoming popular with gay men, who were to be seen openly parading on the promenade arm in arm. Zozimus felt increasingly embarrassed, year by year, when he and his bunch of priest friends were taken by the landladies of their boarding-houses to be gay, and treated with extra tolerance and warmth and special touches like pink towels in the bathroom.

When he retired at the age of sixty, therefore, and received the generous cheque which was his parishioners' farewell present to him, he decided not to go back to Blackpool this year, but to embark on a Mediterranean cruise that would also take in a visit to Egypt and the Holy Land.

– Here have I been priest of Holy Rood all these years, he said: it's high time I went to take a look at the True Cross *in situ*, and all those holy places touched by the blessed feet of Our Lord.

His grey summer cardigan and grey slacks came back from the cleaners. He bought a panama hat, mosquito lotion, a couple of paperback novels by Graham Greene, and two drip-dry shirts, one orange and one green. He left his small, modern presbytery without regret, suddenly real-ising he had always hated its ugliness and bleakness. Nor was he as upset as he had expected to be at parting from his flock. He had been their servant, he realised. He had run around looking after them, and they had felt free to summon him at any hour of the day or night to come immediately to minister to them. He had to listen to their problems, but no one had ever listened to his. That had been the deal. He had not liked to trouble Almighty God too much with the daily details of parish life. He had tried to save Him from being bothered, too, which he thought now might have been wrong of him. Surely God could cope with dullness?

– I'll tell you everything now, dear God, he prayed: from now on I'll have lots to tell You about. You'll see.

He suspected he might not even miss his priest friends, either. Good men, all of them, but noses to the grindstone. Zozimus was feeling his soul expand. He stood on deck as the liner sailed, grasping the rail in both hands and feeling a smile reach from ear to ear.

Egypt was very hot, and did not suit him, though he tried most conscientiously to let it. He was frightened by the desert, its vastness, by its seeming indifference to humanity which hid its voracity. He had never thought of nature as alive, yet he felt the desert waited for him, to devour him as it devoured the camels whose heaped white bones they passed one day on a coach trip. He clutched his plastic bottle of mineral water and thought how easy it would be to die here. His God was not here, for He had taken the Israelites and gone elsewhere. In His place were the heathen gods with animal heads whose names he kept getting muddled up. Too many of them for his peace of mind. Inside the Great Pyramid, sweating up a narrow stone stair with a thousand other tourists, crammed into airless tunnels, he shook with terror and had to repress the desire to cry out. The temples at Karnak and Luxor wanted to fall on him and crush him. The decorated underground tombs, with their painted scenes of voluptuous worldly pleasures, mocked his faith. He was relieved, every night, after each day's excursion, to get back onto the luxurious Nile cruiser, which served ice-cold beer and was air-conditioned. He pretended to himself it was not the pagan gods he disliked so much as the modern culture he encountered on shore: the strange food, the constant hooting of car horns, the loud wailing music emitted from taxi radios, the unofficial guides trying to get money off him, the beggars, all the inquisitive foreign men unable to understand why he was single and had fathered no children. And the heat, which struck at his panama-hatted head with iron fists.

Back on the liner, he gratefully accepted a role he thought he had wanted to cast off. He became a kind of unofficial chaplain to the few Catholic passengers who had chosen this comfortable, slow method of travelling to the Holy Land, and felt he was almost back at home. He shared his copies of the *Tablet* and the *Catholic Herald* with them, and accepted their advice on suntan lotion and indigestion remedies, and in the evenings played them at backgammon, Scrabble and draughts.

Jerusalem, being more Christian than Egypt, was more congenial. The hotel served good plain food of an American sort, and the tour bus showed videos and had a lavatory. Zozimus felt that he should not care so much about these things, but he could not deny they made travelling less arduous and assuaged all the fears of chaos and accident to which the tourist is prey. He had been abroad before, of course, on the annual parish pilgrimage to Lourdes. But France had not felt exotic, or even particularly strange. It seemed to rain a lot in the Pyrenees, just like it did in Gloucestershire, and the French nuns and monks wore plastic macs and rain-hoods over their bulky habits just like English ones did, and the hotels were used to catering for English visitors and understood the necessity of making them feel at home. Lourdes was, very much, an international centre. The shrine itself looked just like any other nineteenth-century Catholic church anywhere in Europe. The famous statue in the grotto, reproduced a million times in parishes across the world, was depressingly familiar.

The Holy Land was not like Lourdes. It was more like Egypt in some ways, being very hot, and brown, and arid, full of clamouring beggars of all ages, suspicious-smelling lavatories, and makeshift cube-shaped houses that appeared unfinished, as though they had no roofs. So Zozimus was grateful for his hotel, which was a marble tower block with room service, and for the tour bus, with its plate glass windows that sealed him off from the troubling outside world, and its artificially cooled atmosphere, and its soft reclining seats, and its headsets that let you listen to taped music or the radio.

One afternoon the bus left him behind. It departed, with its cargo of hot, sleepy passengers, back to the city without him. He had signed up for a pleasure trip to beauty spots along the river, and had fallen asleep, sated by the delicious picnic lunch provided as part of the excursion, in the shade of an oleander bush. When he woke up and realised that the bus had gone without him, he started back on foot, reasoning that he would hitch a lift, or find a phone-box and call a taxi. The road, however, led away from the river Jordan into the desert. He had somehow come the wrong way. He was lost.

There were no cars on this road, certainly no taxis or phone-boxes. He limped along, sweating profusely, under the banging sun. He longed for water, but had none with him.

The terror of the desert that he had first felt in Egypt returned. Burning and flat, it seemed to rise up and mock him, to toss him about like a gnat, to yawn with cruel pleasure and wait for him to fall down and die, alone, far away from anyone who knew him.

Then he saw a mirage. A skinny figure, the wrinkled flesh so sunburned it looked black, came capering towards him. It was a woman. She was so thin that she looked like a boy, with hardly any breasts at all, and her black hair, streaked with grey, cascaded down her back. She waved her mahogany arms at him and loped forward. She seemed to be calling his name.

– My God, now I'm hallucinating, Zozimus croaked to himself: that's it, my time is surely up.

He tried to compose himself, to make a final Act of Contrition, to prepare his soul to meet God. But he had no time. The naked brown woman came up to him and grasped his hands in hers.

– Father Zozimus! Father Zozimus! Fancy meeting you here of all places!

He thought to himself: is this an angel of God? or a pagan spirit trying to lure me into sin? How can she possibly know my name?

She was laughing, her teeth very white in her brown face.

– It's me, Mary, your housekeeper as was! Don't you remember me?

Zozimus gasped. He swayed, weakened by what felt like sunstroke and thirst. As he staggered, she put her arm round him and marched him forward.

– It's just a few steps further along. Come on now, and we'll get you into the shade.

He half-closed his eyes, so that they did not meet the little brown breast so close to them, and let her guide his staggering steps. Then coolness fell upon him. He was some-how, miraculously, in the shade. He heard the tinkle of water. His feet met not the unyielding ridges of desert sand, but the flat hardness of wooden planks.

– Mind the step, Mary's voice sang out into his ear.

She smelled richly of suntan lotion, hot skin, sweat and lavender soap. Zozimus opened his eyes just as she let go of his arm and moved away.

The Oasis. The sign was painted in a white flowing script on a yellow background. It hung over the doorway made

dark and cool by a swinging bead curtain. The dusty courtyard in front was set with tables and chairs, ceilinged by the
tumbling purple flowers of a Judas tree. Tubs of pink
oleanders stood about. The little wooden verandah, up
whose steps he had just come, held a sun-lounger, and a
bamboo table and chairs. A large fridge cooed at one end of
it. A vine wreathed all round the verandah, its green tendrils
imparting coolness and freshness. The sun, kept at bay by
the woven bamboo roof, rippled in wobbly stripes down the
steps.

– Sit down, Mary said: and I'll bring you some water,
and a beer.

He fell onto the sun-lounger and lay back. It smelled of
her. He was lying on her towel. The bead curtain rattled once,
twice, and she was back. Cold water tilted down his parched
throat. He gulped until his stomach was ice. Then he sighed,
picked up the beer bottle, and looked at his ex-housekeeper,
who was now wearing a flowered dressing-gown. She was
barefoot. Her toenails were painted pink.

– There's nothing wrong with a bit of nude sunbathing,
she assured him: one of the reasons I left Gloucestershire was
it wasn't often hot enough there, and people in the parish
would have talked.

Her leathery brown-black skin was richly oiled. Her eyes,
deepset in creases, smiled at him.

– I got a sudden passion to visit Egypt, she said: I'm sorry
for just going off like that, but I knew if I discussed it with
you first you'd have talked me out of it. In those days you
were a very conservative man.

Zozimus leaned forwards, unbuckled his sandals and shook them off. Then he pulled off his socks. He flexed his toes.

– Why Egypt?

– My parents met there before the war, she said: they were always on about it, the gay life they led there, the dinner-dances, the cocktail parties, the hunting, shooting ducks and so on, going riding in the desert. I wanted to see what it was like.

She sighed.

– It had changed. It wasn't like that any more. I wondered if they'd made some of it up. People do, you know.

Zozimus took a long pull on his beer. He unbuttoned his orange shirt a little way, and rolled his sleeves up to the elbows. He drank more beer.

– So what are you doing here?

– It's a nice bit of the country, she said: people come out from the suburbs for the day, they have lunch, a stroll in the desert. Just like you did. I cater for the coach parties that stop down the road in the picnic area by the river. Who d'you think made your soda bread scones? Me! I always made good soda bread, didn't I? Where did you think that picnic hamper came from? Here, of course.

She was smiling, very pleased with herself.

– You mean we're near the city? Zozimus asked: I thought it was miles away. I thought I was lost in trackless desert.

Mary got up from her bamboo chair and went to the fridge for two more beers. She walked so lightly she seemed to be skimming an inch above the floor. He told himself he was light-headed, he'd started seeing things again.

– I don't understand, he said: where did you get the money from to go to Egypt, and then to set yourself up here? Not on your wages as my housekeeper, I'll be bound.

Mary blushed. A brown blush that swept over her brown face.

– That's another thing, she said: I did begin to think that with my talents I was wasting myself a bit. I felt I could have a better career than priest's housekeeper. No offence meant, Father, of course.

– I'm on holiday, Zozimus said: you don't have to call me Father. You'll have noticed I'm not wearing a dog-collar, after all.

Mary offered him a cigarette, which he accepted. He took the matches from her other hand and struck a flame. She leaned forwards to meet it with her cigarette, her dressing-gown falling open, and he saw the deep cleft between her brown breasts, dark and creased.

– I can't really tell you, Mary said: it's not fit for a priest's ears. I don't want to shock you.

– Forty years sitting in the confessional on Saturday nights hearing confessions, Zozimus responded: have left me unshockable. I have to admit I'm curious. Come on now. Tell me everything.

– I discovered I had this brilliant talent for sex, Mary began: I really loved it and I was really good at it. Of course, being single, and being a Catholic, I tried to damp myself down. But once I'd left Blodwell I said to myself: come on girl, you only live once.

– And? Zozimus asked: and so?

– Gentlemen friends, she said: lots of lonely men around, I discovered, as soon as I got on the train for Birmingham. Only too glad to buy me a drink and a meal. Then if I went to bed with them on top of that they were only too happy to contribute towards my travelling expenses.

She ground out her cigarette in the ashtray.

– I fucked my way to Egypt, she said: and then I fucked my way here.

She caught Zozimus' gaze upon her.

– I'm retired now, of course, she said: I bought this bar with my savings, and running it brings me in a tidy sum.

– Oh, Zozimus said.

– When I do it nowadays, she said: I just do it for fun. Not for money. Only with people I really fancy.

She yawned and stretched. She stood up and tightened the belt of her dressing-gown.

– A little supper? she asked: and then we could have a swim.

She cooked lamb kebabs, marinaded in olive oil and rosemary, on the little outdoor grill in the courtyard. Zozimus cut aubergines into thin slices, grilled them, dressed them with olive oil, lemon and garlic. He made a tomato salad while Mary opened the wine. They ate, watching the sun go down and flame red all across the desert. Late at night, they swam in the little blue plastic bubble of the pool, under a string of coloured lights hung between the palm trees set at the corners. Zozimus floated on his back and watched the palm tree fronds flap like torn rags against the dark blue sky. The stars came out. A sickle moon appeared. Crickets whirred and buzzed in the darkness. The cool water felt silky against his skin.

They drank a whisky and smoked a last cigarette on the verandah, looking at the comets which flared across the midnight sky. Then they went to bed together. He didn't know what to expect, never having done this before. Mary's sunburned skin was soft as chamois leather, so much softer to the touch than to the eye. Her mouth tasted of sweet minty toothpaste. He stroked her all over, very gently, and was delighted by her sighs of pleasure. When she drew him inside her, enclosed him, wrapped her legs around him, and began to move her hips in a kind of dance, Zozimus cried out with surprised joy. She was indeed very good at this, and so, he discovered, was he. He tried to tell her how he felt. He quoted from the *Song of Songs*. She put her hand over his mouth.

– No Bible stuff, please. I'm not having any of that.

He spent a pleasant two weeks at The Oasis, before beginning to think that he ought to be getting back to England. He had cancelled his hotel room in Jerusalem, and had let the cruise ship sail off without him on the homeward leg of the trip, but he supposed that he really ought to be making a move. You couldn't spend your entire life just enjoying yourself, could you? And yet he had enjoyed himself. He had helped out serving drinks and meals to the thin but steady stream of customers who turned up, and had had interesting conversations with many of them, he had sunbathed and swum in the pool, he had eaten a lot of delicious food, and he was in the throes of his first love affair.

– So why leave? Mary asked him: stay if you like.

They ran the bar together for the next twenty years. On the day when they both felt old age approaching so fast that death could not be far off, Mary took Zozimus by the hand and led him deeper into the desert, moving so rapidly that he felt they were skimming over the hills of sand like birds. The desert was no longer a terrifying place. It was the place he had come to, the place that had received him, and the place in which, now, he longed to lie down.

A passing lion, finding the bodies, clasped hand in hand in death, dug a grave with its paws, and buried the two lovers. In the night that followed, the wind got up and stirred the desert sands, shifting the dunes into different shapes, until all trace of the burial was obliterated for ever-more.

THE GOLDEN HOUSE

The chapel they called the Golden House was built by the Cardinal, as a result of a vision and two miracles. The vision was Sister Maria's. The miracles were Josephine's. Josephine cooperated with Maria after death in a way she had not always done in life. Maria prayed urgently for her assistance and Josephine provided it. This made Maria love her even more than formerly, and increased her determination to see Josephine beatified then canonised.

Two miracles were needed to convince the authorities, from the Pope downwards, that Josephine was in heaven and able therefore to intercede directly with God.

The first miracle was the return of most of the parts of Josephine's body after they had been stolen by thieves presumably intending to make a fortune by selling them as relics. The dismembered body was dumped outside the convent door one night and discovered by Sister Maria in the morning, just before the Inspectors were due to pay the house an official visit. All that remained of the saint's formerly incorrupt body were her bones: clean, blanched, dry; as though they'd been boiled. The nuns reassembled the body and found that most of the bones were there as far as they could tell, not being surgeons. One of the hands was missing and later turned up in Rome. The little finger of the right hand never reappeared. The Inspectors found the body, the convent and the nuns correct and blameless. They went away and wrote a favourable report. The Cardinal accepted Sister Maria's gift of the head, the torso and one handless arm, but left them with her for the time being, while he consulted his architects over the design of the Golden House.

The second miracle was the discovery, by some boys playing football on the wasteland by the water meadows just outside the city, of a great cache of bones. Sister Maria's nephew was one of this gang. Knowing he would be late home for supper and fearing a whipping, he had prayed to Josephine for help. She had responded by telling him to dig in the dust, and thus he had uncovered a pit full of ancient human skeletons. Sister Maria prayed to Josephine for enlightenment. It came in a vision.

It was well known to everyone in the city that St Ursula and her troop of eleven thousand virgins had passed through the country on their way back from the Holy Land, where they had been helping the Christian armies do battle with the pagans and bring them, at the point of a sword, to baptism. Their current mission was to convert the indigenous

Faithless Ones here in Josephine's home city. St Ursula had rested, with her warrior girls, under the willow trees by the river that flowed past the city walls, declaring it a most sweet and pleasant spot, a perfect place for a picnic. The citizens had accordingly given them breakfast alfresco, bringing them eleven thousand and one croissants, eleven thousand and one dollops of apricot jam, and eleven thousand and one beakers of frothy new milk.

In the vision, so Maria said, Josephine explained these events in detail, while under her feet she busily trampled serpents and devils and pagan blackamoors. Maria knew this resplendent figure wearing a diamond crown and waving a silver sword was indeed Josephine, for her name was written in stars over her right breast. Josephine told Maria that Ursula and her companions had been betrayed by the very heretics and Faithless Ones here in the city they had come to save. Ambushed and slaughtered, as they slept off their delicious breakfast, by the forces of evil, they had not had a chance to baptise a single one of them. As a result, the Faithless Ones had been killed in thousands by the griefstricken Christian citizens, and any survivors driven out. Now Josephine came in a vision to Maria to preach peace, repentance and piety.

Sister Maria and her community of nuns renamed themselves the Little Sister-Keepers of the Bones. They worked day and night sorting and labelling the hill of remains. They prayed for guidance in classification and it came. Faced with mixed bones from eleven thousand virgins plus one, all embracing each other intimately and promiscuously in glorious confusion, they put them confidently into neat piles.

The Cardinal paid for all the reliquaries, saint by saint, as well as the chapel which sheltered them. The leftover bones belonged to the unknowns. The most holy women could be given places, names, and reliquaries. The less celebrated had to make do with being part of the faceless crowd. The division between them was strict, and instantly visible. St Ursula and her thousand chief lieutenants were the big stars of the Golden House. The ten thousand others went up on the wall as bone mosaic. Unfortunately, Josephine's remains got tangled up with those of everyone else. Now there were eleven thousand virgins plus two. Quite where Josephine's bones ended up in the clutter, to be honest, was anybody's guess. Probably she faded into the background, the abstract design of saintly lady subalterns and privates. The Cardinal, switching his focus to the glorious St Ursula, to whom the Golden House was now dedicated, agreed with Sister Maria that Josephine's modest vanishing was typical of her unobtrusive sort of sanctity, and that it would do her cause no harm, in the rigorous and searching canonisation process, for her to be recognised as amongst the most humble and self-effacing of her sex.

Printed in the United States
53175LV00002B/14/A

9 780156 006590